OUTLAW HEART

"Someone shot you in the back?" Catalina couldn't stop herself. She reached out and touched the damaged flesh, silently cursing the man who had done this to him.

"Yep. That was the day I learned never to shoot to wound a man. Always shoot to kill."

"When was that?" Catalina pulled her hand away slowly. It seemed so unfair.

"Fourteen years ago." Jackson stood, and Catalina was free. She didn't move but to massage her aching arms.

"God, Jackson, you were just a baby."

He kept his back to her, and she saw the muscles there tense.

"What happened?" Catalina had seen enough of Jackson Cady to know that he was intelligent, almost human, though he tried very hard to hide that fact. What had brought him to this place? What had turned Jackson Cady into Kid Creede? "Why do you do...what you do?"

He turned then and looked down at her, and she wished he had kept that stiff back to her. Jackson smiled, but there was no humor in that smile. His narrowed eyes burrowed into her, and traveled that length of her body slowly.

"Are you certain you're a virgin, Catalina Lane?" he asked silkily.

Catalina nodded her head, but that didn't stop Jackson. He leaned over her, trapping her still sore arms above her head and placing his lips over hers. They almost touched, and his mouth hovered just above hers so she could feel every breath he took, every beat of his heart.

"How can I know for certain that you're telling the truth?" he whispered.

LINDA JONES

Desperado's Gold

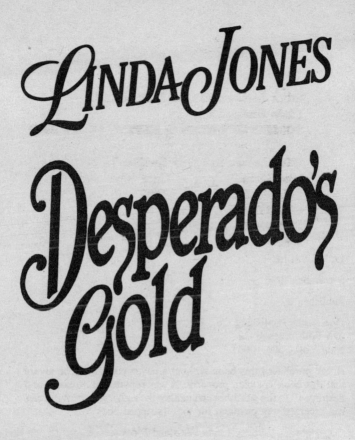

LOVE SPELL ◈ **NEW YORK CITY**

LOVE SPELL®

September 1996

Published by

Dorchester Publishing Co., Inc.
276 Fifth Avenue
New York, NY 10001

Printed in the United States of America.

For Beverly and Linda Sue
Never underestimate a Southern Woman

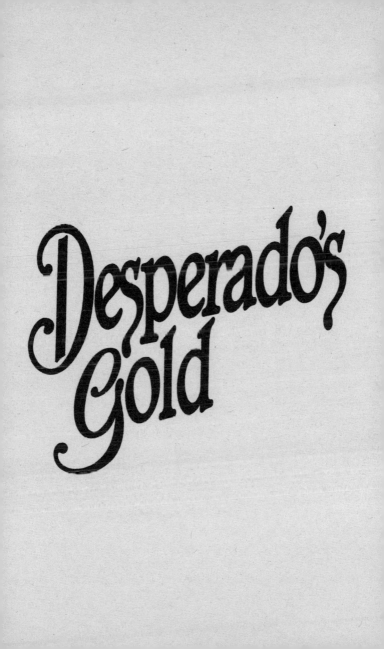

Chapter One

Smoke was pouring from the hood, obscuring the narrow and deserted roadway, and Catalina slapped her palm against the steering wheel. Not now. Please, not now. She loved her white Mustang convertible, and it had never given her a minute's trouble.

Until now. It jerked and surged, and then the engine died in the middle of the Arizona two-lane road that stretched straight ahead and seemingly forever. Catalina steered her cherished vehicle to the side of the road and it rolled to a stop.

Catalina laid her forehead against the steering wheel. She could have cried a little more, but it wouldn't have done any good. Besides, she was all cried out. The tears had poured from her eyes all afternoon, torn from her more in anger than in sorrow. She didn't even know where she was. She'd just climbed into her Mustang and taken off. No destination in mind, but away from the church and all those sympathetic, prying eyes.

She threw open the door and stepped onto the highway, grabbing the full skirt of her wedding dress and reluctantly carrying the burden with her. Her white satin heels were already scuffed, and the gown was likely to be in no better shape by the time she reached the gas station that was still a good ways down the road.

Catalina pushed her wire-rimmed glasses up on the bridge of her nose and looked down the highway as she slammed the car door shut.

She didn't hesitate but walked forward with her skirt in her hands, held just off the asphalt. Her feet hurt. The shoes she wore had been bought with fashion in mind, not comfort, and the heels were a good inch higher than anything Catalina ever wore.

It didn't matter now. She'd been left at the altar. Almost literally. At least Wilson had had the decency to tell her before she'd walked down the aisle. Of course, she'd been ready—dressed in her white wedding gown—and the church had been filled with her friends from Indian Springs and Wilson's friends and family from Phoenix. There were flowers and candles and bridesmaids and a very reluctant groom.

Everything he'd said was true, she told herself as the station down the road appeared to get a bit closer. They were friends, never lovers, but they'd talked that out and decided that was all right. Perhaps more than all right. Perhaps perfect. No passion clouded their disagreements or plans. They both wanted to be married, and they both wanted children, and neither of them had ever been in love. She was twenty-seven years old, and she'd decided that she'd never fall in love. Not like her moony-eyed friends who seemed to lose every speck of common sense they had when they "fell in love." She'd expected that the affection she felt for Wilson would grow, that they would learn to love each other.

Her glasses slid down her nose a little farther, and Catalina pushed them back up forcefully. It was true that her eyes were not very bad, but she always wore her glasses to drive, and to work at the library. Wilson had said he liked the way she looked in her wire-rimmed glasses. Smart. Classy. But Wilson had also said he wanted to marry her. Jerk.

Catalina looked over her shoulder. Her Mustang was far behind, a speck on the horizon, and it was still a good walk to the gas station. It didn't matter, she told herself. She would make it there with no more trouble. What else could go wrong?

At that moment the heel of her right shoe snapped off, and Catalina stumbled off the road, regaining her balance just as she was about to fall face-first into the sandy soil on the shoulder. She picked up the broken heel from the black asphalt and threw it as hard as she could away from the road. There was nothing there but sandy soil and a few scrubby bushes that struggled to survive. She removed what was left of the useless shoe and threw it aside as well. Then the left shoe followed, kicked away with a swing of her leg, leaving Catalina on the side of the road in her stocking feet.

She no longer tried to hold her wedding dress up off the road. The skirt dragged against the asphalt as Catalina plunged straight ahead.

If only Wilson hadn't cried. If he'd been cold and heartless, she could've screamed at him, called him every name in the book. With tears in his brown eyes and real heartache in his voice, he had told her that he couldn't marry her. He did love her, he said, as a friend. As his best friend. But there was this woman . . .

He hadn't even known her a full week, this mystery woman, but he wanted desperately to marry her. And it hurt him horribly to bring pain to Catalina. It hurt *him?*

Why had he waited until the last possible moment to break it off, to cancel the wedding? He'd stood before her in a rented tux that fit him perfectly, with a fresh haircut and a white rose in his lapel. Had he decided to sacrifice himself and go through with the ceremony? His mother was there, all his family was waiting . . . and he just couldn't go through with it.

She had run from the church and taken off in her Mustang before anyone could stop her. Everything she owned was in the trunk. Her clothes, her books . . . that was it. She'd given Kim what little furniture she owned when she'd packed her belongings. Wilson had a great apartment, much larger and better equipped than the one she'd shared with Kim for the past three years. Kim, her best friend and maid of honor. The last time she'd seen her roommate, Kim had been wearing a long, pale yellow dress and carrying a bouquet of mixed flowers. Pretty Kim, who fell in love on a regular basis, and fell out of love just as quickly. And who seemed to like it that way.

The gas station was close at last, and Catalina sighed deeply when she got a good look at the place. At first she wondered if it was even open, and then she saw the figure of a man sitting out front. Parts of the building had once been red, but most of the paint had flaked off, exposing the original white. There were three pumps out front, and a small garage to the side.

And a tow truck out back, she noticed as she came closer. It didn't look to be in much better shape than the building, more rust than paint, but she prayed that it would work. Surely something would go her way today. Surely something . . .

Catalina straightened her spine as she entered the parking lot. She would not lose control now, tempting as it would be to cry on someone's shoulder. My car broke down and my groom left me at the altar and I broke my new shoes. She wondered, briefly, why she thought of her losses in that order. Did her Mustang come before Wilson Ross? Maybe it did.

Ignoring the old man who seemed to be asleep in his chair by the entrance, Catalina threw open the door and stepped inside. A welcome blast of cool air hit her face, and she took a deep, calming breath before she spoke.

"I've had some car trouble," she said calmly to the two occupants of the small room.

A man sat behind a battered desk, looking over what could have been bills or invoices, and a woman perched on a stool in the corner. They stared at her for a moment, saying nothing but watching her with surprised and skeptical eyes. It was the woman, a slender woman with graying brown hair who was maybe forty—maybe not—who spoke first.

"We can help you out, can't we, Stu?"

Stu nodded his head, but he didn't even blink as he continued to stare.

It was the woman who stood and smiled, walking slowly toward Catalina. It was a nice smile, Catalina thought absently, like she really meant it.

"My name's Allie, and this is my husband, Stu. Forgive us for staring. We don't see many strangers out this way anymore. Most of our customers are locals, since the interstate was finished, except when they're filming one of those Westerns down the road. Those movie people," she shook her head slowly, indicating that she just didn't get the Hollywood crowd. "Now, when my daddy ran this place, years ago, it was a bustling place all year round. Tourists mostly."

Catalina realized that Allie was chattering nervously, filling what had quickly become an uncomfortable silence. She took another deep breath of the cool air that circulated through the small office. Besides the desk and Allie's stool, there was a glass-front refrigerator full of soft drinks, a candy machine, and a rack of cigarettes. Catalina stared almost longingly at the frosty-cold glass bottles of soda and realized that she had left her purse in the trunk of her Mustang. All her money, her checkbook, her credit cards, her driver's license . . . everything was abandoned with her car down the road.

But Allie must have recognized the longing in her look. "Have a cold drink while Stu has a look at that car of yours."

Catalina gave Stu directions in a lifeless voice as she sipped a grape soda and gestured lan-

guidly. Allie watched her sharply, se
thing, it seemed, and Catalina de
really didn't matter. She'd killed her
up her apartment—though she was certain
would have her back without hesitation—and
she had been absolutely humiliated in front of
everyone she knew. What did it matter what the
owner of a dilapidated gas station out in the middle of nowhere thought of her?

When Allie offered the key to the rest room
with the suggestion that Catalina might want to
freshen up she took it wordlessly, wondering
why the key was attached to a plywood sign that
said LADIES, each letter a good six inches high.
Was that for the benefit of those with poor eye-
sight? Or did Allie think she was going to forget
whose key it was and slip it into a concealed
pocket of the wedding dress?

Catalina had to step outside to reach the rest
room, and she walked silently past the sleeping
man. His chair was leaning back against the wall
by the door, and, if she wasn't mistaken, he
snored very lightly under a wide-brimmed hat
that covered his face and hair.

Inside the dimly lit rest room, Catalina stared
at her reflection in a cracked and cloudy mirror,
finally understanding why Allie and Stu had been
shocked into momentary silence.

Black mascara ran down her face, smeared
and streaked across her cheeks and around her
eyes. Pale blond hair that had been so carefully
styled that morning had been whipped in the
wind as she tore aimlessly down the highway
torn from a once tidy knot. A single remaini

flower hung precariously just over her ear, angled in a knotted strand of hair. She had even added a purple tinge to her lips with that grape soda, a circle on her lips and just above.

Catalina placed her glasses on the rim of the sink, dampened a length of brown paper towel, and proceeded to scrub her face clean. All the mascara, from her lashes and her cheeks, what was left of her lipstick, and the grape soda. Her eyes still burned and were red-rimmed and bloodshot, but there were no more tears.

She pulled off her panty hose with a vengeance, tossing them into an empty wastebasket with more vigor than was really necessary. She hated panty hose anyway. They were hot and confining, and no matter what size she bought they were either too large and sagged at the ankles or too small and pinched her waist. As soon as Stu was back with the car she'd change out of this cursed wedding dress, slip into a pair of stretch pants and a huge T-shirt and her sneakers, and comb the tangles out of her hair.

The air was a little cooler, the sun a little brighter as Catalina stepped from the dim rest room and slipped her glasses back on. Her life wasn't over . . . not because Wilson Ross had dumped her. Not because she had to stop and rethink her future. Plans could be forgotten, changed, abandoned altogether, just like those panty hose with the blackened feet.

"No more tears, Goldie?"

Catalina's head snapped up at the sound of the ravelly voice. The old man who had been sleep- by the entrance had removed his hat and

16

lifted his head to watch her closely
Indian, dressed in old jeans and a p
with a deeply wrinkled face seemingly
the red rocks in the distance. He was smi g at
her, a wickedly knowledgeable smile, and his
narrowed black eyes twinkled.

"No more tears," she said, to herself as much
as to the old Indian.

She stepped past him, and he pointedly looked
down at her bare feet. "I sell moccasins."

Catalina tried to glance into the cardboard box
at the man's side, but all she could see was another plaid shirt, folded neatly over the contents.

"Maybe when Stu gets back with my car. I
don't have any money with me. . . ."

"Here." He reached into the box without even
looking as his hands disappeared beneath the
plaid shirt and came up with a pair of white moccasins beaded with blue and white.

"They are beautiful," she said, allowing him to
place them in her hands. "I'll pay you as soon as
Stu returns with my . . ."

"One more thing," the old man said, shaking a
finger in her direction. "You need to change your
luck, Goldie." A hand delved into the box, and
again he didn't bother to look. This time he withdrew a yellow crystal, several small crystals
growing together and forming an oblong shape
that fit nicely in the palm of his hand. It caught
the light as he handed it to her. "Wulfenite. Very
pretty. It catches the sun like the gold flecks in
your eyes."

Observant old man, Catalina decided, to have
seen the tiny flecks of gold in her amber eyes.

17

ı hank you," she said, taking the rock he laid reverently on her palm.

"With this rock comes some advice."

Oh, no. She almost said it aloud. The last thing she needed as she sorted through her feelings was the advice of a self-appointed sage. Like it or not, here it comes.

"Open your heart and your mind, and all things are possible."

Simple, heartfelt advice. Not so hard to take after all.

"I have a gift for you," Catalina said impulsively, ripping the diamond engagement ring Wilson had given her from her finger. He would never get it back, and she didn't care if he had to pay on the cursed thing for the next hundred years. "Sell it. Keep it. Eat it. I don't care."

He ignored her statement but took the ring, studying it carefully as he turned it over in his palm again and again.

Catalina took the opportunity to slip inside. She stepped into the moccasins and helped herself to another soda from the refrigerator. Not grape this time. Something clear. Some lemony-limey carbonated drink that she gulped too quickly.

Stu wasn't back yet, and Allie was pumping gas for a regular customer. Catalina knew the man Allie laughed with was one of the regular customers she had mentioned, just by watching the two of them. She couldn't tell what they said, but they bantered easily and laughed again.

A walk. It seemed a stupid idea, after already walking so far, but she wanted to move. Maybe

18

it would clear her head. Maybe she could work all this through while Stu fixed her Mustang. If it could be fixed. It was better than twenty years old, but she'd been so careful to maintain the car after her grandmother had willed it to her. Grandma Lane had always been a real stickler about her Mustang.

The Indian appeared to be sleeping again, and Catalina smiled at the thought of Wilson's diamond ring hidden in that cardboard box of junk and treasures.

There was nothing behind the gas station. Sand and a few scrubby bushes, a stack of tires, tall red rocks like towers in the distance. Catalina was watching those rocks as she set out, pushing her glasses up on her nose to secure them. The sand gave way beneath her feet, but it felt good in the moccasins. It would have been impossible to make progress in her abandoned satin heels, but the moccasins were comfortable and protected her feet.

She lifted her lace-covered skirt with both hands and stalked forward. If only he hadn't cried. Then she could have yelled at him and gotten it over with; released some of this horrible anger that had built up inside her. Who really thought it was a good idea for men to suddenly be sensitive? She was sick and tired of sensitive men who cried at the drop of a hat, men who wanted to get in touch with their feminine side. Wilson was a wimp, and she should be happy to be rid of him.

What had happened to real men? History was her favorite subject, the section of the library she

19

knew best. On slow afternoons she would pull a history book from the shelf and read. It didn't matter what time period; she loved it all. Jean Laffite. Daniel Boone. Eric the Red. Would any one of them have cried to her that they just weren't right for one another?

No. All the real men were gone. Where were the knights? The marauding pirates? The conquerors? These days men cared only about how much money they could amass through a minimum of effort. They watched football and basketball and hockey on television, territorial games safely observed from a comfortable chair. Losers. There were no more knights.

And it wasn't fair. Why hadn't she lived in another time? Just a hundred years earlier. As history went, a hundred years was nothing. And everything.

Catalina realized that she was squeezing the yellow crystal the old Indian had given her, and she unfolded her fingers slowly. A sharp edge had cut into her palm just slightly, and a drop of blood marred one corner of the wulfenite.

She lifted her head and looked to the tallest of the red rocks in the distance. She'd like to climb that rock, just to see if she could get to the top. It was calling her, and she realized as that thought came to her just how bizarre it was. But true, just the same.

The wulfenite was burning her hand, and she looked down. The sun struck it so that it shone with a bright light, and it really did seem to burn her palm.

Catalina dropped the crystal, and as it fell it

got tangled in a scrap of the lace that covered her satin skirt. A cloud of sand rose from Catalina's feet as she tried to shake the crystal free, afraid to touch it again. Then she forgot about the crystal as the cloud grew, churning and whirling, growing wider and taller until it encompassed her completely. She could see nothing but the swirling sand, could hear nothing but the wind that hadn't been there a moment before.

And then the whirlwind stole her breath. She couldn't inhale; she couldn't move. Her glasses were ripped from her face, and Catalina closed her eyes against the sand that surrounded her.

A sandstorm. Here? Now? With no warning? If only she could breathe. The lack of air was making her light-headed. She felt almost as if she were floating, or flying, or drifting without control into the air. It was frightening, even though she told herself that she couldn't be doing any of those things. Her moccasined feet were still firmly on the sand.

Nerves. It was her last coherent thought before the tightness in her chest and the swimming in her head eclipsed everything else. She'd never been prone to fits of nerves. It was just a simple sandstorm . . . there was no explicable reason why she couldn't *breathe.*

Just when she was certain she would pass out from lack of oxygen, the whirlwind subsided. She took a deep breath and opened her eyes, watching the sand around her fall to the ground like heavy snow.

The wulfenite was still tangled in a torn scrap of lace, and she disengaged it carefully. It no

21

longer glowed, no longer seemed . . . alive. Catalina searched the ground around her for her glasses but gave up the search quickly. Buried under the sand, no doubt. No problem; there was a spare pair in the glove compartment.

She looked again at the red rock in the distance. It was as foreboding as ever, but she didn't imagine the towering landmark calling her as it had before. It had just been a very long day. Catalina turned around to head back to the station. There was nothing there. Nothing but sand and sun and those ugly little bushes. Surely she hadn't walked that far! She squinted, cursing the loss of her glasses, and walked in what she was certain was the right direction. Nothing. Not even a speck in the distance.

She veered a little, changing course, then righted herself again. She had left the station and headed straight for the rocks. It had to be there. It *had* to be.

But it wasn't. She walked, confused and just beginning to be scared, for at least a half an hour. Even if she'd missed the station, she should've found the road. She walked a while longer, and still she saw nothing.

With a resigned sigh, Catalina sat down in the sand and decided it would be quite all right to cry again, if she really wanted to. She was hopelessly lost.

Chapter Two

She didn't cry after all, but sat in the sand with her knees drawn up and her arms locked around her legs. The wulfenite, clasped lightly in one hand, was now cool to the touch, so she was almost certain she had imagined its earlier heat.

Well, this was a fitting end to the day, getting lost in the desert. Surely Stu and Allie would have missed her by now. Surely they would look for her, or call the police, or both. Catalina listened for the sound of someone—anyone—calling her name, but there was nothing but silence. It was complete, deep and strangely comforting, even though she knew she should be terrified.

This, too, she could blame on Wilson. She should be at her own wedding reception right now, or perhaps leaving for her honeymoon. Instead she was sitting in the sand, lost and alone and feeling sorry for herself.

The red sun was low in the sky, filling her with an odd kind of peace. Such beauty, all around her. The desert, the towering red rocks, the sky. Sometimes she got into such a rut at the library that she went weeks, months, without seeing anything so beautiful.

And then she saw the rider. A fuzzy figure on

horseback, a dot on the horizon riding away from the setting sun. Catalina didn't move, but squinted slightly as she hugged her knees to her chest and waited to see if the rider would come her way. If he looked like he was going to turn, she would stand and scream at the top of her lungs.

But he appeared to be coming straight at her, slowly but surely, a silhouette against the red sunset.

Catalina stood and brushed some of the sand from her wedding dress. Of course it was in her hair and embedded in her skin, but until she got out of this mess there was nothing to be done for that. Once her Mustang was running maybe she'd head for Phoenix or Tucson. She'd find a hotel, check in, soak in the bath, and order room service. Of course, she'd have to charge it all on plastic, and it would take her months to pay it off, but she deserved to treat herself. She wasn't expected back at the library for another three weeks.

She tucked the wulfenite into the satin waistband of her dusty, sandy, asphalt-stained wedding dress and ignored the pop of a couple of stitches giving way to accommodate the stone that marred the once perfect line of her gown.

Her heart sank a little when she got a good look at the horseman. He probably thought he looked the part of a real cowboy, but he would have been more at home on a Harley. Black boots with shiny silver spurs. Black pants, black duster that hung down to his boots. Black cowboy hat above a shadowed face. All she could see of that face was a closely cropped black beard.

At least the horse wasn't black. That would have been carrying things a bit too far. It was a beautiful animal, a reddish brown that complemented the towerlike rocks in the distance.

He hadn't said a word. The lazy pace of his horse hadn't changed even a beat, and he called no greeting, even when he was almost upon her. Catalina wondered, for a moment, if she'd have to step aside to avoid being run over by that beautiful horse.

"Hello," she offered hesitantly, wondering if she might not have been better off waiting for Stu and Allie to come for her. This man looked . . . dangerous. Not mean, exactly, but calculating. Coldly precise.

"I'm lost," she added when he brought his horse to a halt not ten feet from her.

"Do tell." The voice that answered her was smooth and low.

"Yes. You see, my Mustang died on the highway, and I walked to a station down the road," Catalina said quickly. This man made her nervous. He was too quiet. "But then I wandered off and I couldn't find my way back."

The cowboy swung from the saddle gracefully, as if he'd made that move a thousand times. "There's no station around here," he said suspiciously, closing the gap between them.

"Yes, there is. It's a small place, and not in very good shape, but it's right on that two-lane road that runs from Indian Springs to the main highway."

"Indian Springs?"

Catalina nodded.

"Never heard of it."

Catalina stepped forward, offering her hand. "I'm sorry. I should have introduced myself. Catalina Lane. I'm a librarian from Indian Springs."

The cowboy didn't take her hand, but looked around suspiciously. There was no place nearby for anyone to be hiding, but that seemed to be exactly what he was looking for. He was apparently satisfied that she was who she claimed to be. Catalina could almost see him relax as he removed his hat from his head.

"Most folks just call me Kid. Kid Creede."

Catalina barely heard him. Above the black beard and a slightly too long nose were a pair of the most gorgeous pale blue eyes she had ever seen. Real blue, without any gray or green. Clear and bright and piercing.

"Kid?" she repeated, confused. "Oh, like Billy the Kid."

"Yeah. Except he's dead and I'm not."

Kid. Kid Creede had black hair to go with the rest of his dark ensemble, hanging to his shoulders and touched at the tips with a reddish brown, where it had been bleached by the sun.

"But that's not your real name," Catalina said almost defensively. "What . . ." She grinned as the solution came to her. "Are they filming another movie around here?" Of course. No wonder the man was so gorgeous. He was an actor!

"A what?" he asked, deadly serious.

Catalina nodded her head slightly. She could play along.

He was preparing for a part, immersing himself in the role.

"Never mind," she said, waving her hand dismissively.

"I guess I'll have to take you to the nearest town," Kid Creede said, making it clear that it wasn't going to be a pleasant task. Making it perfectly clear by the tone of his voice that he would prefer to leave her right where she stood. Just her luck, to wish for a knight and get a surly urban cowboy instead.

"I really would appreciate it."

He turned his back on her, placing his hat back on his head. That long duster whipped around his legs, and with every step he took away from her those spurs jingled. His reticence made Catalina want to beat her fists against that stiff back. Really! He could be a little more civil. Chivalry truly was dead. How many more times . . . that day . . . did she need to have that fact drilled into her?

Kid Creede mounted his horse with the same grace he'd displayed when he'd dismounted. He really was at home in that saddle. For a moment Catalina thought he was going to ride off and leave her, and panic welled up inside her. What if no one else found her?

But once he was seated, Kid Creede offered her his hand, and when she took it and stepped into the stirrup he pulled her up to sit behind him.

"I really do appreciate this," Catalina said nervously as she grabbed onto the duster with both hands. She couldn't bring herself to wrap her arms around his waist, even though she would've

27

Linda Jones

felt more securely seated if she had. "I feel really stupid, getting lost. I've just had . . . a very bad day."

His only answer was a grunt, as low and smooth as his voice. He didn't ask her about her "bad day," and he didn't tell her it was no trouble to take her to the nearest town. At least, she consoled herself, he didn't pretend to care. He was honest, in his own rude way. If Wilson had been honest a little sooner, she wouldn't be in this mess.

"I'll be happy to pay you for your time, Kid, after I get back to my Mustang."

There was a short pause before he spoke. "I thought you said your mustang died."

"With any luck Stu will have it fixed before I get back."

Without breaking the horse's stride, Kid Creede turned to look at her. She smiled, just a little, to ease the frown that marred his face.

"I expect no payment, Miss Lane," he said quietly, and then he turned his face and those piercing eyes away from her.

Loco. If he'd known she was loco he would have left her where he'd found her. He tried to tell himself that, though he knew it wasn't true.

Catalina Lane was holding on to his duster, trying very hard not to touch him. That was good. He was already much too aware of her. She smelled too sweet, and her skin looked too soft. And that hair . . . a tangled mess for certain, but it was as golden as the motherlode, and looked as soft as her skin.

But she was definitely loco. Her mustang had died, and some way-station boss was going to *fix* it?

Jackson Cady kept his eyes straight ahead. There wasn't much light left. Soon they'd have to stop for the night. Hell, he had one bedroll, one tin cup, one tin plate. Tonight there would be nothing but hardtack and coffee, and they would just have to share the cup. She could have the bedroll to herself.

A potential job had brought Jackson, better known as Kid Creede, to Arizona Territory again. He liked it here. He didn't have quite the reputation he'd acquired in Colorado, so he felt a little safer. Still, people in the territory knew of him, and many feared him. But Catalina Lane had never even heard of him. If she had, she would've run when he'd given her his name. Everybody who knew of Kid Creede knew he was a cold-blooded killer who didn't even blink as he killed men, women, children . . . never mind that most of the stories weren't true. Well, some of them were true, but he'd never shot a woman before, and he didn't aim to start now. Kids, either, unless you counted that seventeen-year-old who'd drawn on him in Cheyenne. What did it matter that he'd been sixteen himself at the time?

He'd been Kid Creede since the age of fifteen. Been a gunman for a year more than half his life. Jackson Cady was almost completely gone, now, so few people knew him by his given name. He made his living as a hired gun, and had for years. Land disputes, towns gone wild . . . Sometimes he fought on the side of the law. Sometimes he didn't.

But there was always justice in the battles he fought. It was bad enough that he'd been saddled with a reputation that was unwanted and—at least at first—undeserved. He wouldn't allow himself to be turned into just another shootist. A gunslinger with no conscience. The day that happened, Jackson Cady would be gone, and Kid Creede would be all alone.

He brought the horse to a halt and looked around carefully. A rock not much taller than Catalina Lane herself would buffer the wind, were it to rise in the night, and there were no other obstacles. He'd be able to see approaching riders.

Jackson twisted around to assist his passenger to the ground, taking her hand in his.

"You're not going to leave me here, are you?" There was real panic in her voice.

"No. We're stopping here for the night."

"I can't spend the night here," she said stubbornly, refusing to budge from her seat.

"Fine."

Jackson released her hand, grabbed her around the waist, and all but dropped her to the ground.

"Baxter is thataway."

She stepped back as he dismounted. "Baxter is thataway?" she repeated. "Is that all you have to say?"

"I'll be headed there in the morning, and you're welcome to ride along."

"I'd be better off trying to find the highway on

my own," she said, turning her back on him and taking three strides in the direction they'd just come from.

She stopped, and he heard a deep, dejected sigh. It would soon be completely dark, and even the loco Catalina Lane knew that.

"Tomorrow morning," she said, resignation in her voice.

Jackson started a small fire, and then he tended to his gelding. Catalina Lane just stared away from him, lost in her own little world. Loco. Just his luck.

She didn't turn back around until he offered her some hardtack and first crack at the coffee in his single tin cup. She took the hardtack but declined the coffee.

"I can't drink coffee this late," she said, taking the canteen he offered her. "Caffeine and I have never gotten along very well."

Jackson sat near the fire, sipped at the strong, hot coffee, and watched the woman pace. He wanted to ask her who Caffeine was, wondered if he was a husband or a gentleman friend, and what he had to do with drinking coffee in the evening.

"Fancy dress," he said, the words slipping out before he could stop them.

Catalina Lane grabbed the full skirt with one hand and displayed the lace and silk dress. "My wedding dress," she said wistfully. "It cost me a fortune. I know I shouldn't say that. Weddings take place only once, or so I hear, and I shouldn't complain about the cost, even though a librarian doesn't make much."

"What does your husband do? Does he live in . . . Indian Springs?"

Catalina capped the canteen and joined him by the fire. Firelight on satin and lace and golden hair almost mesmerized him, it was so oddly . . . wonderful.

"No husband. He . . ." She stopped and swallowed hard. He could see the gentle workings of her throat. "He stood me up. Changed his mind."

Jackson couldn't imagine anyone leaving this woman at the altar, lunatic or not.

"Why?" he asked softly, immediately regretting his impulsive question.

She looked directly at him, unembarrassed, chin lifted stubbornly and defiantly. "He doesn't love me."

"So? What does that have to do with marriage?"

Catalina smiled. "You're right, of course. I suppose it would have been an even worse disaster if we had married, and *then* he'd changed his mind. Thanks, Kid. Right to the heart of the matter."

Jackson looked away from her smile and into the fire. How she'd come away with that from his comment about love and marriage, he couldn't figure.

"You can have the bedroll," he said sharply. "I won't get to sleep for a while, anyway."

"Caffeine," she said knowingly.

Jackson dismissed her strange comment. "We'll set out early, at first light, and we'll probably reach Baxter sometime in the afternoon."

"The afternoon?"

Jackson ignored her distress and tossed the bedroll a good ten feet away from the fire. Best to get this woman a good distance away from him. He didn't intend to pamper her, or comfort her, golden hair or not.

She lay on the bedroll, still grumbling to herself. He caught a few words, bits and pieces of her conversation with herself that made sense. The word *men* was repeated again and again with more vengeance than the rest of her soliloquy, and so he heard those sharp words clearly.

He could have sworn he heard the angry words *blue eyes* once, but that didn't make any sense. Finally she was quiet, and Jackson did his best to forget that she was there. He stared into the fire and thought about the job that awaited him in Baxter. Sounded like Goodman was involved in another land dispute, but he didn't know much more than that. A letter requesting his presence and accompanied by two hundred dollars had brought him here. More was promised. A lot more.

Once in Baxter, he'd drop Catalina Lane off at the sheriff's office, if there still was one, and be about his business. Once she was there, his unwanted responsibility was done.

"Good night, Kid," she offered softly. Christ! He had almost managed to forget that she was there.

"Good night, Miss Lane."

"Call me Catalina," she said almost dreamily. "Every time someone calls me Miss Lane I think of Lois, and I expect Superman to drop down out of the sky and scoop me up."

Lunatic.

"Good night, Catalina."

"Good night, Kid Creede."

Catalina rolled onto her side and watched Kid Creede. She should have been frightened, or at the very least cautious. He was a stranger, and they were all alone literally in the middle of nowhere. What if he was a serial killer? A mass murderer on the run and hiding in the desert? A sociopath who would kill her in her sleep? None of these possibilities bothered her. They didn't even cause her heartbeat to quicken. Because she knew they couldn't be true.

The fire lit his face, that bearded chin and that sharp nose, but she couldn't see his eyes. His hair fell across his face as he leaned forward, hair that waved just enough. Not curly, not straight. She knew women who would kill for hair like that.

If he'd been grinning and super friendly . . . then she might have panicked. False smiles were the ones a woman had to worry about.

But Kid Creede was so solitary, so lonely . . . so distant. He was a reluctant rescuer, a man who would obviously prefer to be alone here in the desert.

Kid Creede stood and shucked off his duster, the motion as graceful as every other move the man made. Like a cat. But Catalina didn't have much time to admire his grace before she saw a sight that stole her breath away.

Two shiny six-shooters, one on each hip, were revealed as the duster was removed. They were as at home there as the silver spurs on Kid Creede's boots.

She held her breath as he put the duster on the ground beside his saddle. The saddle he used as a pillow as he stretched out his long body. The holster and pistols were not removed.

An actor, Catalina reminded herself. They weren't real weapons, they were props. He wasn't a real desperado; he was a struggling actor. She knew he was struggling, because she was positive she would have remembered that face if she'd seen it before. Kid Creede—whatever his name was—was simply losing himself in some sort of method acting.

Well, she'd have all day tomorrow to find out what Kid Creede was all about. An entire day in the saddle to prod him with the questions that suddenly plagued her.

What was his real name? Where was he from? Was he . . . married?

She rolled away to face the black desert. How utterly ridiculous. She was much too sensible to be attracted to any man while she was still reeling from what Wilson had done to her. Kid Creede would take her to Baxter, wherever that was, and she'd call Kim, and she'd get her Mustang, and . . . and what?

Chapter Three

"So, where is Baxter, exactly?" Catalina leaned slightly to the side, tightening her grip on Kid Creede's black duster so she wouldn't fall. She was tired of looking at his stiff back, tired of enduring the silence. "I mean, what's it close to?"

She thought for a moment that he was going to ignore her completely, but after a long pause he answered in that low, smooth voice that was just short of silky.

"Not close to anything."

"Is it a small town?"

Again there was that pause. "Baxter is a mining town, for the most part, but there are a few ranches in the area. Nothin' fancy, but it's a good-sized town."

A mining town? Couldn't this Kid Creede forget his role for a moment and join her in the twentieth century? A thought that made her heart quicken popped into her already distressed mind. What if he dropped her off in some ghost town . . . and left her there?

"Are there . . . people in Baxter?"

He twisted to look at her, but she couldn't tell what he was thinking. That black hat was low over his eyes, shading the upper half of his face, and all she could really see was the short black beard covering his cheeks, and his mouth, full and wide and . . . very nice, she thought as she pulled her eyes away from those lips.

"Of course there are people there," he said, as if he were talking to a child, or a dimwit. "Do you have a problem with that, Miss Lane?"

"Catalina. And no, I don't have a problem with that. It's just that I know I've heard of Baxter. It sounds familiar, but I can't quite place it, and I've lived in Indian Springs for seven years."

He faced front again, and Catalina was actually relieved. What a disconcerting face he had. Whatever movie he was going to be in, it was going to make him a star.

"What's your real name?"

"Kid will do."

"But it's not the name your mother gave you."

He didn't answer her, and Catalina resigned herself to never knowing the man's real name . . . unless she saw him at the movies. *In* the movies. And then no one would believe her.

He found me in the desert and rescued me, and I never even knew his name. He was preparing for a role, the one that made him famous, and we rode double on a horse across the desert . . . Kid Creede dressed all in black, me in my wedding dress. The ramblings of a dull spinster librarian no one would ever believe.

Her failed wedding seemed so distant now, so unclear. There was no more heartache, no more anger. It seemed she had recovered quickly from losing Wilson. Maybe he'd been right in calling the marriage off. Right now—still lost, though no longer alone—Catalina felt a surge of excitement. What if she never went back to the library? What if she started a whole new life? It was possible. She had no obligations, no family. A postcard to Kim would explain her whereabouts, and all she'd have to do was reclaim her Mustang and start fresh.

"Do you think," she began hesitantly, "that you could help me get a job in Baxter?" If they were filming a movie there, surely she could get a job doing . . . something. She could be a gofer. She could make sandwiches, and sweep, and fetch coffee. Maybe she could even powder Kid Creede's nose.

"What kind of a job?" Kid Creede asked.

Catalina stretched out her legs and hiked her skirt almost mindlessly to her knees, allowing a bit of cool air to circulate beneath her skirts. "I don't know. Really, I'm not particular. I can do anything."

Kid Creede looked down at her calf, then quickly raised his head to face front again. "Sorry, I can't help you. It's been years since I've been there."

"Oh." It didn't really matter. She could try to get a job there on her own, but it would have been nice to have some help.

"I just don't want to go back to Indian Springs right away. My friends will be sympathetic and they'll try to lift my spirits, and I really don't think I can take that right now."

"You'll be able to find something in Baxter."

"I hope so." Catalina shifted slightly, trying to ease the discomfort of sitting for so long on horseback. She wasn't a rider, and even if she had been, it wouldn't have prepared her for this. Two to a horse was very uncomfortable. She squirmed a little more, shifting a little to the left, and then a little to the right. If she ever had to choose a garment to get lost in the desert in, it wouldn't be a full-skirted satin-and-lace wedding dress. Not only was the gown ruined, it was far from comfortable. There was too much material to handle, and it was too snug in the arms and the waist. The moccasins she had bought from the old man outside the gas station were comfortable, though. She lifted one foot and hiked up the skirt again to admire the shoe. White buckskin, adorned with blue and white beads. She turned her ankle, circling her foot slowly. These were much more practical than the satin pumps she had tossed away as she walked the highway.

Kid Creede brought the horse to a sudden stop, and Catalina let her leg drop. He helped her roughly to the ground without a word, and then he dismounted himself.

He wasn't looking at her. He led the horse to a trickle of a stream, and then knelt beside the stream to splash his face with water.

Catalina turned away from him to study the desolate land that surrounded them. They'd been riding for hours, and still they'd seen no one, nothing of civilization. The land was changing, a little. It wasn't sand beneath her feet, but grainy soil. There were white rocks, boulders really, rising from the ground. She could almost imagine that they were only the tips of gigantic buried mountains.

She turned back to the stream and a silent Kid Creede. "I'm so glad we're taking a rest stop," she said, trying to be friendly. "I swear, my butt aches. Even my legs. Of course, I've only been on a horse once, and that was years ago."

Kid Creede stood slowly, unfolding his tall frame in a smooth way that was almost . . . poetic. He tossed his hat aside, sending it sailing with a flick of his wrist to land on a flat white rock near the water. His black duster he simply shrugged off.

Why was he looking at her like that? He stood there, still as a statue, staring at her with those pale blue eyes.

And then he started walking toward her, long strides that brought him to her quickly. He took her chin in his hand, cool, easy fingers against her skin, and tilted her face up. And she knew that he was going to kiss her.

And she wanted him to. Heaven help her, she wanted this man, this stranger without a name, to kiss her.

She parted her lips when they met his, closing her eyes and abandoning all her reservations simply to feel. His warmth, the softness of his lips, the big hands that stole around her softly to rest against her back. Kid Creede was so tall, so big, that she felt dwarfed in his arms. She didn't feel helpless, but sheltered. Warm.

When he touched her tongue with his, Catalina wrapped her arms around him, holding on for dear life. She could feel her heart pounding, and the blood rushing through her veins, and a strong and strange sensation grew deep within her. If she didn't hold on tight, she would surely sink to the ground.

He took his lips from hers but continued to hold her. Catalina opened her eyes and looked up into his. Those pale blue eyes were still piercing, but softened somehow.

"I've never kissed a man with a beard before," she whispered, expecting him to release her.

But he didn't release her. He smiled, a small and almost wistful smile, and then he kissed her again. Harder this time, more demanding. Catalina wanted to lose herself in this kiss as she had in the last one, but the intensity frightened her. His mouth left hers and trailed across her cheek and down her throat, and the hands at her back expertly and quickly unfastened the first several of the tiny buttons that ran from the back of her neck to well past her waist.

"Stop that," she said weakly, and the hands at her back stilled as Kid Creede brought his face back to hers.

His eyes were half closed, his lips parted slightly, and that sight alone made her insides quicken. She wasn't completely stupid, though she felt like it at the moment. The kiss had been wonderful, and she had lost herself, and now Kid Creede believed that she wanted to make love to him on the rocky ground. At this moment, with him looking at her like that, she almost did.

"I can't," she said simply.

He gave her another of those small smiles. "Of course you can, darlin'."

He abandoned his efforts at her back and brought his hands to her sides. Catalina gave him a nervous smile, but her relief was short-lived. Kid Creede grabbed her skirt and starting hiking it up.

"Stop it," Catalina ordered in her strongest voice, a poor effort that was no more than a rasping whisper. "I'm warning you . . ."

Kid Creede placed his face close to hers again, and now she saw something more than desire in his eyes. She saw anger, and that frightened her. "You're warning me?" he whispered.

Catalina didn't give him another warning. She twisted to the side, grabbed him just as she'd been taught in the self-defense class she and Kim had taken, and flipped a man who was well over six feet tall ass over head to land on his back at her feet.

Kid Creede stayed on the ground for a long moment. The dust around him settled over his black shirt and pants and in his hair and over his face. It occurred to Catalina, briefly, that if she was going to run, now was the time to do it. But where would she run to?

When Kid Creede finally moved all he did was sit up and dust off his shirt. "What the hell did you do?"

"I told you to stop," Catalina said defensively. "I warned you . . ."

"Yes, you did."

"I'm not . . ." Catalina offered him her hand, but he stayed put and refused to accept her help. ". . . I mean, I'm sorry if I gave you the wrong impression."

Desperado's Gold

"The wrong impression? You've been waving your . . . your legs in front of me all morning. What was I supposed to think?"

Catalina was no longer frightened of the man who continued to sit on the ground. The desire and the anger were gone from his eyes, and he looked . . . resigned, there at her feet.

"I was just trying to cool off a bit. You have no idea how hot these long dresses can be."

Kid Creede hiked up one knee and stared at her with skeptically narrowed eyes. Finally he took her offered hand, and she pulled him to his feet.

"I didn't mean to . . . well, never mind, Kid."

"Jackson," he said, turning his back on her. "Jackson Cady."

Jackson stepped into the saddle and grudgingly assisted Catalina Lane into her position behind him. If she would just sit still for the rest of the trip . . .

It had been bad enough last night, when he'd thought her to be a lady. A lunatic lady, but still a lady. But today, when she'd squirmed behind him, trying not to touch him but finding that an impossible task, he'd been painfully aware of her. Showing her limbs, as she had, and speaking crudely. Aching butt. Sore legs. No lady would dare say *butt* or *leg* aloud in mixed company. For all he knew, a lady didn't even *think* of her own butt, or anyone else's.

And she'd kissed him back. She'd wanted him to kiss her, and she'd opened up to him like a flower in the desert after the rain . . . almost.

He'd been too long without a woman. That was

why he felt so strongly attracted to this woman, why he'd believed she was willing. Hell, more than willing. Once he got to Baxter he'd make a stop at Alberta's place . . . if it was still there. If the town had survived, he had no doubt that Alberta would have survived as well.

In a land where few women had settled, but for a handful of miners' and farmers' wives, places like Alberta's were necessary, and they profitted and flourished as the towns did.

How long had it been since his last visit to Baxter? Five years? Maybe longer. Old man Goodman had needed his help fending off squatters. He hadn't had to do any shooting, just make an appearance and spread his name. An easy job.

Alberta's place had been small, but she'd had four girls, a couple of gaming tables, and a stock of strong liquor. Jackson didn't gamble, and he limited himself to no more than one shot of whiskey. In his business he couldn't afford to get sloppy.

But right now he definitely needed an evening with one of the women, an evening in one of the upstairs rooms.

He wondered if Juanita was still at Alberta's. Tall and dark and by far the most openly seductive woman he had ever known, she had all but claimed him as her own on his last trip to Baxter. He didn't hold out much hope that she would still be there. She'd probably snared some miner who'd hit it rich and moved back East, or to San Francisco. He seemed to remember Juanita talking an awful lot about going to San Francisco.

Alberta herself was strictly a businesswoman.

From what he remembered, she didn't even like men much, and he'd never known her to entertain a customer. Not a bad-looking woman, as tall as Juanita and almost as dark, but wider in the shoulders and the hips. Alberta had a distinctive hip-swinging walk that could be spotted a mile away and a coarse voice that didn't fit her fair face. Not beautiful, but regular and free of scars and deep wrinkles.

Catalina started squirming again, brushing her thighs against his hips, brushing his back lightly . . . with her breasts? Christ, the woman was trying to make him as loco as she was.

"Could you please sit still?" he snapped.

All movement ceased. "Sorry," she said in a low voice. "I was just trying to get comfortable."

"Well . . . stop it. You're not going to be comfortable until we get to Baxter."

She sighed deeply but remained still. "Jackson. That's a nice name. I like it much better than Kid."

Jackson made no response, even though she paused, as though waiting for one.

"Where are you from, Jackson?"

She just couldn't leave well enough alone. She couldn't simply be still and quiet until they reached Baxter.

"Colorado, mostly."

" 'Mostly'?"

Jackson didn't feel that question warranted a response, so he didn't offer one.

"Where in Colorado?"

Damn, she was persistent. "I lived in Creede

45

from the time I was eleven or twelve until I was fifteen."

"And after that?"

Jackson shrugged slightly. He didn't want to be having this conversation with this woman. "I traveled around a lot."

"Is that where you got your nickname? Kid Creede? From the town where you lived?"

Jackson was tired of talking; he was tired of answering Catalina Lane's endless questions. He was going to have to scare her off.

"Creede is the place where I killed my first man, when I was fifteen."

"I see," she said, no fear but a healthy dose of amusement in her voice. "In a shootout on the street?"

Damn her, he could hear the smile in her voice, that whiskey-eyed witch.

"Something like that."

"And how many men have you killed since then?" she asked lightly.

"I stopped counting ten years ago."

"Oh, really, you must have a number. Every decent gunslinger has to be able to say, 'I kilt eighty-seven men, two of 'em jest for lookin' at me cockeyed.' "

He resisted the urge to turn in the saddle and look at her. "Not quite eighty-seven, and I never shot anybody for lookin' at me cockeyed." She should be scared, terrified, not amused. But the only thing that had terrified Catalina Lane had been the kiss. He could touch her and she'd be trembling, while she all but laughed at the violence that had filled his life.

"Catalina Lane, you're a strange woman," he observed, shaking his head.

"I'm strange?" She leaned to the side. He could feel the weight on his duster shift. "I'm not the one riding around in the desert pretending to be a . . . a . . . a fictional character out of the past. Really." She slipped from her perch and grabbed onto his waist with both hands to keep herself from falling to the ground. She clung to him tightly for a long moment, and he was almost certain she was holding her breath.

"Wait a minute," she said as she righted herself and loosened the arms around his waist. "Kid Creede wasn't a fictional character. Aisle nine, almost to the end, bottom shelf. I can't believe I almost forgot. It's the only book I ever saw him mentioned in, and he's a minor historical figure, certainly. Why are you making a movie about him?"

Jackson shook his head. It was lucky that she had stopped him before anything more than a kiss had happened. He didn't want to be saddled with a lunatic. What the hell was a movie?

"Let's see. Kid Creede. Got caught up in a land war in . . . in . . . Baxter! Jackson, you could have told me, though I've decided you're not the most talkative man I've ever met. Is the movie about the land war? Does Kid Creede have a big part or a small one? Let's see . . ." She shifted in her seat, and Jackson resisted the urge to tell her—again—to be still.

"I don't think there was more than a paragraph or two, and there was no picture. Kid Creede was

47

killed in Baxter, wasn't he? Ambushed by . . . by
. . . I don't remember."

He knew she was loco, but the words sent a
chill down his spine. Ambushed in Baxter. It was
a risk he'd lived with most of his life, particularly
when he got involved in these land disputes. But
it wasn't pleasant to hear it voiced as a fact.

"Catalina." He said her name in a calm voice,
displaying none of the fire she ignited in him . . .
one way or another. "If you don't shut up, I'm
going to dump you on the ground and let you
walk the rest of the way."

"You wouldn't dare," she said sulkily.

His silence must have been sufficient response
to that, because once again Catalina Lane was—
thankfully—silent and still as death.

Chapter Four

"This is great," Catalina said, leaning to the side so she could get a better look at the town that stretched before them. "It looks so real."

Kid Creede, Jackson Cady, said nothing, but she heard an uncustomary deep sigh.

The town of Baxter had been perfectly re-created. The few people she saw were in costume, and the single dirt street was lined with hitching posts and buildings—adobe and wood—that looked eerily authentic. There was a saloon to the right, with wide terraces on the second and third floor. A general store, sprawling and busy, was directly across the street from the saloon. A costumed lady in a calico dress swept out of the general store, took one look at Catalina and Jackson and, with her nose in the air, turned her back just as Catalina waved energetically.

Jackson stopped in front of the saloon, and Catalina glanced up at the sign that hung over the door. It appeared to be freshly painted, a sign of the prosperity of the place, she supposed. The general store sign was properly weathered, as were most of the others on the street. But there it was, Alberta's Saloon, painted in red on white and hanging over the batwing doors.

He helped her to the ground and in a moment was beside her, his movements fast and smooth. Those pale blue eyes took in everything, searching the almost deserted street and the windows that faced it.

"Thanks for the ride, Jackson." Catalina tried to smile, but her escort wasn't cooperating. He all but ignored her, and she felt, for a moment, as if she didn't even exist for him. "Who should I see about a job?"

He did glance at her then, with a calculating gleam in his eyes. "You could check at the general store, or see if the hotel needs any help with the laundry or the kitchen."

Neither of those options seemed very exciting, and Catalina frowned. "Anything else?"

He nodded to the batwing doors. "You could always go to work for Alberta."

Catalina looked toward the saloon. "I did learn the cancan when I was twelve or thirteen. I don't remember exactly what year it was. Dance class," she added. "It might be fun to work in a real Old West saloon. Do you think I could wear one of those costumes? You know, red silk and black stockings and a feather in my hair?"

Jackson closed his eyes and shook his head slightly. Why did he have to look so irritated? As if she'd done something wrong? "I'm sure Alberta would be happy to have you, and if you want a red and black costume, I'm sure she'll arrange to have one made. Alberta is very . . . accommodating where her girls are concerned."

The doors to the saloon swung open, and a busty woman who looked to be approaching

50

middle age burst through. Her costume was nothing like the simple calico the lady from the general store had worn. Her ample breasts looked about to spring from the tight bodice of Catalina's dream red silk dress. She had a tiny waist, but her hips were wide and swung as she stepped onto the boardwalk, the motion as certain as the continued sway of the doors.

"Kid Creede, you old dog." She greeted Jackson in a husky voice, opening her arms wide. "Where the hell have you been keeping yourself?"

Jackson removed his hat and stepped forward. "Here and there," he said softly as the busty woman wrapped her arms around him and gave him a chaste kiss on a bearded cheek.

Catalina squirmed impatiently, abandoned there beside Jackson's horse and filled with a sudden awareness of her appearance. She knew she must look a mess. Her dress was dirty, and her hair hadn't seen a comb for two days. She could use a bath, too.

She felt a little better when the woman released Jackson.

"Alberta, this is Catalina Lane. She's looking for a job here in Baxter."

Alberta turned her calculating eyes to Catalina, but her perusal didn't last long. Another woman burst through the doors with a squeal that pierced Catalina's brain.

This woman, dark-skinned and with a gorgeous head of flowing black hair, threw her arms around Jackson just as Alberta had, but she held on and continued to squeal. She wrapped her long, skinny legs around Jackson's and offered her lips to him for a kiss.

He didn't hesitate. He gave her a long and passionate kiss, eyes closed and mouth open, that made Catalina's stomach do a sick flip. Alberta was watching them with a satisfied smile, and then she turned her eyes back to Catalina.

"So. You're looking for a job?"

Catalina ignored the spectacle Jackson was making of himself and faced the impressive Alberta. She had a soft and pretty face, and brown hair that was tightly curled and piled high on her head. Still, there was something in her eyes . . . something hard. Jaded.

"Yes," Catalina said confidently.

"Why?"

Catalina licked her lips. "Well, to be honest with you, I was supposed to be married yesterday, but the man I was supposed to marry . . . changed his mind. There's no place I need to be for a while, if ever, and I'm looking to make a change in my life."

Alberta smiled. "To be beholden to no man."

Catalina nodded.

"To take charge of your own life."

Catalina nodded again. Alberta tipped her head slightly, tucking in her chin in a way that was almost girlish . . . and slightly bizarre on the aging woman. "Have you no family, Miss Lane?"

Catalina shook her head.

Alberta's smile was broad. "Honey, we're all here for the same reason. Can you see me as some farmer's wife with a passel of kids?" Fortunately, she didn't wait for an answer. "We'll get you cleaned up in no time, dress you in some suitable clothes . . ." She looked Catalina up and down. There was approval in her eyes as she nodded her head.

Catalina allowed the woman to take her arm. "I think you'll do nicely," Alberta purred.

Catalina looked at Jackson's back. He was still kissing that . . . that tramp. "You mean, I'm going to be an extra?"

Alberta looked a little puzzled, wrinkling her brow and pursing her full lips, and she continued to hold Catalina's arm, gently but firmly. "We can always use an extra girl."

As Catalina passed Jackson and the dark-haired hussy, she pretended to trip, and her shoulder thudded against Jackson's back.

All her force, and he barely moved. But he dropped the trollop and turned his head to Catalina, silently staring down at her.

He knew she'd done it on purpose. Catalina could see that in the set of his damp mouth and the fire in his hooded eyes.

"Thank you, Kid," she said sweetly, "for not leaving me in the desert to perish of thirst."

He could have said "You're welcome," or "No problem," or even a surly "Sure." But he said nothing.

The slut wound her arm through Jackson's and glared at Catalina. "Come on upstairs, Kid. I've missed you so much," she cooed.

Jackson leaned his body toward the tramp, resting a portion of his weight on her shoulder. Catalina carefully restrained a sigh. She should've known; he was too good-looking not to be attached.

"Tonight, Juanita," he said, in that silky voice that suddenly made Catalina's toes curl. "I've got business to see to."

What might've been a smile started to cross his lips. "Maybe I'll see you tonight as well, Catalina Lane."

Catalina smiled brightly, ignoring the challenge in his voice. She could give this harlot—she had a name, now: Juanita—a run for her money. And Jackson was interested. He was definitely interested in her. It was that competitive streak within her—the one that was always getting her into trouble—that made her refuse to back down.

"Maybe you will."

She could clean up, and dress in one of those skimpy outfits—well, skimpy compared to the wedding dress that now seemed about to choke her—and put on a little makeup and fix her hair.

Alberta chuckled and Juanita glared, narrowing her black eyes. Jackson just raised his eyebrows and blinked quickly a couple of times.

"Maybe you will," she repeated, turning away from Jackson Cady and allowing Alberta to lead her into the dim saloon.

Jackson stabled his horse at the livery and walked to the prearranged meeting place. By now, the man who had sent for him would know he was in town and would be waiting.

It was a ramshackle little house off an alley, built onto the back of what had been a dressmaker's shop five years ago. That building was vacant now. Must not be much call for fancy dresses and such in a mining town.

Of course, Catalina Lane would be needing new things. Dresses and shoes and ribbons . . . all the things women had to have. Alberta would likely take care of all that for Catalina. For her new girl.

Is that what she was? A soiled dove? Jackson had never claimed to understand women, but he never would have thought . . . it never would have occurred to him that Catalina was that kind of woman. Like Juanita and Alberta. If he had offered to pay her there in the desert, would she still have done . . . whatever it was she had done . . . and put him on his back?

He walked through the alleyway with an unexpected smile creeping across his face. She'd surprised him, and he had to admit he respected that. Admired her, even. If she'd cried or screamed, he would have been disgusted with her and with his own lack of control. But she'd taken care of herself. Catalina Lane had done what any number of men had tried and failed to do; she'd flattened Kid Creede.

And tonight she'd most likely flatten him again. The smile faded as he faced the door and knocked rapidly. Thinking about the woman was going to get him killed, if he didn't watch it. There was a time and a place for giving his attention to women. Any woman. Places like Alberta's.

The door swung open, and Jackson laid his right hand over one six-shooter, ready to draw if necessary. But the old man who opened the door looked familiar, and even greeted Jackson with a weak smile.

"Come on in, Kid," the old man said shakily, watching closely the hand that still hovered over his weapon.

"Walter, isn't it?" Jackson asked crisply, stepping into the dimly lit room. Goodman's right-hand man, if he remembered correctly. And he always did. The last five years hadn't been kind to Walter. His hands shook, and he'd lost a lot of weight. The man had been thin to begin with.

"Where's Goodman?" Jackson asked, searching the darkened single room.

"Right here."

The voice of the man who answered from the dark corner was too young and too cocky to belong to Ben Goodman, and Jackson drew one six-shooter and dropped his stance slightly.

But the figure in the corner raised both hands in a gesture of peace. "I know you're expectin' my old man. I wasn't sure you'd come if I let you know it was me who wanted to hire you."

The man stepped forward, and Jackson reholstered his six-shooter. Little Harold Goodman, only he wasn't a kid any longer. What was he now, twenty-three or-four? He still looked like a kid, but he wasn't gangly, as he had been five years ago. There was a bit of muscle on that thin frame, and Harold was trying to grow a mustache.

"You're probably right," Jackson said, no emotion in his voice.

"Have a seat." Harold dropped one hand and pointed to a rickety-looking chair placed before a small table in the center of the room. Quickly, the younger man stepped to the table and took a similar seat himself. There was a bottle of whiskey in the center of the square table, and two glasses. Harold poured two full measures and took a healthy swallow himself before Jackson sat down. Jackson didn't drink, but lifted the glass and watched the play of light from a single low lantern through the amber liquid. The color of Catalina's eyes.

Damn! The thought had come out of nowhere, and he couldn't afford that. He banged the glass down on the table, and whiskey splashed over the warped wood.

"What do you want, Harold?" he snapped.

Harold smiled. "I would like to retain your services."

Jackson rocked the glass back and forth, maintaining an appearance of calm control.

Harold leaned across the table, bringing that idiotic smile closer. "The ranch has really grown since you were here last. A few people moved on, and I bought them out. A couple of mines have done right well for me, in addition to the ranching. The place has prospered since Pa died."

"When?" Jackson asked quietly. Ben Goodman had been a decent fella. Ambitious, but fair and kind-hearted. Harold seemed to have inherited his father's ambition, but without the temperance of fairness.

"Pa? Oh, he died just over three years ago," Harold said, no hint of sorrow in his voice. Jackson wanted to throw the whiskey at his fingertips in the boy's face, but the restraint he'd developed over the past sixteen years wouldn't allow it.

He didn't have to work for the boy, though.

"What do you want?"

"There's this one ranch that borders us to the west. Hell, old Doc Booker barely makes a living off the place. It's not suited to ranching, and he won't mine it. I want it. I want it, and the old bastard won't sell."

"What do you want me to do?"

Harold's smile widened. "Kill him."

Jackson pushed the whiskey glass to the center of the table and stood slowly. "Sorry. I can't help you."

"What do you mean you can't help me?" At last, Harold's grin faded. He stood quickly, spilling his own whiskey. It rolled across the table and seeped into the dry wood.

"What do you not understand?" Jackson stepped away from the table. This trip had been a waste of time. He could never work for Harold Goodman.

"You're a hired gun! You've killed dozens of people! What's one more?"

Jackson had long ago quit trying to defend himself. People would always believe what they wanted to believe, no matter what he said. He wasn't an assassin.

"You'll have to find someone else, Harold."

"That's Mr. Goodman to you, Kid."

Jackson smiled. "Whatever you say, Mr. Goodman." He couldn't contain the sarcasm that crept into his voice. Harold would never be the man his father had been, not even if he ended up owning all of Arizona Territory.

"Don't you walk out on me," Harold insisted shrilly as Jackson turned away. "Dammit, you'll regret it if you do."

Jackson slammed the door on Harold's protests. Damnation. All this way for nothing. And Harold might be a problem, until Jackson decided it was time to leave town.

He listened for the door behind him to open as he walked down the alley, but all was silent. Harold wasn't completely senseless, after all.

The trip to Baxter didn't have to be a total waste of time. Alberta's was a great place to spend a day or two, or maybe even a week. There was Juanita . . . and Catalina.

Catalina Lane, golden-haired and loco and the prettiest thing this side of the Mississippi. It would definitely take more than a day or two to work her out of his system.

She worked for Alberta now. He had a pocket full of gold and silver coins, and she couldn't say no. She couldn't toss him on his back, either . . . unless that was where he wanted to be.

Catalina sank deeper into the old-fashioned tin tub that sat smack dab in the middle of her room and closed her eyes. She'd never been so thankful for a simple bath before . . . but then, she'd never been quite so dirty before. Her hair was washed and her skin had been scrubbed pink, and still she lingered in the cool water, reluctant to rise.

With her arms draped over the sides of the tub, she surveyed the room she'd been assigned. There was a high bed that looked incredibly soft, and it was covered with a deep green silk comforter and dotted with pillows—large and small—in gold and shades of green. The dresser looked like a real—and very well-preserved—antique, and there was a cheval glass in one corner.

Alberta's was a miraculous re-creation of an old saloon. Even the old tub she sat in, and the outhouse she'd been forced to use. That was carrying things a bit too far, in her opinion. Maybe the director was an eccentric, forcing all the actors to live their roles twenty-four hours a day. Catalina frowned, thinking of one of those performers.

That floozie Juanita was a terrible actress, and her legs were like toothpicks. What did a man like Jackson see in a woman like that? Catalina didn't even try to answer that question. She'd seen the way Juanita had clung to Jackson, had seen the way they kissed. Physical attraction. Sex. In real life or in the movie? Catalina sighed and rubbed her temples with pruning fingers. The line was fading, and she didn't know what was real and what wasn't anymore. All she knew for certain was that Jackson Cady had saved her, and that he was a really good kisser. Catalina raised one leg into the air. All those long walks, the aerobic classes . . . she'd never been able to trim her waist as much as she wanted, but her legs were all right. Next to Juanita's chicken legs, they'd really look good.

The door swung open, and the chicken-legged hussy herself sauntered in, a small stack of clothes in her hands. Green silk and black lace, from what Catalina could see, with black stockings and a pair of black boots like Juanita's sitting on top of the neat stack.

"Alberta asked me to deliver this." Juanita had a slight accent, and you had only to look at her striking face to see that she was of mixed blood. Mexican, certainly, and perhaps some Indian blood as well. Except for her legs, she was beautiful, with pouting lips and black eyes, and really great breasts . . . and a tiny waist. And that hair, black and silky and hanging straight to her waist. She tossed the costume on the end of the bed and turned to leave.

But at the door she stopped and twisted her head to look down at Catalina. "Stay away from Kid Creede," she warned. "He's mine."

"Oh, are you engaged? Married?" Catalina asked casually. "He didn't mention it."

A sly smile passed over Juanita's lips. "No. Not yet. But we will be soon. He's taking me to San Francisco."

"Funny, he didn't mention that, either."

The fact that Juanita's smile didn't falter at all unnerved Catalina a little. The hussy was so sure of herself . . . maybe it was true. Maybe Jackson and Juanita would be leaving Baxter for San Francisco when the movie was done. After all, she had just met him the day before, and there was certainly no reason for her to be so obsessed with the man. He was good-looking, that was all, and he had saved her. Wasn't that some sort of syndrome? She'd read about that somewhere: falling for a man who had rescued you. A doctor, a fireman, a policeman . . . an actor who pretended to be a long-dead gunman.

"He's a nice guy," Catalina said with a sigh. So,

he really was taken. Not a very faithful boyfriend. That kiss had been wonderful, and if she hadn't put a stop to it . . .

Juanita laughed harshly. "A nice guy? Kid Creede? He's a killer, a man who looks out only for himself. But he has money, and he's clean, and he treats me with respect. That's more than I can ask of any man."

Catalina could think of no proper response to that. He was clean? And had money? A killer? There was no mention of love, and Juanita had obviously been speaking about Kid Creede, the gunman, not Jackson Cady, the actor. A chill started at the base of Catalina's spine and worked its way up as Juanita slammed the door behind her.

Something wasn't right here. The cameras weren't rolling. In fact, she hadn't seen a single one. Or a single person out of costume. Or a phone or a car or a director. And still all the actors played their parts. Method acting? Or were they all nuts?

Including Jackson?

Chapter Five

She'd been dressing forever, it seemed, and she was almost finished.

Her bath had been followed by a hot meal delivered to the room by a scantily dressed woman only slightly less surly than Juanita. This one— she'd mumbled the name Winnie—was fleshy and plump, and her brown hair was thin and poorly styled. Still, she wore next to nothing, and when she moved too quickly the low neckline of her flimsy dress fluttered and an entire breast was bared. Catalina considered telling Winnie that she needed a pin or a scarf at her neck. Surely she wasn't aware of the display. And then Catalina was certain that the exposure was no mistake.

Evidently she was to be dressed a little differently from Winnie. Layers and layers of clothing, including several pieces she didn't quite know how to put on. There was a thin lace-trimmed chemise against her skin, and a pair of bloomers. Bloomers! Ribbed stockings, black and thick, came well over her knees, and there was a pair of ankle-high black lace-up boots that were just a bit too large.

The corset was the killer. Winnie, no friendlier

than she'd been when she'd delivered dinner, was there to assist, and she pulled the strings so tightly, Catalina could barely breathe. There was a definite benefit to the device, Catalina thought with a smile as she looked into the cheval glass. No wonder Juanita and Alberta had such small waists. No aerobics required.

The dress was emerald green and black lace, and was cut so low her nipples all but showed. Her breasts were pushed up, giving the illusion that she had cleavage. No, she amended as she faced the mirror. With the tight corset and the low-cut dress she *did* have cleavage.

The emerald green skirt came just to her knees. The length was certainly far from daring, but the skirt was full and swished when she walked. With a bounce in her step Catalina practiced walking back and forth, crossing the room again and again. What would Jackson think of her in the costume?

Alberta herself fixed Catalina's hair, and Catalina was grateful. Winnie, who had corseted her so tightly, might have snatched her bald-headed before she was done.

But Alberta brushed her hair almost tenderly, leaving the slightly curling tresses hanging down her back. The longer strands that sometimes fell across her cheeks were pulled back, and Catalina got her feather—a black plume that brushed one cheek when she turned her head quickly.

Alberta took on an almost motherly attitude as she helped Catalina apply the strange makeup. Lip rouge, she called it, and a white powder she dusted lightly over Catalina's face.

When she was done Alberta leaned back and smiled. "You look lovely, Cat."

Inwardly, Catalina cringed. All her life people had tried to stick her with that nickname, and she hated it. "Catalina, please."

Alberta obviously didn't like being corrected. Her gray eyes hardened, and her smile faded for a moment. Then it was back. "Never mind about that. You'll knock 'em dead."

"I'm really not much of an actress," Catalina confided.

Alberta patted Catalina's arm. "I know. The best thing to do is to clear your mind. Don't act; don't try to pretend. Be yourself. That's what they like."

That's what they like. Apparently someone in charge would be downstairs. A director or a producer or . . . someone.

"Be myself," Catalina repeated, nodding her head slightly.

Alberta opened the door for her, and waited for Catalina to leave the sanctuary of her room. For some reason she felt sick to her stomach, as if something were terribly wrong. Was this stage fright?

The saloon had changed in the hours she'd been upstairs. It was dark outside, and the place was lit with lanterns and gaslights. It was noisy, and the bottom floor that had been all but deserted that afternoon was now filled to capacity.

Catalina stood on the stairs and surveyed the scene below. Smoke hung over the room like a low cloud, and the tables were occupied by more actors in costume. None looked as fine as Kid

Creede, of course. She searched the room for him first. He would certainly stand out in a crowd like this. Catalina wrinkled her nose as the smell of unwashed bodies reached her.

They appeared to be mostly miners, covered with dirt and sweat, bearded and dressed in well-worn work clothes. Not one of them had a nicely trimmed beard like Kid Creede's. Their facial hair grew unattended, bushy and—she was certain—filthy.

There were two other girls besides Juanita and Winnie, and they laughed too loudly as they leaned close to apparently drunken actors.

"Go on." Alberta prodded her from behind, with a hand on her shoulder.

"What kind of movie is this?" Catalina asked, her words meant only for herself.

Juanita was on the other side of the room, sitting in a filthy miner's lap. She smiled, as if she were smiling at Jackson. Her smile was that bright. The miner whose lap she occupied seemed thrilled, as did the surrounding patrons . . . actors, Catalina corrected herself.

"What should I do?" Catalina whispered her question to Alberta, who was losing her patient and motherly look.

"Be friendly. Mingle. Have a drink. Any one of these men would be thrilled to buy you some refreshment."

Catalina looked at the glasses and bottles of whiskey that dotted every table. "I really shouldn't drink," she confided. "I have no tolerance . . ."

"Go!" Alberta whispered harshly.

Catalina stepped cautiously between drinking men seated at tables crowded close together. They leered at her, and one bold man touched her leg, grabbing at her and just missing. He got a slap on the hand for his trouble, but all he did was laugh raucously.

Just as she was about to reach the bar—what she would do when she got there she didn't know—a man grabbed her and pulled her onto his lap.

"You're new," he said into her face. What foul breath he had! And she could see bits of his dinner in his beard. God, she hoped it was dinner, and not lunch . . . or breakfast.

"Release me," she said quietly.

The ignorant miner continued to smile. That was no special effect; he had only three visible teeth. "Oooh, we got us a real lady here at Alberta's."

"Let me go."

"Lemme buy you a drink, and I'll do that," he countered. His grasp was tight.

"All right," Catalina agreed calmly. She would have a drink, find the director, and get an explanation for this bizarre place.

The miner, who introduced himself as Milford, did release her when the bartender placed another glass of what appeared to be whiskey on the table. Probably tea, or at least watered-down bourbon. Catalina found herself perched on the edge of a chair much too close to Milford, and she lifted the small glass and downed it in one swallow.

It burned all the way down. Her eyes watered,

and she began to choke. The miner clapped her on the back until she could breathe again, laughing throughout the embarrassing episode.

Catalina lifted watery eyes to Milford. "Who is the director of this debacle?"

His eyes were blank. "What?"

"The director. Who's in charge?"

He nodded, finally comprehending her simple question. "That would be Harold Goodman. He owns . . ." Milford waved one arm grandly. "Hell, all of Baxter, but for this place."

"Is he here?" Catalina asked calmly. Finally, someone who could explain all of this to her.

"Right this minute?"

"Yes, Milford, right this minute." Her head was already swimming. From the too tight corset or from the whiskey? She didn't know and didn't care. Another glass of whiskey appeared before her, and she downed it.

Milford seemed to be searching the room. "Nope," he said after a futile search. "I don't see him here right now, but I 'spect he'll be in shortly. It's Saturday night," he added with some special meaning.

Catalina wrinkled her brow. "No, it's not," her words slurred slightly, against her will. "It's Sunday. Yesterday was Saturday."

Milford was shaking his head, and Catalina decided not to bother arguing with him.

She pushed herself away from the table, and the room tilted and spun. Grabbing onto the edge of the table, Catalina fell into Milford's lap.

"Sorry," she said as she rose unsteadily to her feet.

"No apology necessary."

Catalina wandered away from Milford's table. Where was Jackson? He should be here. He could introduce her to the director. He could point out Harold Goodman.

A series of friendly miners . . . actors . . . pulled her onto their laps and placed glasses of whiskey in her hands. Apparently, the only way to escape was to drink the vile stuff.

Another actor arrived, and this one was dressed like a gambler. Red silk vest, thin mustache, slick grin. Juanita lit on him as soon as he walked through the swinging doors. Catalina watched as the tramp latched herself onto the actor with the dark blond hair and actually rubbed herself against the man. Disgusting.

Finally she found herself back at Milford's table . . . back in Milford's lap. She perched on a bony knee and closed her eyes so the room would be still.

She refused the glass he pressed into her hand.

"Harold Goodman came in a few minutes ago," Milford whispered as though they shared a deep secret.

"Where?" Catalina looked around the room, but her eyes wouldn't focus. If only she had her glasses.

Milford pointed to the batwing doors, which were swinging nauseatingly as a weaving miner exited. Catalina knew the man who stood just to one side of those doors had to be the director. He was the only man in the room who wasn't filthy. He was dressed as a cowboy, but his clothes were clean and he carried himself differently. Like he was an important man . . . or at least thought he was.

Catalina clasped Milford's head in her hands, trying to make him be still. "Introduce me."

Milford was more than happy to take Catalina's arm and lead her to the most important man in town. He made the introductions almost formally, as if they stood in her grandmother's parlor.

When the introductions were done and Milford had been dismissed by the director, Harold Goodman took Catalina's hand.

"You're new."

Catalina was thinking that he was awfully young to be a director, but then maybe he had money, or his father was famous, or he was one of those child geniuses.

"Yes I am," she said, trying to speak clearly. "And I really would like to speak to you. There's something very strange going on here."

There was a buzzing in the room, or else a buzzing in her head, or both, and she covered her ears momentarily.

"Too noisy in here for you, Catalina?" he asked, leaning in to speak into her ear.

Catalina nodded. "It really is. Do you think there's some quiet place we can talk?"

Harold Goodman smiled, and it wasn't at all pleasant. He looked rather like a weasel when he smiled. "Your room, perhaps?"

"Sure," Catalina started toward the staircase at the back of the room.

Alberta waited at the foot of the staircase, a feline smile on her face.

"I see you've met our Cat," she said to Goodman, ignoring Catalina and offering both hands to the director.

"Yes. She's lovely." Goodman kissed the back of Alberta's hand. "Wherever did you find her?"

"She was a gift from an old friend."

Catalina tried to interrupt, but they ignored her. First of all, she hated to be called Cat, and secondly she was not a *gift*, and thirdly . . . she forgot what came thirdly.

"Go on up," Alberta said to Goodman. "She's in the green room."

Goodman nodded to each of them and started up the stairs.

Alberta gave Catalina a smile that was very unlike the one she'd given Goodman. It was almost mercenary. "Very good, Cat. Getting your claws into Harold Goodman before he's even had a chance to mingle with the other girls. You'll do well here."

"I just want to . . ."

"Don't worry," Alberta whispered, leaning close and placing an arm around Catalina's shoulders. "The girls say he's real quick."

Catalina came to an abrupt halt at the bottom of the staircase. "He's what?"

"Quick. Done in a flash. You'll be back down here before you know it."

"We're just going to talk."

Alberta shook her head. "Hell, if I know Harold, he's naked and ready as we speak. All you have to do is lie down and . . ."

Catalina took a step back. "I can't."

"What do you mean, you *can't?*" There was no

71

more maternal charm in Alberta's eyes.

"I mean, I never have before, and I can't just . . ." Catalina waved a hand at the deserted staircase. At that moment the chubby girl who had tied Catalina's corset walked past, a miner on one arm. They walked up the stairs, and the miner's hand dropped down to squeeze Winnie's ample butt.

"I'm not a hooker," Catalina whispered loudly. "I'm a librarian."

"Girlie, you owe me," Alberta said harshly. "For the room, and the bath, and the meal, and the clothes on your back. You can and you *will* entertain my customers."

Catalina closed her eyes. She was hearing everything wrong because she'd had too much too drink. "I can't. I've never . . . I was waiting for my wedding night, and I know that's unusual in this day and age, but it's really important to me."

"You're a virgin?" Alberta asked in a low voice, her anger gone.

Catalina nodded. Alberta understood. Everything would be all right.

"You've never been with a man before?" Alberta asked, as if to clarify that Catalina knew what a virgin was.

"No," Catalina said, leaning against the banister. "There's been a terrible misunderstanding here."

Alberta smiled and looked over Catalina's shoulder. "Walter, tell your boss to get dressed and come downstairs."

"Thank you," Catalina said, relieved. That had been close. Too close.

"It never occurred to me, that after traveling with the Kid . . . oh, well. Come this way." Alberta took Catalina's arm and led her to a door at the back of the room, almost behind the stairs. She took a key that was hanging from the sash at her waist and unlocked the door, shoving Catalina through.

It was a parlor, Catalina thought distantly, garishly decorated. Red and gold dominated, with red velvet chairs placed around the room, gilt-framed mirrors on the walls, tasteless cherubs—gold and marble—gracing small tables throughout. There was a plush red carpet on the floor, and one long couch upholstered in red and gold brocade. Even the walls were red and gold, covered in what could only be called whorehouse wallpaper.

How on earth could they have expected her to sleep with the director? How could Alberta claim that she *owed* her? Before she knew what was happening, the bartender was at her elbow, and Alberta was gone.

Catalina didn't like the way the man looked at her, or the way he held her arm. She tried to wrest away from him, but the man held fast. A smile would fool him. She relaxed and turned a grin to the goon. She had knocked Jackson to the ground, and she could certainly handle this joker.

Catalina turned her back on the massive creature and tried to flip him. Something was wrong. Her hands were tangled up and he was immovable. A rock. He only clasped her tighter.

Alberta was back with two other men, and they

led Catalina to the front of the room, herding her like a stubborn cow.

"What do you think you're doing?" Catalina asked, trying to break free. One man tied a long black scarf to her wrist, and then tied an identical one to her other wrist. "Would you stop?" She tried for a commanding tone but fell far short.

The barbarians were tying scarves at her ankles now, and she got in one good kick. The bartender yelped loudly, and Catalina smiled down at his bushy head.

She was pressed against the wall, and first one scarf and then the other were tied to two gold rings mounted into the wall at shoulder height. Her legs were jerked apart and tied in the same way to rings almost hidden in the carpet, until Catalina found herself spread-eagled and effectively immobilized.

Her feet were on the ground, but she was unable to move them. Her arms were spread wide, sticking out at right angles. For the first time in her life, she just knew she was going to faint. The corset, the whiskey, the fact that she was tied to a frigging wall . . .

The room was filling quickly. Harold Goodman walked into the room still tucking his shirt into his pants, a less than happy look on his little boy face. He plopped down onto the brocade couch and leaned back almost sullenly, propping one boot on his knee. A few of the miners wandered in, but they hung near the back of the room. The gambler she had seen Juanita latch on to entered the room and took a chair facing her. He looked like a caricature, with his oiled hair and carefully trimmed mustache and silk vest. Like a gambler in a bad western.

A miner slapped him on the shoulder and asked, "How you doin', Lucky?" in an overly friendly tone. The gambler, Lucky, was less than pleased to be touched and acknowledged by the lesser man.

The thought that finally sobered her was the certainty that they had done this before.

"Gentlemen," Alberta said smoothly, stepping to the front of the room to stand beside Catalina. "What we have here is a bona-fide virgin. A rarity in these parts, to be certain." She glanced over her shoulder to Catalina and smiled. "And isn't she lovely, our golden Cat. Untouched and pure. Her skin is soft and smooth, as though it's never seen the sun. Her hair is abundant and silky. . . ." She went on, selling Catalina, pointing out all her virtues. And then Alberta turned back to the audience. "The bidding will start at two hundred dollars."

Catalina pulled against one of the scarves, trying to yank a gold ring from the wall. It wouldn't budge. "You fat bitch," she muttered loudly. "This is very illegal."

Harold Goodman quickly bid two hundred dollars. Another man entered the room. A sheriff. Thank God! A real sheriff, with a badge on his vest and a gun at his hip.

"Sheriff," Catalina said, trying to keep the tremor from her voice, "arrest this woman."

The sheriff spoke up. "Two hundred and fifty."

"You filthy pig!" she shouted.

The bidding continued, climbing in increments of ten and twenty and fifty dollars. A few miners spoke up early on but soon dropped out of the bidding completely. The sheriff, Goodman, and the gambler continued.

And then Jackson appeared in the doorway. She had never been so glad to see any person in her entire life.

"Help me," she whispered hoarsely, her eyes fixed on his face.

He leaned against the doorjamb and crossed his arms over his chest. "Four hundred dollars," he said in that silky voice of his.

"You . . . you . . ." Catalina sputtered, aware that somehow . . . some impossible way . . . this was all real. It was the details that finally convinced her. The underwear she wore. Milford's missing teeth. The hand-rolled cigarettes the gambler smoked. The horrid whiskey that had gone to her head. "Kid Cretin," she all but spat, and several miners who had removed themselves from the bidding laughed. "You got me into this mess, you damn well better get me out."

He didn't move. The gambler looked back over his shoulder to the doorway and waved his hands in surrender. He was out. The sheriff looked nervous and backed away a step as he withdrew himself from the game. Neither of them wanted to bid against Kid Creede. Only Goodman and Jackson remained active.

Goodman bid five hundred dollars for her, but she saw beads of sweat on his face that hadn't been there a moment earlier.

Jackson stepped into the room, his spurs jangling softly with each slow step. He stopped in the center of the ostentatious parlor, removed his hat, and ran his fingers through that long dark hair. When he raised those pale blue eyes to her, Catalina thought she really would faint.

He was no actor. He was Kid Creede. A hired gun, a killer. And he was bidding on her virginity like it was a fine horse or a piece of art.

"One thousand dollars," he said in a low voice. "But I want her for the week."

Goodman sputtered. "I don't have that much with me."

"I do," Jackson said smoothly. That was directed at Alberta, a businesswoman if ever there was one.

Alberta lifted her arms to Jackson, palms upward as if asking for a hug. But he didn't move. "Kid," she said huskily. "She's all yours."

"I want the blue room," Jackson said, his eyes on Catalina Lane's face. Finally she was scared. Being lost in the desert hadn't frightened her. His reputation hadn't moved her at all, but at this moment those whiskey eyes were wide and full of terror.

"I've put Cat in the green room." Alberta stepped forward, blocking his view of Catalina.

Jackson lifted his eyes to the woman who had auctioned off her new girl without a qualm. "I want the blue room." He didn't raise his voice. He didn't have to. "Clean sheets, a hot bath, and both keys."

Alberta smiled. "There's a single key to each room, Kid, I assure . . ."

"Both keys," Jackson repeated, and Alberta's

smile faded. Behind him, he could hear the last of the patrons leaving the parlor, shuffling their feet and whispering softly. He knew some of them turned their heads to get one last look at Catalina. He didn't like it. Not at all.

"Of course, Kid." Alberta swept from the room, and he was once again afforded a full view of Catalina Lane displayed against a gold and red wall. With each breath she took her breasts heaved, and her pale face was flushed with color. Christ, she was the most luscious sight he had ever laid his eyes on.

Jackson stepped slowly to the sofa that was positioned directly in front of Catalina and lowered himself with ease. What now? Now that he had her, what was he going to do with her?

"Are you going to get me down?" she said breathlessly, a slight slur in her voice. Jackson smiled. She was drunk, as well as frightened.

"How much have you had to drink tonight?"

"What difference does it make? Are you just going to leave me here?"

Jackson shook his head slowly, and her face paled.

"If you'll just help me get out of here, I'll pay you back. Every penny. There's been a terrible mistake. I don't belong here. I don't even know how I got here."

"I found you in the desert and brought you here myself, Catalina. Pretending to be loco isn't going to work anymore."

She pulled fruitlessly against one scarf, turning her head away from him for a moment. "What is the date, today?" she whispered harshly.

"I don't know. It's September, I think." The date? What was she trying to pull now?

The efforts at freeing herself stopped, and Catalina faced him again. She looked down into his face, wide-eyed and frightened. He wanted to tell her not to worry. But he didn't.

"The year, Kid," she said, licking her dry lips. "What year is it?"

She was going to try playing the lunatic again, trying to scare him away. "Last time I checked it was 1896."

"Eighteen ninety-six," she repeated. "That's not possible."

Jackson didn't answer her. He wasn't going to play this game. As soon as the blue room was ready, he was going to cut her down and carry her up those stairs. No matter what she said.

"Listen to me very carefully," she said slowly. "When I was left at the altar, when I was a librarian in Indian Springs, when I wandered away from the gas station . . . it was 1996."

Jackson placed his hands on his knees and leaned forward slightly. "This isn't going to work, Catalina," he assured her.

"I swear it's true," she said desperately.

Jackson leaned back, never taking his eyes from the picture before him. He could almost swear that she believed what she was saying to be true. No one could lie that convincingly.

Alberta swept into the room, and Catalina's eyes jerked up. She was almost more frightened of the madam than she was of him. Almost.

"The blue room is ready," Alberta said, placing a single key in his hand. Jackson waited, letting the key lie on his open palm. He didn't even look at Alberta. A moment later she laid the other key atop the one he held. "Your bath is ready, and I took the liberty of placing a bottle of my finest whiskey and a bowl of stew by the fireplace."

"Your finest whiskey would eat a hole right through this rug." Jackson tapped his foot lightly. The stew probably wasn't much better, but Catalina would need something to eat.

"Do you need any help with our Cat?"

"It's Catalina, you stupid cow." Her face paled as soon as the words were out, and Catalina pursed her lips and watched the madam, waiting for a reaction.

For a thousand dollars Alberta was willing to take all kinds of abuse. She continued to smile, ignoring the insult.

"I think I can manage," Jackson assured Alberta, hoping it was true. She'd flipped him once, but she'd caught him off guard then. That wouldn't happen again.

He untied the lower scarves first, leaving the knotted silk at her ankles. Then the rings to her sides, again leaving the knots at her wrists. He kept his body close to hers as he worked, pressing Catalina against the wall, giving her no opportunity to run or to get a good hold on his arm as she had in the desert. He expected her to fight him, to struggle, but she was deathly still, even when she was finally free.

"I'd be careful if I was you," Alberta warned. "Harold was right pissed."

Jackson looked down into Catalina's face. Pale and trembling, she stared at him with her fear and confusion crystal clear in her eyes. Whiskey eyes, with flecks of gold, he noticed, like sparks of light. Gold dust and whiskey.

Then he lifted her unceremoniously and tossed her over his shoulder. The scarves that were still tied to her wrists and ankles hung to the floor, and she finally began to struggle.

"Put me down," she insisted. "You can't buy a person. Not for a night or a week or a lifetime."

Alberta whispered, words meant for Catalina but reaching his ears. "Don't worry, Cat," she cooed. "Better the Kid than Harold Goodman. Talk about the blind leading the blind . . ."

Jackson left the parlor, taking long, slow steps that carried them into the main room of Alberta's saloon. He was accustomed to curious eyes, but not to the catcalls that followed him through the room and up the stairs. Catalina was still, at least, finally giving up her futile fight.

The blue room was on the third floor and had a door that opened up to a small balcony that overlooked the street. It was at the end of the hall, approachable from only one direction.

The bathwater was steaming, and a fire had been lit in the fireplace. On a small table sat a full bottle of whiskey and a bowl of stew. Neither one looked particularly appetizing.

The bedspread, a sapphire blue satin coverlet, had been folded back, and clean sheets gleamed brightly in that dark corner of the room.

Jackson tossed Catalina over his shoulder to land on the soft bed, and she bounced once lightly before she tried to leap from the mattress.

He was on top of her before she could get very far.

"Kid Cretin," she called him again, and he tried to hide a smile as he tied the scarves that were still attached to her wrists to the headboard. She did try to fight him this time, but with all his weight on her she could barely move, much less struggle.

When both her hands were tied, he sat on the side of the bed and looked down at her. She tried to kick at him, and Jackson stretched across her legs, stilling that movement.

"Now, I can tie these scarves at your feet to the foot of the bed, or I can leave them loose. That's up to you."

She froze immediately, and Jackson sat up again. Catalina's legs didn't move, and he gave them a good, long look. Nicely shaped legs, encased in tight black stockings.

"I was telling the truth, Jackson," she said, her voice pleading. "Please, I don't belong here."

Jackson stood and turned his back on her. What the hell was he going to do with her now that he had her? He couldn't leave her here, and he certainly couldn't take her with him. He'd bought her for the week, so that gave him a little time to consider the possibilities.

He locked the door first, and placed both keys on the top of the dresser. Then he placed a chair beneath the doorknob. He wouldn't put it past Alberta to have three keys. She'd given him that second one too easily.

Then he took off his gunbelt and draped it across the footboard. His hat went sailing to the chair at the door, and he started unbuttoning his shirt. It had been too long since he'd had a real bath, with soap and hot water and a soft towel for drying afterward.

He couldn't even hear Catalina breathing, she was so quiet. Jackson turned his head and caught her staring at him with those wide eyes and trembling lips. Finally terrified of Kid Creede.

"Don't worry, darlin'," he said with a smile, shucking off his shirt as he turned to her. "I'm just going to take a bath." He leaned over the bed, purposely placing his face close to hers. "I don't bed virgins."

Chapter Six

Catalina stared at the ceiling, trying to ignore the muffled sounds of Jackson Cady undressing. His boots dropping to the floor, the rustle of heavy-duty fabric as he removed his pants. Each breath she took was an effort as she tried to make sense of what had happened.

Eighteen ninety-six. It was impossible, but undeniably real.

Open your heart and your mind, and all things are possible.

The old man's words came back to her, along with her wish to live in another time, the glow of the wulfenite, the sandstorm that had stolen her breath. And stories. Stories she'd heard in her years in Indian Springs, of locals and tourists who claimed to see into the past, there near the ancient red rocks. She'd never taken those claims seriously, but had explained them away as delusions brought on by too much sun, too much excitement, and way too much imagination.

But what if there was a door there, a door that allowed some to see into the past . . . and others to step through?

She heard the splash of water as Jackson stepped into the tin tub, and the satisfied sigh that followed, and Catalina turned her head to watch him. His head rested against the rim of the tub, and he'd closed his eyes. Jackson Cady. Kid Creede. One of the last gunslingers to make a name for himself in the West. One of the last gun-fighters to die in a bloody shootout on a dusty street.

"You have to leave Baxter," she said softly, and Jackson opened his eyes and glanced at her.

"Not before the week is out," he said, turning his face away from her and picking up a bar of soap from the floor.

Catalina scooted up into an awkward sitting position, thankful that Jackson had at least left her legs free but mortified to find herself in such a predicament.

"I know it's hard to accept that I come from 1996, but it's true. You must believe me. Kid Creede was killed in Baxter, ambushed and shot a dozen times. Maybe if you leave town that won't happen."

Jackson ran the bar of soap over his arms, giving that task all his attention.

"Are you listening to me?"

Jackson dropped the soap into his bathwater with a splash and turned a hardened face to her. "You can stop this . . . this loco act of yours. I've already told you I don't bed virgins, so there's no reason to pretend . . ."

"I'm not pretending!"

"Besides . . ." Jackson lowered himself slightly into the water and closed his eyes, "I can't leave Baxter until I decide what to do with you."

What to do with you. Those words had a

slightly ominous ring to them that Catalina tried to ignore.

"Take me with you," Catalina suggested quickly, knowing—in spite of her current awkward situation—that staying with Jackson was best for her. She couldn't possibly remain here at Alberta's, and what else was there for her in Baxter? Nothing. She had to reach a big city, a place where she could blend in while she decided what to do.

"No." Jackson's hesitation before he answered was brief, but was long enough to give Catalina hope.

"I'll earn my keep," Catalina said quickly. "I'll cook, and wash your clothes and, if you teach me how, I'll build a campfire at night and make coffee. It'll be like having a maid on the trail."

Muscular arms rested on the sides of the tub, and that bearded face stared straight ahead. Away from her. "What makes you think Alberta will let you go?"

"She has nothing to say about it. Alberta doesn't own me."

"I'll wager she thinks different," Jackson said softly, and Catalina knew he was right. The madam had told Harold Goodman that she was a gift, for heaven's sake. Alberta had felt her claim strong enough to auction Catalina off like a slave.

"We can sneak out . . ."

"We'll be watched."

"Surely the great Kid Creede . . ."

"Is no match for Alberta when she's got her mind set on something."

Catalina tried to roll one aching shoulder. She

couldn't possibly stay in this embarrassing and painful position all night. "You could find a way . . ."

"If I had a mind to."

He turned his face to her, and caught her with those piercing pale blue eyes. Heaven help her, she'd never seen eyes like that before. Cold and bright and distant . . . and incredibly haunting. And in those gorgeous eyes was the truth.

"You don't want to take me with you, do you?" she asked, her breathy voice barely carrying across the room.

Jackson leaned back his head and closed his eyes. He couldn't seem to bear looking at her for very long. "Not particularly."

"So you're going to leave me here?"

"Most likely."

Catalina sagged back and rested against the headboard. Trapped. Somehow she'd traveled one hundred years into the past, and now she was trapped in a bordello where she was likely to stay for as long as Alberta desired it.

No way. With Jackson's help or without it, she was going to get out of this place before the end of the week. She could steal a horse and make her way back to the place in the desert where Jackson Cady had found her. She still had the wulfenite, tucked into one of the moccasins, though she didn't know if that was necessary or not. She didn't know, not really, if she *could* go back. Maybe she was stuck here, in 1896.

Well, if she was, she wasn't going to be stuck in a bordello, *entertaining* miners who probably didn't bathe more than once a month, if at all.

87

While Jackson leaned back in the water and ignored her, Catalina studied him. Even though he had every intention of abandoning her, she couldn't allow him to be shot down in the street. She likely would've died in the desert, waiting for Stu and Allie to rescue her. They weren't even born yet, and there was no highway, no gas station. She would have died of thirst if he hadn't found her and carried her to Baxter.

And he was a beautiful man, all dark and muscled and graceful. She'd never noticed grace in a man before, but Jackson displayed it in every move he made. He was like a cat, slow and strong and deadly certain of himself.

He twisted his head toward her, just slightly, and barely opened one eye. "How old are you?" he asked gruffly.

"Twenty-seven, just last month," Catalina said, refusing to turn her eyes away from his face. He'd been thinking about her, sitting there in the cooling water, just as she'd been thinking of him.

"How does a woman who looks like you do manage to reach the advanced age of twenty-seven and remain a virgin?"

"First of all, twenty-seven is hardly an advanced age, Kid." Catalina shifted on the bed, trying to get comfortable. That was an impossible task. The corset was too tight, her arms ached from wrist to shoulder, and the stockings were beginning to itch. "As for how I managed to remain a virgin . . ." She paused and shifted again. She'd had this discussion with a couple of close girlfriends over the years, but never with a man. No man had dared to ask.

"I was raised by my grandmother," she looked Jackson in the eye as she began to speak. "My very old-fashioned Southern grandmother. She was my father's mother, and the only family I had after my parents were killed."

"What happened to your folks?" he asked, and Catalina could almost convince herself that he really cared.

"A plane crash. A small private plane that my father's company owned. They were going to a football game."

Jackson's wide mouth was tightly closed and he frowned at her. "A . . . what kind of a crash?"

"A plane . . . never mind. It was an accident. Anyway, I was eight, and I went to live with my Grandma Lane. She enrolled me in a private all-girls' school in Spring Hill, and that's where I stayed until I graduated."

Jackson nodded his head slightly. "Ah," he said with a wry lilt in his voice. "An educated woman."

Catalina ignored him. "So, I really didn't have much contact with boys until college."

"You went to college?"

Catalina nodded, smiling at his obvious disbelief. "But by then it was already too late. My grandmother had ruined me."

His frown was almost back. "How?"

Catalina tried to ease his frown with a smile of her own. "I grew up hearing fairy tales, stories of true love and happily ever after. Princes and princesses, knights and damsels in distress. Magic."

Jackson picked that moment to plunge his

head into the bathwater. When he brought it back up it was too quickly, and droplets of soapy water flew through the air, almost—but not quite—reaching the bed. He leaned his head back and rested it against the rim of the tub, eyes closed and water running in disappearing rivulets down the hard planes of his face. It was almost as if he were avoiding looking at her.

"Do you believe in magic?" he asked softly when he finally spoke.

Catalina thought of all that had happened to her in the past two days. Did she believe in magic? Even if she hadn't before, she certainly did now.

"Yes. I guess I always have. I waited for years, waited to feel that magic, to find my prince charming, my knight in shining armor . . . but he never came."

"The man you were to marry . . . wasn't he your prince?"

"Wilson? Wilson Ross was no prince. It's just that I had given up on magic. Given up on the belief that there's one special man for me. That I would meet my prince charming and fall madly in love and have a fairy-tale wedding and a special wedding night." Catalina felt suddenly uncomfortable having this discussion with Jackson Cady. She hadn't even told Kim this much. Kim, who had more than once encouraged Catalina to have a one-night stand and get it over with.

"Anyway," she said casually, "that's why I'm still a virgin at the advanced age of twenty-seven."

He cracked one eye open and turned it in her

direction. "You don't look twenty-seven," he said suspiciously.

Catalina could only imagine how old some women must look at twenty-seven after living in the West for years. Endless sun, and childbearing, and hard living took its toll. "Well I am. How old are you?"

Jackson closed that cold eye. "Thirty-one."

A smile crossed Catalina's face, and for a moment she forgot the pain that seemed to attack every bone and muscle in her body. "You don't look thirty-one. Are you sure you don't mean *forty*-one?"

His wide mouth smiled, though he didn't bother to open his eyes. "Pretty sure," he answered.

Catalina sat up a little taller, trying to ease the increasing ache in her shoulders. "You're not going to leave me tied up like this, are you?"

Jackson sat up himself, giving Catalina a clear view of his wide chest, wet and covered with a light sprinkling of black hair. "That depends. Are you going to run?"

"To where?" she snapped, unnerved by the sight of so much of his skin.

"Are you going to attack me again?"

"Attack you? When did I attack you?" Her patience was wearing thin. Jackson lifted his eyebrows, in a manner much too amused for Catalina, and with his hand in the air demonstrated a flip-flop motion.

"Oh, that," Catalina said with less venom. "Not if you behave yourself."

"Well," Jackson placed both hands on the sides

of the tub and stood without warning. Catalina closed her eyes tightly and turned her head, but not before she'd seen more than she cared to, and not before she'd had her suspicion that Jackson was gorgeous from head to toe confirmed. "I already told you I don't . . ."

"Bed virgins," she finished for him, holding her eyes so tightly closed that she saw red stars. "I know."

She heard the splash as he stepped from the tub, listened to every step of his bare feet on the floor. Twice he passed close to the bed, and when he was near Catalina squeezed her eyes shut even tighter. Both times she heard him chuckle. She wanted to strike out at him for laughing at her, but she remained silent. He was her best hope for getting out of Baxter alive and with her virginity intact.

Finally she felt his weight on the bed, and his hands at her wrist.

"You can open your eyes, Catalina," he whispered huskily. "I'm decent."

"That's debatable," she answered, opening her eyes cautiously.

Maybe he was, technically, decent. He had his pants on, at least. But his chest was bare, and it was so close to her face as he leaned over her to untie her bonds that she could have leaned forward and touched his still damp skin with her lips.

He was certainly not the first man she had seen without a shirt. Good heavens, there was a pool at the apartment, and it was well used. But she had never seen a body so perfectly formed. Not overly muscular, like those body builders who loved to flex their muscles whenever she and Kim had gone to the pool for a swim, not thin and pale like the more sedentary guys she'd seen—like Wilson. Jackson's body—and she'd just recently gotten a glimpse of a good bit of it—was perfect.

His long dark hair was wet, but he'd towel-dried it and it didn't drip on her. Still, damp strands brushed her face and her indecently exposed cleavage as he leaned to the other side.

He was no fool. She remained immobile as long as he held his body so closely over hers.

"There's stew, if you're hungry."

Catalina closed her eyes to still the rolling nausea that shook her at the mention of food. "No," she said. "Oh, definitely no."

She took a deep breath and opened her eyes. A pale, thin scar on Jackson's side caught her eye, and a newly freed hand reached out to touch it briefly. "What happened?"

"I was shot," he said tersely.

"Oh." It was a breath, a whisper in the quiet room. Of course he had been shot.

"Here, too," he said sharply, turning his back to her. There was a nasty puckered scar high on his back, inches from his spine.

"Someone shot you in the back?" Catalina couldn't stop herself. She reached out and touched the damaged flesh, silently cursing the man who had done this to him.

"Yep. That was the day I learned never to shoot to wound a man. Always shoot to kill."

"When was that?" Catalina pulled her hand

away slowly. It seemed so unfair.

"Fourteen years ago." Jackson stood, and Catalina was free. She didn't move but to massage her aching arms.

"God, Jackson, you were just a baby."

He kept his back to her, and she saw the muscles there tense.

"What happened?" Catalina had seen enough of Jackson Cady to know that he was intelligent, almost human, though he tried very hard to hide that fact. What had brought him to this place? What had turned Jackson Cady into Kid Creede? "Why do you do . . . what you do?"

He turned then and looked down at her, and she wished he had kept that stiff back to her. Jackson smiled, but there was no humor in that smile. His narrowed eyes burrowed into her, traveling the length of her body slowly.

"Are you certain you're a virgin, Catalina Lane?" he asked silkily.

Catalina nodded her head, but that didn't stop Jackson. He leaned over her, trapping her still sore arms above her head and placing his lips over hers. They almost touched, and his mouth hovered just above hers, so she could feel every breath he took, every beat of his heart.

"How can I know for certain that you're telling the truth?" he whispered, and then he kissed her, hard lips against her trembling mouth. Catalina tried to push him away, but she had no strength . . . and she was no match for Jackson Cady when he was wary of her.

She allowed her pinned arms to relax, and the pressure there lessened. His lips softened as well, and Catalina lifted her chin to taste more of him, forgetting what a threat he was to her.

Jackson trapped both her wrists with one hand and trailed the other hand down her arm . . . slowly . . . his fingers dancing against her skin. She burned where he touched her, and she ached for more of him. Her heart beat so fast, she was certain he could feel it; could hear it, it pounded so hard. There was no way to catch her breath, to ease the pressure that was building inside her. Catalina felt as if she might actually explode.

He released her wrists and wrapped his arms around her, slipping his big hands under her and clutching her tightly. She was almost certain she heard a low, deep moan coming from somewhere deep inside Jackson, and she captured that sound with her parted lips. Her hands came slowly to the back of his head, and she wound her fingers into his damp hair and pulled him toward her, wanting his lips ever tighter against hers, wanting his sweet tongue to dance with hers all night.

But Jackson pulled away from her, taking his lips from her as he continued to hold her close. "You don't kiss like a virgin."

"I'm sorry," Catalina whispered.

Jackson was gone, his hands and his lips and his weight gone in a flash. He turned his back on her again, and stood at the side of the bed, motionless. Like a cold marble statue. Catalina sat up, her fingers touching her lips tentatively. What was that? What had happened to her?

* * *

Jackson doused the light, careful not to look at the woman lounging on the bed. Unfortunately, he was assured that she was a virgin. Her breath had come so fast after just one kiss, and he had seen the confusion in her whiskey eyes when he'd pulled away from her. She was feeling that confusion for the first time.

His little plan had backfired. To hear her ask him, in her soft voice, what had made him choose the life he led was more than he could bear.

A rough kiss, to change her train of thought. A careless hand, to remind her of what her fate could yet be. Confusion, to make her forget her tender questions.

But he'd been as caught up in the caress as she had. He'd never before touched an innocent, and he wouldn't start now—except for that kiss. So pure, so unjaded. So open, Catalina Lane was. He could have her, and it wouldn't be rape. She would give herself to him without a qualm, but he was unwilling to have her.

She offered too much.

He'd rather face her questions, were they to come up again, than endure another kiss like that one. Perhaps he'd even tell her—in a weak moment—that he hadn't chosen this life. It had chosen him.

"Jackson?" Her voice was uncertain, like that of a lost child afraid of the dark. He could turn, he knew, and see her there on the bed, lit by the moonlight that streamed through the balcony door. He kept his back to her.

"Where will you sleep?"

Where will I sleep? Between your legs if you don't be quiet. "On the floor," he said shortly.

"Oh." He heard the rustle of her dress, another lost sigh, and then she was quiet.

He waited without moving, standing with his back to the bed for several long moments. Surely no more than a few minutes passed before he heard the deep, even breathing of a sleeping Catalina.

Then he turned. She was lying on her side, her knees pulled up just slightly. Golden hair, silver in the moonlight, fell over half of her face. How had she fallen asleep so quickly? Some nights he didn't sleep at all, and he never slept for more than an hour or two without waking.

Catalina slept the sleep of an innocent, and he reminded himself that that's exactly what she was. She was innocent, and beautiful, and loco . . . and not for him.

He placed the blue coverlet over her sleeping form, and she stirred slightly. There was a frown on her face, and she twisted her torso a bit . . . and then she was deep asleep again.

Pure. That was the word that came to him as he watched the moonlight on her face. She was pure and good, and she deserved her magic.

Chapter Seven

Catalina woke in pain. The damn corset was going to have to go, and now. The pinch of the uncomfortable undergarment was almost matched by the pain in her head—from too much of Alberta's whiskey—and the ache in her arms and shoulders. She wasn't accustomed to being trussed to a wall or a bed, thank you very much.

She lifted her head and surveyed the blue room washed with a pale morning glow. It looked different by the light of day, even the faded half light that illuminated the rough texture of the wooden floor and the man who slept upon it.

Her head was clearer than it had been the night before, in spite of the headache. Still, none of what had happened made any sense. The harder she tried to find some sanity in the events of the past forty-eight hours, the more her head hurt.

Jackson's tub still sat near the fireplace, and Jackson himself slept on the floor, as he'd said he would. Even in sleep he seemed aware. Catalina wouldn't have been surprised if he'd lifted his head and greeted her with a cool and calm good morning. But he didn't. He slept on, with nothing but a single sheet between his bare back and the wooden floor.

She slipped her legs over the side of the bed, as slowly and quietly as possible, and stood. Jackson's slightly too long nose twitched, but that was the only movement he made. Catalina reached behind her and started working the buttons down her back. Why hadn't she removed the damned corset last night? Too drunk, too scared, maybe both. She hadn't wondered, when she'd been assisted in dressing, how she would undress on her own. She knew now that Alberta had never intended for Catalina to remove the costume alone.

She slipped the green silk off, sliding her arms as quietly as possible from the sleeves. The bodice of her dress dropped to her waist, and she started working the corset. The stays were digging into her flesh. No wonder the contraption hurt her so much!

The corset came free, and Catalina tossed it to the floor. Never again. Not even for a tiny waist would she subject herself to that. She took several deep breaths, enjoying that freedom, and then looked down at Jackson to find him staring at her.

"You could've said something," she snapped, pulling the green silk up over her chemise.

"Good morning," he said softly.

"Too late." Catalina turned her back on him. She heard him stretch and rise behind her, heard the pop and crack of joints accustomed to sleeping on hard surfaces.

Before she could tell him that she wanted—

Linda Jones

that she *demanded*—a change of clothes and a trip to the outhouse, there was a knock at the door. Alberta—she would bet her life on it—and the madam had probably been listening at the door, waiting to hear their voices.

Jackson grabbed her shoulders and forced her to sit on the edge of the bed.

"What do you want?" he yelled sleepily as he quickly worked the laces at her ankles and slipped the black boots off her feet.

"I just wanted to check on you two, and make certain that everything was to your satisfaction, Kid. May I come in?"

It was Alberta, with that false smile in her voice.

"Give me a minute," Jackson almost drawled, his lazy voice belying the quickness of his actions. His hands were at her thighs, and before Catalina could protest he was rolling down her black stockings. One he threw toward the door, the other he tossed so that it landed over the foot of the bed near his gunbelt.

With his hands under her arms he jerked Catalina to her feet, and the green silk was stripped from her body in a flash, to be tossed to the floor.

"Stop that!" Catalina whispered harshly. "What on earth are you . . ."

Jackson silenced her with a finger to his lips. He was, Catalina knew, her only ally in this world, and she obeyed his silent order.

"Come on, Kid. Open the door."

"Damnation, Alberta. The sun's barely up."

"I have to make certain that my Cat's all right."

Catalina opened her mouth to deliver an angry

reply, but Jackson's hand clamped down over it before she could make a sound. His eyes warned her, and she sighed as Jackson lowered his hand slowly.

A knife appeared there, recovered from a hidden sheath in one of his boots that had been dropped by the bed. It was rather plain, with a worn wooden handle and a long, narrow blade, and he handled the weapon with frightening ease.

Jackson threw the blue coverlet at Catalina, and she wrapped herself in it as he stood over the rumpled bed and cursed. Then he held his hand over the pristine sheet and ran the sharp blade of his knife across his thumb.

Several drops of blood fell to the sheet beneath his outstretched hand as Catalina watched, dumbfounded. She all but cowered in a corner of the room, holding the coverlet to her like a cocoon that could protect her against all this. Jackson snapped his bedding from the floor and tossed it on top of the bloodstained sheet; only then did he lift his head to look at her. He mouthed the words *stay there and be quiet,* and then he stomped to the door.

The chair at the door he removed quietly, not once making so much as a whispering scrape of wood against wood. He removed both keys from the dresser, dropping one into his pocket as he inserted the other into the lock.

"What the hell do you want?" he demanded, throwing the door open to reveal a smirking Alberta.

Catalina didn't move, even as Alberta's eyes fell

on her and she received a chilling smile. She didn't know what Jackson was up to, not exactly, but he was definitely up to something.

"Is there anything you need, Kid?" Alberta turned her attention back to Jackson.

"Yeah," Jackson said softly. "Breakfast. My laundry done. A decent dress for Catalina. One I can take her on the street in, if I choose to. And a tub of fresh, hot water. For Catalina." He turned his head slowly, away from Alberta, to look at Catalina and smile. A vacant smile, but charming just the same. Part of the show. "Oh, yes." He walked away from the door and whipped the sheets off the bed, balling them up as he returned to the door. "Clean sheets."

He thrust the soiled sheets into Alberta's reluctant arms, and then he slammed the door.

Catalina Lane was staring at him as though *he* were the one who was loco. Her coverlet had slipped a little, in her distraction, and the lace from her chemise peeked through.

"I should've thought of that last night," he muttered, turning his back on her to lock the door.

"Should've thought of what?"

Jackson turned and looked at her again, and it appeared she hadn't moved at all. He leaned back against the door and crossed his arms over his chest. "I have a reputation to think of, you know. I can't let it be known that I spent the night in the same room with a woman I paid a thousand dollars for . . . and didn't touch her."

She looked thoroughly disgusted with him, and that was just fine. There was no need for her to realize that he still didn't know what to do with her, that Alberta would be suspicious if she thought Kid Creede hadn't gotten what he'd paid for, and if he decided to take Catalina with him . . .

Stupid idea. There was no way he could stand to be on the trail with Catalina Lane and not have her. And he wouldn't take her, not even if she asked . . . which she wasn't likely to do. The virgin princess, waiting for her prince charming.

Her eyes fell to his chest, and her mouth dropped open. Jackson looked down to see what Catalina was no doubt gaping at. His thumb continued to bleed, a trickle at most, and the blood ran down his hand to his wrist.

"For heaven's sake, Jackson," she said, forgetting her anger to cross the space that separated them. "That was a dumb thing to do."

"She'd expect blood . . ."

"I don't care what Alberta expects," Catalina snapped, taking his hand in her own smaller one. Small and white and soft . . . and strong. She held on even as he gently tried to pull away from her.

"We'll have to clean it right away, and again when the hot water comes."

"It's just a scratch . . ."

"It is not a scratch. It's a cut. Really, Jackson." She bent over his injured hand and he kept his eyes on the top of her golden head. Hair as soft as the hand that held his own, and as rich with gold as any ore. For the span of a few heartbeats he allowed her to hold his hand and enjoyed the odd warmth, the moment of rare peace. Nothing would touch him right now. Nothing ugly or mean. Death was held at bay for a while, for a few precious seconds.

Catalina led him to the tub and plunged his hand under the cold, soapy water. She washed the thumb gently, cleansing it and drying it and then, as he sat on the edge of the bed, bandaging his thumb with a strip torn from the hem of one of Alberta's blue curtains. The coverlet in which Catalina had wrapped herself had fallen from her shoulders to be abandoned on the floor, there by the tub, and she didn't seem to miss the protection it had offered. She sat beside him in her chemise and drawers and gave her full attention to the cut on his thumb, a cut he wouldn't have given a second thought.

"There are a few details we need to discuss," Jackson said when she finished with the bandage.

"What kind of details?" Catalina rose and walked away from him, nervous once her chore was done.

"Outside this room, call me Kid."

She turned and looked across the room to him, a question in her golden eyes. "Why?"

"Few people know my real name, and I'd like to keep it that way. When we're alone you can call me whatever you will." He wouldn't tell her that he liked the sound of his given name on her lips.

She started to smile, but that smile faded quickly. "Jackson, you have to get out of Baxter. I know you don't believe me, but I really *do* come from 1996, and you really *are* supposed to die in an ambush in Baxter. I don't know exactly when, I don't even know if it was in 1896, but you've done so much for me I can't allow you to . . ."

She ignored the hands he raised, asking her silently to cease her prattling, so he ordered it in a voice that left no room for argument. She stopped for a moment and proceeded to argue with him anyway.

Jackson rose slowly from the edge of the bed, and the look he gave her quieted her nonsense at last. "You don't have to try to convince me that you're loco. I knew that was true the moment you opened your mouth. I've told you, I won't touch you. Your precious virginity is safe. . . ."

"Until you leave me here," she said, pouting almost seductively.

"I haven't made my decision about that just yet."

Catalina stood there in nothing but her chemise and a short pair of bloomers and stuck her tongue out at him, like a child who'd been denied her candy.

"Lovely," he muttered.

"Why don't we leave today?" she asked impatiently. "Have you taken a job here? Quit. Leave it. They can find someone else."

"I've already turned the job down."

"Good. We can leave today," she said with finality.

Jackson shook his head. "Not just yet. Alberta will be watching us closely. Maybe in a couple of days . . ."

"You may not have a couple of days!"

She was the most infuriating, the most insufferable, the most beautiful woman he had ever seen. And she had the best pair of legs. Long and slender, but shapely.

She caught him staring and picked up the coverlet from the floor to wrap herself once again. "What kind of job would bring Kid Cretin to Baxter, anyway?" she asked sharply, transparent in her attempt to take his mind off her great legs.

"Harold Goodman wanted me to murder some old man so he could take his land," Jackson said flatly, all the while slowly raising his eyes from her legs to her face.

She looked properly shocked. "Out-and-out murder? Thank heavens you said no."

"He wasn't willing to pay my price," Jackson lied, wanting nothing more than to widen the distance between them. Catalina was naive; she wouldn't understand or condone what he did.

Catalina hugged the coverlet to her body and turned her eyes away from him. "Would you have done it," she asked softly, "if Harold Goodman had offered you more money?"

He opened his mouth to say yes, to convince her that he was no better than his reputation, but he couldn't. The lie stuck in his throat.

"You wouldn't have," she said, relief and assurance in her voice. "Are you going to warn the old man?"

"Hell, no," Jackson said gruffly. "This is none of my affair."

Catalina took a single step toward him but was smart enough to stop more than an arm's length away. "But it is your affair," she whispered. "Goodman'll just hire someone else. You can find

106

the old man and warn him today, and tonight we can sneak away from here. . . ."

"No."

"Really, Jackson. You're so stubborn." She hadn't given up. He could hear her own stubbornness in her voice.

They could have argued all morning, but Juanita arrived, sleepy and yawning, bearing breakfast and a neatly folded sand-colored dress, plain and well-worn.

"Good morning, Kid." She greeted him with a warm smile, an invitation in her black eyes. An invitation he needed badly to accept. Staying with Catalina was surely going to kill him.

Jackson stepped into the hallway, ordered—*ordered*—there by Catalina. He heard the scrape of the chair as she placed it beneath the doorknob. He should be relieved to have a few minutes of peace, a respite from the woman's constant irritating presence.

It was still early for the employees and the patrons of Alberta's. The hallway was deserted, and as he made his way down the stairs to the second floor, Jackson realized how aggravating the unnatural quiet was. He had to admit, he'd been easily annoyed since finding Catalina in the desert.

Juanita was awake. Hell, even if she'd been sound asleep, he would have knocked on her door.

Jackson was almost certain Juanita would still be in the room she'd occupied five years ago. She'd told him more than once that she'd decorated it herself. He'd thought then that the pastels and lace didn't suit her, but he'd kept that opinion to himself.

That room was on the second floor at the end of the hall, and once Jackson had made up his mind he didn't hesitate. With Juanita beneath him, he would work Catalina Lane out of his system once and for all.

He had raised his hand to knock when he heard the forced squeak of bedsprings. And then again, and then again. For a moment he thought that perhaps Juanita had moved to another room, but then he heard her laugh. A low laugh, followed closely by a deep moan. Definitely not Juanita. Juanita's customer.

Jackson turned away, more frustrated than ever. Somehow he was certain it was all Catalina's fault.

Alberta's saloon by morning's light, free of cigar smoke and laughter and drunken shouts, appeared innocent enough. Tables with upturned chairs on their surface. A clean-swept floor. The smell of oil. Either Milo stayed up late to clean or he was an early riser who had already done the job.

Jackson walked slowly down the stairs and flipped over one of the chairs. He sat with his back against the wall and propped his boots on the table where his chair had been moments earlier.

It had finally happened; he was cracking. Losing his mind, along with the control that had kept him alive this long. There was no other explanation for his behavior. Why did he feel responsible for a lunatic who accepted a job in a whorehouse and then refused to do her job? Why did he feel obligated to stay away from her, when he should stalk up those stairs right now and *demand* what he had paid for?

And why in hell did he want her so bad?

Jackson lit a cigar and tried his best to forget that Catalina was, at this moment, sitting naked in a tub of water in his room. *His room.*

He finished his cigar, thinking about Catalina's legs. He sat there for a while longer, thinking a bit more. Not just about her legs. Strangely enough, he could close his eyes and see her as clear as day. He fingered the blue bandage on his thumb, remembering the swell of the breasts he had watched as she'd carefully doctored the scratch. No one, that he could recall, had ever cared much for his welfare. The only doctoring he'd ever received had been either paid for, delivered by another of his own kind, or forced at the end of his Colts. He couldn't remember ever seeing a concerned frown like the one Catalina had shown him.

He had waited long enough, Jackson decided as he all but jumped to his feet. Surely Catalina had finished with her bath by now. He climbed the stairs slowly, still fingering the bandage on his thumb, frowning in spite of himself.

The door opened as he reached the second-floor landing, and he instinctively turned his head. The door to Juanita's room was open, and she stuck out her head and smiled at him. A hand snaked through the opening, and she crooked a finger at him.

Jackson turned away from the stairs and toward Juanita.

"I thought I heard you in the hall earlier," she whispered as he neared the door.

Through the crack in the door, Jackson could see her sleeping customer, facedown on the bed. Pale tousled hair, paler butt. A red silk vest had been carefully hung over the back of a chair, and dark trousers were neatly folded on the seat of that chair. That gambler, Lucky, slept soundly on Juanita's squeaky bed.

Juanita was wearing nothing but a red silk robe, thin enough for him to see every curve of her body. Her face was flushed, her hair loose and tumbled around her face and shoulders, and with her smile she offered him what she had just given Lucky.

"Were you looking for me?" she asked after a short silence.

Jackson fingered the blue bandage unconsciously. "Yeah, but you were busy."

Juanita slipped through the door and closed it slowly behind her. "There's an empty room upstairs," she offered. "It's not very fancy, but it has a bed." To emphasize her suggestion, she pressed her body against his.

Her face was flushed, anxious, her lips parted invitingly. She rubbed her leg against his, and her robe fell open. Juanita offered herself openly, without reservation.

And he didn't want her.

She had just come from another man. And, in spite of himself, Jackson could see Catalina's smile. Hell, he felt like she was *watching* him.

"Maybe later," he said, stepping back and away from Juanita.

She followed him, her smile fading just a little. "Why not now?"

Jackson turned, but he could hear her right behind him, and then he felt her hand on his arm as she followed him up the stairs to the third floor.

At the top of the stairs Juanita turned left and tried to pull Jackson with her. Jackson turned right, and Juanita didn't let go. She clung to him, even as he inserted his key into the lock.

Catalina stood on the balcony and watched the slow, irregular parade of churchgoers beneath her. She'd finally gotten her trip to the outhouse, having refused Jackson's offer of a chamber pot. A chamber pot! How disgusting. The outhouse seemed almost civilized in comparison.

She'd also had a long hot bath, after ordering Jackson from the room. He'd left her alone, locking the door and taking both keys with him. Catalina followed his example of the previous night and placed that same chair under the doorknob while she'd bathed. She had no doubt that Jackson would've been able to get past that, if he'd wished, but it wouldn't have been easy.

Amazing, what a luxury a hot bath and a change of clothes had been. The tan dress Juanita had provided for her was a little too big, and prim as any lady's. Long sleeves fell just past her wrist, and the plain round collar was quite modest. The full skirt touched the floor when she

111

walked across it. At least she didn't look like a hooker anymore.

Only after she was fully dressed had she removed the chair that blocked the door, wondering as she slid it away where Jackson was, and why he'd been gone so long.

With her hands grasping the rail, Catalina leaned forward. A man looked up and smiled, but his head was quickly yanked down, his wife's fingers pinching one ear. Catalina smiled. What must they think of her, these women who lived a completely different lifestyle from her own? Now and then. In the present and the future.

She accepted the fact that she'd traveled back in time a hundred years, and the questions that had assaulted her at first were dismissed. It made as much sense as questioning her very existence, or the existence of the soul. It was real. She was here, and the people around her weren't dreams or ghosts; they weren't hallucinations. They were as real as she. In fact, she was the one who didn't belong. If she thought about it too much, she'd be as loco as Jackson accused her of being.

She had wondered only once if she'd be able to make her way back. There was nothing for her in 1996. No family, few friends, a low-paying job. She had even less here, but the possibilities were endless.

Catalina knew she couldn't stay in Baxter. Even if the entire town didn't think she was a prostitute, she was always aware of the importance of getting Jackson away from this place. If she had to drag him by that long hair of his, she'd get him away from this town as soon as possible.

She heard the key in the lock and turned to face the door, anxious—for some inexplicable reason—to see Jackson Cady's face.

She leaned against the railing and stared through the open balcony door, through the blue room, to a still and solemn Jackson. It was ridiculous, but her heart beat faster just to look at him, and her mouth was suddenly dry. It had been that way almost from the first moment she'd seen him, and now that she knew what it was like to be kissed by Kid Creede . . . Jackson Cady . . .

But he had made it clear that he had no interest in virgins. Catalina's belief that there was one special man for her had been renewed, was stronger than ever. Had she traveled back in time to find him? Was Jackson the man she had dreamed of all her life?

"I do believe," he said lazily, still standing in the open doorway, "that's the ugliest dress I've ever seen."

Catalina smiled brightly, grabbed the full skirt with both hands, and curtsied deeply. "Thank you, sir." He couldn't ruin her good mood with his insults.

But her smile faded quickly when Juanita appeared behind him. The hussy placed her hand on Jackson's arm.

When she'd delivered the dress and breakfast earlier Juanita had been dressed. Now the harlot wore only a thin robe that gaped open almost to her navel. Her hair was mussed, her face was full of color—it didn't take a lot of imagination to picture what had just taken place.

Linda Jones

"I'll see you later?" the slut asked in a low voice that carried to the balcony quite well.

Jackson turned his head just slightly. "Sure," he said easily, just before Juanita raised up on her toes to kiss him. He not only allowed the harlot to kiss him, he opened his mouth as Juanita did.

Catalina could stand no more. She turned swiftly and returned her attention to the street below. How could he! And right under her nose! She closed her eyes and took a deep breath. No corset to impede that simple act today.

She had no claim on Jackson, she reminded herself. None at all. He had saved her . . . twice now . . . and had continued to make it clear to her that he had no use for inexperienced women. He preferred tramps like Juanita.

Her heart skipped a beat when the door slammed shut, but she didn't turn around. She didn't turn around when she sensed him in the balcony doorway, or when she heard his soft step behind her.

She didn't even look his way when he stood beside her at the rail, but took a small step away from him.

"It's not *that* ugly," he said contritely, and Catalina realized that the man had no idea what he'd done. So, she could add insensitivity to the growing list of his faults.

She took a deep breath and turned to him, careful not to let her unreasonable jealousy show. "I've been thinking, and I have a plan."

He showed little interest in hearing her plan, but she continued anyway.

"This afternoon we find the old man Goodman wants killed and warn him about what's going on. Tomorrow morning we make a stop at the general store and stock up on supplies. Discreetly, of course. Alberta mustn't suspect what we're up to."

"We're not up to anything, Catalina." There was a hint of warning in his soft voice.

She ignored that comment. "All I ask is that you take me to another town. A larger town would be nice, maybe Phoenix or Tucson."

"I don't intend . . ." he began.

"I don't intend to stay in Baxter. I'm leaving, with or without you," she snapped.

He turned those pale blue eyes on her, the set of his mouth was harsh. "You wouldn't make it ten miles on your own."

"I can be very resourceful."

That got a grin out of him, which only infuriated Catalina more. "You know nothing about me."

"I know you're a twenty-seven year old virgin with a tendency to get lost and to concoct wild stories along the way. I know you can flatten a man, when you've a mind to, and have a singular distaste for chamber pots and corsets." He leaned his face closer to hers and cracked another smile. "I know you mumble in your sleep and dearly hate to be called Cat. I know . . ."

"Enough," she said sharply. "Will you take me with you or not?"

He pulled his eyes away from her and looked down to the street below. "I haven't decided."

115

"Well, make up your frigging mind," Catalina snapped.

He turned his head slightly, so that he caught her eye. His long hair fell in black, chestnut-tipped waves that caught the sun. "Make up my what?"

"Make a decision, Jackson." Catalina turned away from him to stalk into the blue room.

Only after she was gone did Jackson search the rooftops and windows on the opposite side of the street. Careless. He was never careless. He should have searched those areas before he'd stepped onto the balcony.

He should've taken Juanita up on her offer, but in spite of himself he'd continued to see Catalina's face. Smiling, as she had when he'd opened the door. Sparkling eyes, golden hair, anxious lips. It wasn't enough that in his heart he knew he could never touch Catalina Lane. He still wanted her, more than he'd ever wanted anything. And, for some reason he couldn't quite grasp, he wanted Catalina to know that he hadn't touched Juanita.

He wouldn't mention it, one way or another. It was none of her concern.

Still, he'd felt a strange kind of guilt when Catalina had seen Juanita in the doorway. She had obviously suspected the worst; her smile had faded so quickly.

He could hear her, stomping through the room they'd shared, her booted feet banging against the floor as she took quick, angry steps. She was talking to herself again, and that wasn't a good sign. He couldn't make out much, other than the hotly spoken words *Kid Cretin* once or twice.

There was no way he would survive a long journey in her company. She brought out the worst in him, awakened insecurities and a strange protectiveness that he didn't understand. And didn't want to understand.

But he knew just as well that he couldn't leave her in Baxter. Alberta had laid claim to her, and it would take a goodly number of miles to break that claim.

He stopped in the doorway and watched her pace, unaware that he studied her. He'd called her dress ugly, and it was. But Catalina looked beautiful in it. Like a flower he'd seen once, growing out of a cluster of rocks on a rugged hillside. Beauty where there should be none. Her face glowed, radiance where there should be pallor.

Catalina stopped pacing and stared at him, that damned question in her eyes. She looked to him to help her, to protect her, to give her more than any person had asked of him. Jackson was afraid he didn't have that to give.

But he couldn't refuse her. She had a hold on him that was undeniable . . . and he had to find a way to free himself of that hold. No one owned Kid Creede, least of all a woman.

"All right," he said, his voice displaying none of his emotion, cold and smooth as always. "I'll get you out of Baxter."

Her smile warmed him, but he dared not show it. "Thank you, Jackson. I don't know what I'd do without you. And the old man? We'll warn him?"

Jackson shook his head. "I don't . . ." he began.

"Please," she begged. "I won't rest if we don't at least warn the poor man."

"And if you don't rest, I don't suppose I'll be able to rest either."

Catalina shrugged her shoulders and smiled almost sheepishly, and Jackson had his answer.

Chapter Eight

He couldn't have been more than five feet five inches tall, and his shock of white hair and deeply wrinkled face marked him as an old man. His clothing was clean, but as tattered as that of the miners who frequented Alberta's, and the hat he had removed and tossed onto the seat of his wagon was merely functional, wide-brimmed and shabby. This was the rancher Harold Goodman wanted murdered?

Jackson scowled—no surprise—as they advanced on Doc Booker. The old man was apparently unaware of their approach as he prepared to climb into the seat of a rough buckboard hitched to two horses that could only be called nags.

Catalina tried to hurry, no easy feat in the long, hot dress she wore. Jackson had learned, rather quickly, who Doc Booker was, and that he always came to town on Sunday for church services. They had to speak to the man now, or else make the long trip to his ranch.

If Jackson was right, and Alberta was indeed watching them closely, that could prove to be difficult.

Doc Booker started, literally jumped, when he

noticed they were nearly upon him. The man pressed his back to the buckboard, and his eyes grew wide with fear as he riveted them on Jackson. It was an understandable fear, one Catalina had briefly shared.

Then the fear faded, and a sad acceptance stole over Doc Booker's face.

"Kid Creede," he said, a trace of an accent much like Grandma Lane's in his gravelly voice, marking him a Southerner. "I reckon I know why you're here."

Jackson didn't ease the man's fears, as Catalina thought he should have, but continued to stride forward. She took quick steps to keep up with him. Why didn't he say something?

"The Goodman boy wants my little ranch awful bad, but he's too chicken to do the dirty work himself." There was slowly growing anger in the old man's voice. "But then, that's how you make your livin', isn't it Kid? Doin' other folks' dirty work for them. I hope you're gettin' paid plenty for this deed."

All fear was gone now, and the man faced Jackson with defiance in his eyes, looking up as the gunman came closer. Doc Booker had no weapon that Catalina could see, and still he faced the infamous Kid Creede without any sign of his earlier panic.

Jackson stopped just short of running over the old man. "So you know?" he asked quietly.

"Of course I know," the old man spat. "Why do you think he had to bring you in? Do I look so fearsome that none other than the great Kid Creede can manage to do me in? Some of Harold's ranch hands are old cronies of mine, just like his pa was. If he coulda got one of them to do the job for him, he wouldn't need you, now would he? I have a few friends left in this territory, and they let me know what's what."

Jackson looked Doc Booker up and down, and then looked past the short man into the buckboard. "And you still travel unarmed?"

"I'll not shoot any man, not even a soulless bastard like you, Kid."

Catalina saw the fingers of Jackson's right hand twitch at that insult, and she stepped forward.

"We came to warn you," she said calmly, trying to catch Doc Booker's eyes. Still the two men stared at one another. "Ja . . . the Kid turned down the job, and he wanted to make certain you knew you were in danger before we leave town. Certainly Harold Goodman will hire someone else, but it should take a while."

Doc Booker pulled his eyes away from Jackson and stared at Catalina. They were of the same height, and stood almost nose to nose. "You must be Alberta's new gal. Cat, is it?" There was no welcoming softness in his voice, but the same condemnation she had seen in the faces of the people of Baxter as she and Jackson walked the street.

"My name is Catalina," she said tersely, "and I am *not* Alberta's gal."

"Let's go." Jackson grabbed her arm and pulled her away. "Are you happy now?"

Catalina took a quick look over her shoulder and found Doc Booker watching their retreat with a puzzled expression on his face. There was no longer anger or fear there, but confusion and even a bit of softness. Perhaps he'd expected to die when he'd seen Jackson approaching, and now he watched them walk away.

"Did you have to tell him we were leaving town?" Jackson's question was whispered, even though there was no one nearby to overhear their conversation.

"Who's he going to tell?"

Jackson shook his head slightly and sighed. A rather disgusted sigh, Catalina decided.

There were few people out on a Sunday afternoon. Those who were on the street cast sideways glances at the couple who argued quietly as they hurried down the boardwalk. Catalina could almost smile: the gunfighter and the prostitute. She would have to be more careful in the next town. Appearances were so very important, social skills everything.

How would she support herself? What skills did she have that would aid her in the nineteenth century? As a housewife, her skills were all but nonexistent. So much had changed in a hundred years. What about business? There were few opportunities for women, but certainly in a larger city, with the knowledge she had . . . she brushed those worries from her mind. She would think of something.

Jackson stopped abruptly and yanked Catalina back into the shadows as she stepped past him.

"Over there," he whispered.

Catalina tried to follow his line of vision, but she saw nothing. "What?"

"There by the livery."

Catalina looked across the street and down several buildings. A man stood just inside a dark doorway. She wouldn't have seen him if Jackson hadn't told her just where to look.

Jackson turned her to face him and tilted his head down. Those pale blue eyes were cold and hard. "That's Alberta's bartender, Milo, watching my horse."

"How can you tell?" Catalina whispered. She'd seen no more than a figure darkening the doorway; but then, she didn't have her glasses.

"Milo is the biggest man in town, and there's no mistaking that bushy head of his. He didn't follow us to meet Doc Booker. I would have known."

Catalina had no doubt that was true. "So, he's making certain we don't leave?" She remembered Milo well, the burly bartender who had held her down so she could be trussed to a wall.

"He knows we can't leave Baxter on foot." Jackson leaned down, placing his nose almost on hers. "Dammit, Catalina, how the hell am I going to get you out of here?"

There was a tightness in her chest that had nothing to do with Jackson's closeness. What if he left her here? What if Alberta made it too difficult for him to take her? Would he ride away without a word?

"I won't leave you," he whispered, though the words seemed torn from him against his will. He'd recognized her terror and attempted to ease it, though his responsibility for her was as reluctant as ever.

"Promise me," she whispered.

"I don't make promises."

"Promise me," Catalina repeated, her fear of being left alone at Alberta's making her heart beat fast and her breath catch in her chest.

"I don't . . ." Jackson began, and then he hesitated. "I've never . . . Kid Creede's word isn't worth a plug nickel."

Catalina smiled. She saw the uncertainty in his eyes, the softening of his hard lips.

"But Jackson Cady's word is as good as gold."

Jackson pulled his face away from hers, took her arm roughly, and practically pulled her toward Alberta's. Her statement had only made him angry, angrier than she'd ever seen him. His cool control was gone.

They hadn't gone far when that control came back. His step slowed and his grip on her arm eased. Still, he didn't look at her, but guided her at a slower pace.

"We'll have to pretend we're getting along right well," he said softly.

"We have to pretend? I thought we were . . ."

Jackson's glare silenced her. "Alberta needs to think I'm getting my money's worth, that you're deciding you like your new job."

Could she ever hope to fool someone like Alberta? She'd been told, more than once, that she'd make a lousy poker player. Deception was not her game.

"She won't think I'm earning my way if you continue to see Juanita." Catalina tried to keep the jealousy out of her voice, but it wasn't easy.

"That's none of your business."

Catalina stopped in the middle of the board-walk and yanked back the arm Jackson grasped. He spun on her, a warning on his face that she chose to ignore.

"How do you think it looks?" Catalina whispered harshly, though there was no one close by to hear her, "when you spend the night with me and then go to that . . . that tramp first thing in the morning? It's humiliating, that's what it is."

"Juanita and I are very old friends. . . ."

"Hah!" Catalina scoffed. "She's a whore. God only knows how many men have screwed her."

Her voice had risen as she spoke, and she heard a loud gasp from a woman who was walking down the boardwalk, hidden from her view by Jackson. Great; how many laws of society had she broken in those two sentences?

The woman—Catalina thought it might have been the same woman who had snubbed her as she rode into town—stepped off the boardwalk and into the street to avoid passing Catalina too closely.

It didn't help matters any that Jackson was smiling, that he seemed to find the entire scene terribly amusing.

Catalina resumed walking, refusing Jackson's assistance, brushing his hand away as she passed him and he tried to take her arm again.

"Well?" she asked, staring straight ahead.

"Well what?" Jackson asked calmly from just behind her.

"Juanita," she hissed.

"I'll think about it," Jackson said softly, as if his mind were elsewhere.

He had the good sense to stay well behind her as she entered Alberta's and made her way through the saloon and up the stairs. He'd damn well better not leave her here, and he'd damn well better not touch Juanita again. Another wave of what could only be jealousy washed over her, and even though she recognized it for the senseless emotion it was, she couldn't shake it. Heaven help her if she was truly falling for a man like Jackson Cady.

He wasn't asleep, of that Catalina was certain. His eyes were closed, and he hadn't said a word since they'd returned to the blue room. He reclined casually on the bed with his ankles crossed and his hands behind his head, his breathing slow and even. But he wasn't asleep.

Her anger faded as she sat and watched Jackson pretend to sleep so he wouldn't have to talk to her. None of this was his fault. He'd really been quite . . . decent where she was concerned. Too decent, maybe.

Jackson Cady wasn't nearly as tough as he would have the world believe, but he wasn't a man to be taken lightly. He'd lived the kind of life she could only imagine. Hard. Violent. Unpredictable.

But he was more than a gunslinger. He was a flesh-and-blood man with a secret, tender spark in his cold eyes that only she could see.

She wanted, at that moment, to lean over him and kiss him. One more of those searing kisses that could lead to so much more. The effect of a simple touch was stunning; but then, it was new to her. It was no wonder that women in love lost every speck of common sense.

Was it the same with men? she wondered. Did they think of one woman to the exclusion of all else? Was the need to touch so deep it was painful?

What would it take to convince Jackson that she could give him something that tramp Juanita never could?

The thought of that hussy made Catalina lose her smile, as well as the warm contentment that had crept over her as she'd watched Jackson. She didn't know how to fight someone like that.

The realization that she wanted Jackson—that he was the man she had waited for all these years—was almost a relief. After all this time, after dreaming and giving up and almost settling for a loveless life with Wilson Ross, she had found what she'd always wanted.

That smile began to creep across her face again, and she bit her lower lip nervously, uncertainly. That remarkable knowledge was just the first step. There was still Jackson's stubborn assertion that he didn't bed virgins to contend with.

Jackson sat with his back to the wall, a single untouched glass of whiskey in front of him. Where the hell was she? She'd all but pushed him from the room, insisting on her privacy to prepare for the night ahead.

She'd resisted at first, and then had accepted his command that she make an appearance in the saloon in a frighteningly quick turnabout.

Hadn't given it a second thought since then, apparently. Could she convince Alberta that she wasn't a prisoner, but a willing employee? Catalina Lane did tell a good story when she set her mind to it.

As always, he sat alone. Juanita had tried to engage him in conversation, sitting in his lap and asking him to buy her a drink. He'd bought her one glass of Alberta's deadly whiskey, and then sent her on her way. She'd tried again, as she had that morning, to make him promise to come to her. Twice in one day, asked by two different women for a damned promise! He owed them nothing, least of all his word.

Juanita had recovered quickly, and now stood at Lucky's shoulder. The gambler who had bid on Catalina. The gambler who had spent the night in Juanita's bed. Why did he feel so much anger over the fact that Lucky had wanted Catalina, and none over his night in Juanita's bed? He didn't think on it much. Didn't want to.

He saw her first, as she stepped down the staircase, and he couldn't suppress a slow grin. Alberta had dressed her new girl in gold satin and black lace. The gold suited Catalina, hugging her body as if it had been sewn on. The neckline plunged daringly, trimmed with black lace that was stark against the pale globes of her breasts.

There was a bright smile on Catalina's face as she walked slowly down the stairs, and her eyes remained on him all the way. With each calculated step, her hips swung just enough. With each breath she took it seemed as if her breasts would burst free. Jackson's smile faded. Damnation, she didn't have to take the charade this far.

He found he was holding his breath, and he didn't release it until she was almost upon him. "Hello, baby," she crooned as she sat on his knee and wrapped her arms around his neck. "Did you miss me?"

Jackson finally tore his eyes from her and scanned the room. Every eye was on them . . . on Catalina, to be specific. The eyes he met turned quickly away, afraid of any challenge that might be there.

He turned a scowling face back to Catalina "Baby?"

"Sorry," she said breathlessly. "Darlin'. Did you miss me . . . darlin'?"

Did she know what she was doing to him? He was already hard, and if they hadn't been sitting in a room full of people, he would have taken her right there, pulled her down on top of him, virgin or not.

"Perhaps you should smile," she suggested, whispering into his ear, finishing her sentence with a quick nip of her teeth on the lobe.

He placed his arms around her waist and pulled her close so he could whisper back, "You've gone too far, Catalina Lane."

"You like?" she whispered back.

She wanted to know if he liked what he saw or not? Jackson didn't answer.

"Isn't this what you had in mind?"

She pulled her head away from his ear and placed the tip of her nose against his. Now he could see the amusement in her eyes, there in the dancing flecks of gold. Amusement and . . . something else he didn't want to identify.

"I should put you over my knee right now and whale the tar out of you," he threatened.

"Ooohh," she crooned, pursing her red lips. "Kinky."

"Catalina," he began, with a warning tone to his voice. "What exactly are you doing?"

"I'm only doing what you told me to do, Jackson." She whispered his name, her lips almost on his. She faltered a little, and he could see the flash of indecision in her eyes. What did she want from him?

He laid his lips lightly against her ear. "I told you to pretend to like your job; I didn't say you had to perform your new duties in front of an audience." He didn't pull away immediately. She smelled so good, clean and sweet, and her golden hair brushed his face. Catalina was soft and warm beneath his hands. No corset tonight, just skin beneath the gold silk he touched.

She didn't move away, but laid her head against his shoulder, curling into him just slightly. If he didn't know better, he would think she was trying to seduce him. When she began to trail her fingers along his neck he almost came out of the chair.

"What's the matter?" she whispered, lifting her head and placing her face close to his. The tip of her nose touched his, and her lips—reddened, full lips—almost touched his mouth. He wanted to kiss her, right here, right now, but it wouldn't have been enough.

"Make the rounds," he said, drawing his face

away from hers before he gave in to temptation and kissed those red lips.

"What?" The seductive huskiness was gone from her voice, and Jackson smiled.

"You're not going to sit on my knee all night, you know. Alberta will expect you to drink with her customers, spread that smile around, wiggle that nice ass for the men who are just waiting for my week to be up."

Catalina lifted her eyes and surveyed the room, obviously not liking what she saw.

"Don't worry," he said softly. "Everyone knows you're mine for the week. No one will challenge that."

"No one?" she asked uncertainly.

He smiled and gave her a gentle shove. She sounded like a lost little girl again, in spite of her fancy dress and made-up face. "No one," he assured her.

He watched her walk away, giving him several backward glances as she approached the crowded center of the room. It had seemed like a good idea at the time, but when he saw a miner pull her into his lap he had to force himself to stay seated.

Catalina looked over the disgustingly grubby miner's shoulder to find Jackson staring at her. She wanted to stick her tongue out at him, or give him the finger, but she did neither. She turned to the miner, her friend Milford.

"Let me buy you a drink," Milford offered with a wide grin.

Catalina smiled but shook her head. "No liquor

for me, Milford. My head's still reeling from last night."

"Just one," he begged. "You can sit on my knee and drink it as slow and easy as you like." Toothless Milford was staring openly at her breasts, grinning like a fool, all but drooling into his whiskey.

Catalina shook her head slowly. Jackson could have let her stay at his table. Surely Alberta didn't expect anything more from her tonight. Yet Jackson had all but ordered her to mingle with these miners and cowboys who wanted to ply her with whiskey and paw her.

Maybe the gold dress she'd requested from Alberta hadn't been such a good idea after all. She'd only asked for something seductive for Jackson, for his benefit, and she hadn't given a moment's thought to the other patrons of Alberta's. She wanted him looking at her, not that hussy Juanita. And then what? She wanted Jackson to get what he had paid for.

She met his glare over Milford's shoulder. He wasn't smiling, and she couldn't force herself to give him a seductive grin to show him how easy this all was. She'd never before met a man who made her want to melt, who made her want to touch and kiss and explore all night. Had she come all this way . . . all this time . . . just to find Jackson? And if that was true, would she be a fool to let him slip away?

A new and rougher hand on her arm made her look away from Jackson and up at the man who pulled her to her feet. It was Harold Goodman, that little weasel, and he was leering at her with very bleary eyes. The man was well on his way to drunk.

"Join me at my table, Catalina," he said, his grasp at her wrist tightening.

"That's very sweet, but . . ." Catalina stopped speaking when he laid a hand over the swell of her breasts above the low neckline trimmed with black lace. She knocked his hand away, but he raised it again to brush his fingers over the same skin.

Catalina looked over her shoulder, waiting for Jackson to help her. But her brief glance toward Jackson squashed any hopes she might have had for rescue. He sat calmly at his table, apparently unconcerned for her safety.

Catalina looked up into Harold Goodman's face and smiled sweetly. "Well, I guess it wouldn't hurt to have just one little drink."

Goodman presumably attributed her change of heart to his charming ways, and the grip at her wrist eased. That was what Catalina had been waiting for. She twisted so that her back was to him and flipped him over her shoulder. Harold Goodman landed on top of Milford's table, and it fell to the floor with a crashing, wood-splintering thud, the spindly table legs giving way.

She didn't even give Goodman a second glance, but turned her eyes to Jackson. He was suppressing a smile, and so she forgave him . . . just a little. He raised his still full glass to her, as close to a salute as she was ever likely to get from him. He knew that she was capable of taking care of Goodman. She'd tossed Jackson to the ground, once.

Juanita had the gall to saunter over to Jackson's table, and to sit on his knee while Catalina watched. Jackson's eyes didn't leave Catalina's face, but he didn't push Juanita away, either. And he still hadn't agreed to stay away from that tramp, as she'd asked just that morning.

Catalina was at the table before she had a chance to think about what she was doing, and had a handful of Juanita's black hair in her hand before the bimbo even knew she was there.

Juanita yelped as Catalina pulled her to her feet. "Did you see that?" Catalina asked quietly, placing her face close to Juanita's. There was surprise there, and anger, and Catalina wondered too late at her hasty act. She didn't need another enemy in Baxter—not that she and Juanita had ever been friends. But it was too late for second thoughts.

Juanita looked to the center of the room, where Harold lay, still. Catalina followed her eyes, and watched as Alberta helped Goodman to his feet. The madam was flustered for the first time since Catalina had met her. She was a very unattractive woman without her air of confidence.

Catalina turned her attention back to the hussy in her hands. "If you don't want that . . . or worse . . . to happen to you, stay away from Kid Creede."

"You can't do this . . ." Juanita said breathlessly, her words denying the fear in her eyes.

Catalina loosened her grip, and then she released Juanita's hair and stepped back. What had Jackson done to her? She had never attacked any person, except in self-defense, in her entire life. All those acts of self-defense had been since she'd come here. Since Jackson had found her in the desert. She stared down at him. He hadn't moved at all, and there was no way to tell what he was thinking, not when those eyes were so cold and distant.

She stepped back, her eyes flitting from Jackson to Juanita. And the one thought she couldn't shake was that she didn't belong here.

"I don't feel well," she said weakly, taking a step back and toward the stairs. Alberta was headed her way, confidence back and fire in her eyes. Harold Goodman had a lot of money and was no doubt a good customer. The madam's hands were doubled at her sides, and Catalina didn't have to think very hard to imagine what her punishment was going to be.

But Jackson rose and stepped between them, blocking Alberta from view.

"Go," he said in a menacing voice, pointing to the stairs.

Catalina didn't need any more encouragement. She turned, spinning on the heels of her black boots, and ran up the two flights of stairs without looking back.

All she heard of the quiet conversation in the saloon beneath her was Jackson's quiet statement, "I'll take care of it." She didn't have to look back to know he was right behind her.

Chapter Nine

Catalina slammed the door behind her, too ashamed to face Jackson. She was making an absolute fool of herself over a man who'd made it clear he didn't care for virgins. *I don't bed virgins*, he'd said without a hint of uncertainty in his voice. He preferred women like Juanita, and made no bones about it.

There was no future for them. She didn't belong here; they never should have met, and she certainly shouldn't have fallen in love with him.

Her heart skipped a beat when she heard the rattle of the doorknob. It twisted slowly, but the door didn't open, and then she heard the scrape of Jackson's key in the lock. He was locking her in.

She listened for his footsteps walking away from her, but there was only silence. Catalina stood with her forehead and a palm against the door, knowing that Jackson waited on the other side. What did he think of her now? He'd called her loco more than once. Is that what he thought? Would he really be so grateful to be rid of her?

"Are you all right?" The whispered question drifted clearly through the wooden door, Jackson's silky voice free of humor or anger or frustration.

"I'm fine. Just sorry I made such an ass of myself."

She waited for him to walk away, as she had before, but he remained where he was. An earlier thought echoed through her head. *In love with him.* All her life she'd waited for that feeling, and when it came it was at the wrong time, in the wrong place, and for a man who was destined to die a violent death.

"Go on to bed," he said gruffly. "I won't be in until . . . late."

She wanted to ask if he was going to Juanita, if he would return to the blue room at all that night, but she was afraid she knew the answer. She had seen the way the two of them had looked together, the way Juanita touched Jackson, the way he kissed her. She didn't ask, because she didn't really want to hear him say it. The very idea hurt too much.

"All right," she said softly, and then she did hear those slow, steady steps, even and soft, as Jackson walked away from her.

He was determined to stay in Baxter until it was safe to take her away. That was her fault. She'd all but begged him to take her with him, pleaded with him not to leave her here alone. How long would he insist they wait? The entire week? Longer? He might not have that much time.

Catalina walked onto the balcony and grasped the rail, taking a deep breath of cool, crisp air. A miracle had brought her here . . . to fall in love with Jackson Cady just to watch him die? She couldn't stand by and allow that to happen, and she couldn't convince him that she *knew* what his destiny was.

If she wasn't here in Baxter, maybe he wouldn't stay. He'd already turned down the job that had brought him here, and he had no ties . . . no reason to stay. He'd never expect her to run, given her fear of traveling alone. Once she was gone, maybe Kid Creede would move on as well.

That would definitely be for the best. Best for Jackson, at least. She would miss him. More than she missed anyone she'd left in the twentieth century.

It had to be something instinctive, something primal, that drew her to him. It was like discovering another, new part of herself. Knowing that she was going to have to let him go, Catalina wished that she had never uncovered that particular wonder.

The crowd moved steadily down the street, almost slithering. The black night was brightened by torches carried high above their heads, and Catalina leaned forward slightly to get a better look. She squinted until the figures lit with firelight were clear. The woman who had stepped into the street to avoid her that very morning was in the lead, along with a preacher. The mob that followed was made up mostly of women, although there were men there as well.

As they neared Alberta's, a lone voice rose singing "Shall We Gather at the River," and soon the entire crowd joined in, much too loud and horribly off key. Catalina took a small step back, removing herself from any light the torches cast as the mob stopped in front of Alberta's to face the front of the saloon like the army she was certain they were, ready to fight.

She could see, through the slats beneath the rail, the vigilantes below.

"It's the Lord's day!" the preacher shouted, and the hymn stopped in mid-verse. "These abominations must be stopped!"

She couldn't see, but beneath her Catalina heard footsteps on the boardwalk.

"Millicent!" Alberta shouted. The madam's cheerful voice gave Catalina chills. "Looking for your husband? He's inside. Come on in."

The woman beside the preacher stepped back, and Catalina assumed the pious sourpuss was Millicent. Suddenly she felt sorry for the woman. What could she do in this time? Leave him? For what? Did he come home drunk every night, with the smell of cheap perfume on his skin? Was that why the woman, Millicent, had hated Catalina at first sight?

The voices below were lowered, and then were raised again, and a torch was raised threateningly, as if the bearer intended to toss it onto the boardwalk. Catalina began to search for the quickest way out of the building, and wondered if she could manage to swing from this balcony to the one below and then to the ground. That was the sort of thing that looked so good in the movies but seemed impossible when you looked down from the third floor and tried to imagine actually hanging over the edge.

But it was a decision she didn't have to make.

Linda Jones

The sheriff intervened, and after a few hotly spoken words the crowd moved away.

Moments later the miners and cowboys filed out of the saloon, grumbling as they were all but herded by the sheriff. It looked like Alberta's had been closed down for the evening, though Catalina had no doubt it would be business as usual the next day.

The greasy gambler was the last to go, headed alone for the boardinghouse down the street. Catalina was a little disappointed. He had been the object of Juanita's attentions, when the hussy hadn't been fawning over Jackson. Catalina had hoped the gambler would be spending the night with Juanita, but it appeared the trollop was available for the evening. Available for Jackson.

She remained on the balcony. Jackson had told her to go to bed, but she couldn't sleep. Not now. There were plans to be made.

If she could save Jackson by leaving, she had no choice. Maybe she could make her way back to the place where he had found her, grasp the wulfenite tight, and return to 1996. The idea left her cold. There wasn't much to go back to. Just an hour ago the possibilities awaiting her in this world seemed so intriguing, so endless. She hadn't realized what part Jackson had played in that excitement until she was faced with the actuality of going on alone.

She heard the key in the lock and turned to face the door. It opened silently, and Jackson turned his eyes immediately to the bed. Then he lifted his head and saw her there.

He looked like the desperado he was supposed

140

to be, dressed all in black, with that growth of hair on his face and those long locks that fell to his shoulders. Catalina could see how he could strike fear into men's hearts. But there was no fear in her heart at the moment.

Jackson kicked the door shut, and that was when Catalina saw the bottle in his hand. He grasped the almost full bottle by the neck, and as he turned whiskey splashed onto the back of his hand.

"You're awake," he said, setting the bottle on the table and lighting the lamp.

Catalina nodded and stepped to the door. Jackson avoided looking at her as he sat at the table and studied the bottle as if there was something fascinating there.

"I hope none of that's for me," Catalina said as she stepped off the balcony and into the room. "I had entirely too much last night."

Jackson shook his head, and still he didn't look at her. "Nope. It's all for me, darlin'."

Catalina closed the balcony door and locked it, and then pulled the drapes closed. Jackson was sitting in the chair that he had placed under the doorknob the night before, and Catalina knew he would eventually place it there again. Barricading them in. Locking the world out.

Catalina took the few, difficult steps that separated them. A hundred years. Had she traveled so far only to leave without tasting what she'd found?

"We could leave tonight," she suggested softly. "Surely Alberta won't suspect."

"Alberta's got men watching this room and the

livery around the clock." He did lift his eyes to her then, studying her with as much intensity as he had the bottle that sat before him. "You're a valuable commodity she can't afford to lose."

"But we could get away, somehow."

Please say yes, she begged silently. *Please don't make me leave here alone.*

But Jackson was shaking his head, and studying the bottle as if he wasn't sure if he wanted it or not. "Sorry. It won't work."

She knew what he really meant. His words told her what she didn't want to know. What she already knew. That there was nothing for them.

Her hands were trembling as she placed them on his shoulders. "Jackson . . ."

He lifted the bottle then and took a long swig. "Get to bed, Catalina," he said softly, a resigned gruffness in his voice.

"Kiss me good night?" Catalina leaned forward, and Jackson turned his head so their lips met briefly. It wasn't what she wanted, but it was better than nothing, a touch of lips that tasted like whiskey and warmed her from the inside out. She tried to prolong the kiss, but Jackson turned away from her, breaking the contact.

She stood behind him to slip out of the gold and black dress. All he had to do was turn around. But he didn't, and he wouldn't, Catalina knew. She dropped the nightgown—a special request, like the gold dress—over her head. A near sheer white gown fit for a fairy princess, it was a bit too long and pooled around her feet. The sleeves were cut wide and fell over her hands, and danced when she lifted her arms. The bodice was cut daringly deep, a v-neckline that plunged almost to her navel. It was a nightgown made for seduction, not for sleeping in, and it was going to be completely wasted.

Jackson wasn't likely to respond. He lifted the bottle to his lips once again.

"Jackson?" Catalina stepped past him to the bed. If he took any notice at all of the seductive nightgown, he didn't show it. His manner and expression were almost weary, or else bored. Either way, he was definitely not interested in her, as she had been so certain he was. Somehow she'd blown it; ruined her chance with Jackson. "I'm sorry I screwed everything up tonight."

He lifted his head only briefly, then looked down again. "Go to sleep."

"I just don't want you to . . . hate me." Surely she could leave him with some good memories of her, even if he didn't care for her as she did him. Even if he didn't love her.

He lifted his head slowly, gazing into her eyes. "I don't hate you, Catalina. If I sometimes seem like I don't know what to do with you, it's because I've never known a woman like you before."

"A loco one?" she offered with a smile.

"You're not loco," he said softly. "I've just never spent any time with ladies . . . except for women like the ones who work here in Alberta's."

At least he hadn't mentioned Juanita by name. "Haven't you ever thought of getting married? Settling down with a nice girl and having children?"

"You've forgotten who you're talking to," he said angrily, lifting the bottle again, hesitating reluctantly. "Kid Creede. What kind of *nice girl* wants to settle down with a gunslinger?"

Catalina sat on the edge of the bed. "Don't sell yourself short, Jackson. You could start all over. It's a big country . . ."

"I told you, when you asked, that I didn't know how many men I'd killed," he interrupted her. "That's not true. I tried to stop counting, but I couldn't." He licked a drop of whiskey from his lower lip. "Thirty-one," he said softly. "A life for every year of my own. Rather prophetic, don't you think? I can't put that behind me. I can't forget."

Catalina stood, wanting, *needing* to go to him, but he stopped her with his raised hand. "No. Stay where you are."

Catalina lowered herself slowly.

"Don't try to make me anything more than I am. Or anything less. Could you look a man in the eye while you shot him in the heart?" For a long, terrible moment Jackson's pale blue eyes held her. He wasn't avoiding her now. Catalina knew that Jackson wanted her to know exactly what he was. No illusions. "I've done it."

Less reluctantly than before, Jackson lifted the bottle to his lips.

"Tell me," she whispered.

"Tell you what?"

"Why?"

Jackson reached out and doused the light, leaving them in complete darkness. "Good night, Catalina."

* * *

He sat in the dark, taking frequent sips of the cheap whiskey that he normally—no, always—avoided.

No one had ever asked him *why* before.

Catalina tossed and turned on the high bed, and only after his eyes had adjusted to the complete darkness could he make out her form there. The curve of her hip as she lay on her side. An arm raised slightly as she shifted, trying to find comfort.

As hard as it would be to keep Catalina with him and not touch her, he knew he couldn't leave her here. She trusted him. In spite of everything she knew, Catalina Lane trusted Kid Creede.

No, he corrected himself. She trusted Jackson Cady.

Her ridiculous story that she was from 1996, that he would be ambushed in Baxter, he dismissed without much thought. He'd always been careful never to place himself in a position where he might be vulnerable. That hadn't changed. Right now he had Harold Goodman to worry about, but that didn't weigh heavily on his mind. He was more concerned with how he could get Catalina out of Baxter without taking on the entire town than facing Harold. By the time the boy managed to hire another gunfighter he would have Catalina well away from this place.

And then what?

He never should have told her his name. She was able to separate Jackson Cady from Kid Creede, so that he was forced to remind her who he was . . . what he was.

Finally she was still, her breathing even. She

wanted to know *why*. He wanted to know why she cared. Why she was jealous of a whore. Why she trusted him.

Jackson rose slowly, leaving what little was left in the bottle sitting on the edge of the table. His resolve was wavering as he stepped toward the bed and Catalina. He unbuckled his belt and draped the gunbelt, with the six-shooters still in their holsters, over the footboard.

Catalina was curled up on her side, hugging the edge of the bed. The evening was warm, and she had folded the blue coverlet to the end of the bed, covering herself with only a thin sheet that came to her waist.

Jackson sat slowly and easily on the opposite side of the bed and eased off his boots. The first boot he set gently on the floor, but the second dropped from his clumsy fingers and hit the floor with a dull thud. He waited, remaining perfectly still, to see if he had awakened Catalina. But she didn't move, didn't even stir.

The shirt he wore he slipped off silently and dropped to the floor by his boots. And then he stretched out beside Catalina, sliding his legs slowly under the sheet until they all but touched hers, and rested his head on the pillow. Her hair was right there, fresh and clean and golden, and he reached out to touch a strand that lay on her pillow, careful not to disturb her.

"When I was fifteen," he whispered, his voice so low it was no more than a hushed breath, "I was mining in Creede, Colorado, with Gus. Augustus Philpot. Gus was always looking for gold, and we'd been all over Colorado and Nevada. Finally it looked like we had struck it rich."

Jackson fondled the strand of hair between his fingers. "I dreamed of gold. Not the things we would have, but of the gold itself. Bright and shining and . . . magic."

He hadn't thought of Gus in years . . . and now he remembered why. It hurt too much. Gus had been the only family he'd ever known. His parents had died when he was six, and he'd run away from the orphanage in Chicago three years later, figuring life on his own couldn't be any worse than it was there.

He'd been wrong, finding out soon enough what real hunger was, and what it meant to be terrified, with no home, no family, nowhere to run. But Gus had taken him in, taught him to work hard, taught him to dream of gold. . . .

"They tried to buy the mine, at a price that was way too low, and Gus refused to sell. He was too happy about the strike to wonder what they might try next. Fenton and Kent Walker. Brothers with a reputation I knew nothing about, until later.

"They shot Gus down in the street. He didn't have a chance. He never wore a gun, and he never saw them coming." Jackson closed his eyes and he could see it: Gus's body twitching and bloody.

"I don't remember everything." His voice slurred slightly, and Jackson was reminded that without the false bravery of the whiskey he wouldn't be telling any of this even to a sleeping Catalina. "But I killed them both. Two guns. Six bullets in each of them." He could still hear the screams as the guns blazed, and remembered that he hadn't realized until the deed was done that the screams had been his.

"Turns out they were real badmen. Ours wasn't the first mine they'd taken over by killing the rightful owner. Gus wasn't the first unarmed man they'd killed."

Jackson slid closer to Catalina, until his legs brushed hers. He spoke soft words into her hair. "They had friends and three brothers, who came after me when word got around what had happened. They laughed when they saw that I was nothing more than a skinny kid . . . but they didn't laugh for long. It's amazing how brave a man can be when he doesn't care if he lives or dies."

He moved a tentative hand to her side, unable to resist the urge to take in some of her softness and warmth. "And that's how it happened, Catalina Lane. That's how Jackson Cady became Kid Creede."

Shifting his weight gingerly, Jackson settled himself against Catalina's back. It seemed like a story about someone else, it had happened so long ago.

Catalina continued to breathe evenly, but it took a real effort. Another tear slipped from her eye and slid across the bridge of her nose to land on her pillow.

He never would have told her those things, never would have shared so much of himself if he hadn't believed her to be sleeping soundly. And so she resisted the urge to roll over and wrap her arms around him and cry on his shoulder and tell him how sorry she was.

It wasn't right. Jackson had never had a chance for a normal, happy life. Never had a chance to know love.

His leg brushed against hers, rough twill against her bare leg, and with his chest against her back Jackson held her. His touch was soft, undemanding, comforting, and Catalina knew he needed that comfort as much as she did. More.

He fell asleep—or passed out—and Catalina let out a deep sigh. The weight of his hand on her side increased, and the breath that touched the back of her neck slowed.

She did love him, and if he would let her, she would teach him to love her. A healing love, a love that would make him forget the past. But she didn't think she would ever get the chance, and a fresh tear fell to her pillow.

Chapter Ten

Catalina opened her eyes slowly. She knew it was morning. A tiny beam of sunlight peeked through a break in the heavy curtains. Time to leave. If she could sneak away from Jackson now, he would have no reason to stay in Baxter.

His chest was against her back, as it had been the night before, but the hand that had rested on her side now lay on the bed in front of her, and a possessive arm encircled her. One leg, covered with the white sheet, rested heavily over hers. She could feel each warm breath Jackson exhaled, there at the top of her spine.

The thin shaft of sunlight touched the almost empty bottle that still sat on the table. She knew the only reason Jackson had confided in her, the only reason he held her now, was the effects of the contents of that bottle. It had broken through his shell, shattered the wall he kept between them, and she knew that when he woke he would distance himself from her again.

Maybe she could slip from the bed without waking him. Maybe not. Catalina decided not to try. For now, while he held her, she would stay.

Catalina remembered the short paragraph about Kid Creede almost word for word. It had painted him as a heartless killer and had told of his death with no regret or passion. Shot a dozen times on the street of Baxter in broad daylight. She shivered at the thought of the warm body that held hers devastated in such a way.

Jackson would certainly have quite a hangover when he did wake. Maybe she didn't have to leave right away. If she could keep him in this room and nurse his hangover, she would have another day. One more day with Jackson, in the safety of the blue room. Tomorrow morning would be soon enough to leave. She knew him well enough already to know that his bender had been a one-time occurrence. There would be no repeat performances, and no more nights sleeping in his arms.

Her eyes drifted closed as Catalina found herself trapped in the comforting warmth of Jackson's arms surrounding her. There was a deep ache accompanying that comfort. An odd combination, but undeniable.

Jackson murmured in his sleep and pulled Catalina solidly against his chest, and she knew there would be no escape this morning.

The whispering click of a key in the lock woke Catalina from a deep sleep. She sat straight up, and Jackson's hand fell from her side as he groaned—a low, rumbling groan from deep in his throat.

Catalina reached for the pistol nearest her feet and pulled it from the holster. It was so much heavier than she'd expected it to be that it sagged as she drew it toward her. But by the time the door swung silently open the six-shooter was held securely in two hands and aimed at the door.

Alberta made a tempting target, and the madam took a single step back as she entered the room and found Catalina pointing one of Jackson's Colts at her midsection.

"Hold on there," Alberta said, a small tremor in her husky voice. "I was just gettin' worried. It's near to noon, and there ain't been a peep from this room."

Catalina didn't lower the weapon, but rested her thumb on the hammer. She didn't trust Alberta as far as she could throw the substantial woman. With good reason. Jackson had been right about the third key.

The bed shifted, and behind her Jackson took a deep, waking breath. A slow hand snaked over her side and rested on her wrist, and Catalina expected Jackson to take the six-shooter from her. But all he did was gently move her thumb from the hammer.

"Double-action, darlin'," he said calmly, sleepily. "All you have to do is pull the trigger."

"I was worried about you two, that's all," Alberta said breathlessly. Her hand remained on the doorknob, and her eyes hadn't left the bed.

Alberta tried to take another step back, but Jackson stopped her with a softly spoken, "Not just yet, Alberta."

His hand moved slowly away from Catalina's wrist, his fingers trailing along her arm. "The key," Jackson said idly. "Leave it on the dresser."

Alberta stepped quickly to do as he ordered,

and then returned to the open door. "Anything else?"

"Yes," Catalina said before Jackson could send the woman on her way. "A plate of biscuits and honey, and a pot of coffee. And a hot bath."

"Another one?" Alberta snapped, and then she pursed her lips tightly. "Anything else?"

Catalina hesitated, enjoying watching Alberta in a weakened position. Of course, she could never actually shoot anyone, not even the madam who had auctioned her off like an animal. But Alberta didn't know that.

"I guess not," Catalina said as she rose slowly from the bed, the gun still trained on the doorway. Alberta shut the door quickly, and only then did Catalina allow her arms to drop.

She took the third key from the dresser and locked the door, and then she turned to face Jackson.

He fell back onto the bed with a groan and covered his eyes with both hands. "Thunderation, what have I done?"

Catalina replaced the key and returned to the bed with the heavy weapon hanging at her side. "What have you done?"

"I don't drink," he mumbled.

Catalina slid the Colt into the holster and sat on the side of the bed. He really did look awful—paler than usual and oddly unfocused for Kid Creede.

"Well," she drawled, "last night you certainly did."

Jackson lifted a hand slightly and glared at her with one bloodshot eye.

"Poor baby," Catalina cooed.

One more day. She should have no trouble keeping Jackson off the street for today, as miserable as he was. But tomorrow morning, before the sun was up, she would go. And she could only pray that Jackson would be right behind her. He didn't deserve to die like that . . . the way the history book said he'd die. He deserved another chance.

"You know . . ." Catalina leaned over his outstretched body. He was covering both eyes again, shutting out the light, or the sight of her, or both. "It's not too late for you to start over."

She thought for a moment that he hadn't heard her, or else he was going to ignore her completely. The hands didn't move, and his breathing didn't change. He took long, deep breaths, even and almost meditative.

"This is a huge country. You said yourself that few people know Jackson Cady is Kid Creede. Think of it, Jackson. You could go back east, or to the northwest. Even to Canada."

"Shut up, Catalina," he grumbled.

"No." She leaned forward so her face was just above his. "It's a good idea. Think about it. . . ."

Jackson shook his head slowly. "For God's sake, leave me alone. What makes you think I want to change my life? I like things just the way they are. Men respect me. Women love me. I make good money. . . ."

Catalina grabbed his wrist and pulled the palm away so she could peer into one eye. "Men fear you. Whores love you. And money never made anyone happy."

She stared into one pale blue bloodshot eye for a long, silent moment, and then he turned the tables on her. Jackson broke free of her tenuous grasp, grabbed her, and flipped both of them so that her back was flat against the mattress and he was pressed against her from chest to ankle.

"Are you a whore, Catalina?" he rasped. There was a chill in his voice and a look in his eyes that frightened her.

"You know I'm not."

Jackson ignored her and lowered his head to her neck. His lips were harsh as they trailed from just beneath her ear down to her shoulder. "Are you sure, Cat?"

There was nothing between her breasts and his bare chest but the thin nightgown. She could feel the beat of his heart, the heat of his skin next to hers.

But that doesn't mean I can't love you. She wanted to say those words aloud, but she didn't dare. Tomorrow morning she would be gone, and she would probably never see Jackson Cady again.

She took his head between her hands and pulled his lips away from her skin. Those pale eyes stared down at her, the blue as clear as a spring sky unbroken by clouds. This morning those perfect eyes were marred with a sprinkling of red veins, and dark circles that she'd not seen before.

Catalina pulled his face to hers, and put her mouth against his. He resisted for a moment, and then she felt his lips relax, soften, molding to her own lips—against his will, she was certain. Her hands slipped to the back of his head, to tangle in his hair, to hold him so he couldn't pull away. She parted her lips and brushed her tongue against his lower lip, lightly, no more than a whisper of a touch.

They could have today. If they had nothing else, they could have today. To remember, to treasure.

But Jackson pulled away from her abruptly and leapt from the bed. "You'll be the death of me yet," he mumbled, running his fingers through his hair.

Catalina didn't move. She couldn't have even if she'd wanted to. "You don't have to walk away, Jackson." Those were such hard words to say. His kisses told her that he wanted her, but he'd made a point of steering clear. She knew he preferred more experienced women, like that tramp Juanita, but she could almost swear that he wanted her.

"Yes, I do," he answered her crisply, turning away and leaving her aching and brokenhearted on the bed. "I told you before. I don't bed virgins."

Catalina stood at the foot of the bed and chewed her bottom lip as she looked down at the sleeping Jackson. What if he recovered too quickly? He did everything else very efficiently, and she could only assume that efficiency would include recuperation.

They'd had their baths, even though Jackson had to be prodded. He'd just *had* a bath, he insisted. But Catalina had explained to him

Grandma Lane's first step to recovery from anything, including a hangover: a nice hot bath. A
few deep breaths. Close your eyes and think of
your favorite place. It had been her cure for almost everything, from a headache to a sprained
ankle to the simple anguish of a bad day.

He'd insisted Catalina bathe first, and she'd
done so quickly so the water would still be warm
for Jackson. He'd waited on the balcony until she
called him, and even then he'd hesitated, sticking
his head into the room first. Had he expected to
find her standing there stark naked? Had he expected that she would try to seduce him, even
after he had rejected her?

Of course, she had waited on the balcony for
Jackson to finish his bath. Once in, he must have
decided he liked Grandma Lane's cure after all,
because he took an awfully long bath.

And then he had stretched out on the bed fully
dressed and gone to sleep, one arm flung over his
eyes.

He stirred, just a little. A knee was raised and
lowered slowly, and then he turned onto his side.
What if he woke up and decided to leave the
room? How could she stop him?

Catalina paced at the end of the bed, silent in
her wool-stockinged feet.

"Would you please be still?" he muttered.

Catalina stopped in her tracks and stared down
at Jackson. His eyes remained closed and his
wide mouth was set in a frown that looked almost . . . painful.

"Thank you," he grumbled.

Placing her hands on the footboard, Catalina

made herself be still. Jackson rolled onto his back and opened his eyes slowly, to no more than narrow slits.

"How did you do it?" he grumbled.

Catalina leaned forward slightly. "How did I do what?"

With the heels of his hands digging into the mattress, Jackson pushed himself into a sitting position. "You know . . . when you tossed Harold Goodman over your shoulder."

"And you," Catalina added with a smile.

"And me."

"It's really just a matter of balance and leverage. Center of gravity and all that. Judo," she clarified. "Kim and I took a class in self-defense at the Y."

Jackson ran his fingers through his hair, smoothing back the black mass. It was then that Catalina saw the widow's peak and—she was almost certain—a small streak of white at his right temple.

He swung his legs over the side of the bed. "I'm not even going to ask who Kim is, or where the Y is . . . or *what* the Y is. I don't even know why I asked. It's just that I was having this dream . . ."

"How do you feel?"

"Rotten."

Catalina was almost happy that he felt rotten. Surely he wouldn't leave the room now. "Maybe you should go back to sleep."

Jackson was shaking his head before she'd even finished the sentence.

"You'll feel much better tomorrow if you rest all day today," Catalina said as cheerfully as she could. Her answer was a glare as biting as any insult.

"I can't possibly get any rest with you making so much damned noise."

"What noise?"

"Those damned skirts make more racket than anything I've ever heard. Swishing and crinkling or something, like somebody's dragging a burr across my brain. You have a step as graceful as a buffalo, and just as light."

Catalina's mouth dropped open, and then she clamped it shut. Of all the nerve! A buffalo! True, her grandmother had once accused her of walking through the house like an elephant. Ballet lessons had begun shortly after that.

"It couldn't be that you're overly sensitive due to the bender you went on last night?"

Jackson shook his head. "Not at all. I'm just tired from the trip. That's all."

"If I sit, will you go back to sleep?"

Jackson raised his head and looked straight at her, into her, and the pain she saw in his eyes went much deeper than any hangover. "Why do you care?"

"I don't. At least, no more than I would care for any human being who looked as terrible as you do right now." Catalina took the few short steps that separated her from the table and chair and seated herself slowly. "How's this?"

Jackson stared at her for a moment, and then he fell back against the bed. "Great," he said gruffly. "Just don't breathe too loud."

He was asleep in minutes, and Catalina smiled. She wouldn't move, if that was what it took. She wouldn't breathe at all, if it meant Jackson would be safe for one more day.

Jackson walked down the steps slowly, his eyes searching the room as always, looking for anyone who showed too much interest in his approach . . . or not enough. It looked to be the same old crowd, drinking and playing cards and turning on the charm for Alberta's girls.

His head still hurt, but it was tolerable enough. He couldn't remember the last time he'd spent the entire day in bed, or the last time he'd slept for so long. Last night's drinking and the loose lips that had followed would not be repeated. Not tonight. Not ever.

At least Catalina hadn't heard his drunken confessions. The last thing he needed or wanted was her . . . or anyone else's . . . sympathy.

But he had strengthened his decision where Catalina Lane was concerned. There was no way he could leave her at Alberta's. Like it or not, he was going to have to take her with him. In a few more days, after he'd rested a bit, they would light out early in the morning, and he'd take her to Phoenix. He didn't want to take on Alberta's men, but he would if he had to.

And maybe, if he rode hard enough and long enough each day, he'd be able to forget how soft she was, how she tasted, how she offered herself to him.

Alberta met him at the foot of the stairs. You'd never guess, watching that composed front, that she'd been scared witless by Catalina earlier that day. Another reason he couldn't leave her here.

Alberta would have her revenge, one way or another, but she was smart enough to wait until he was gone.

"Evenin', Kid." Alberta all but blocked his way, and he stopped while still two steps from the bottom.

He said nothing, but nodded his head slightly.

"Where's my Cat?" Alberta asked softly. "I hope you haven't exhausted her completely, keeping her in that room all day long."

Jackson stepped down one calculated step. "Catalina will be down in a bit. She was fussin' with her hair when I left."

Alberta stepped aside and allowed Jackson to pass by, but he heard her fall into step behind him as he made his way to his table. Even though the room was crowded, his table at the back of the room was vacant. Everyone knew it was reserved for him, and no one wanted to test his patience.

Jackson sat with his back to the wall, and Alberta took the chair next to him, signalling the bartender with a wave of her hand. She said nothing until the big man set two filled glasses in front of them, and she lifted hers to sip almost daintily. Jackson's glass sat untouched.

"So?" she said, leaning in slightly. "What do you think of her?"

Jackson turned his face to the smiling woman and gave her a cold glare. "Catalina?"

Alberta nodded. "Of course, Cat. I have a feeling she's going to make me a fortune."

"Could be," Jackson said in a low voice.

"Is she . . . adapting well?"

Jackson's eyes swept the room again. These would be Catalina's customers, were he to leave her here. "Seems to enjoy herself well enough, if that's what you mean."

Alberta's smile widened and she leaned back, satisfied. "That's exactly what I mean. I have no doubt you're spoiling her terribly, of course. She's bound to be disappointed once she gets into the regular routine here."

Jackson could do no more than grunt noncommittally.

"How long are you planning to stay, Kid?" Alberta asked so casually, Jackson knew that was her real purpose for singling him out.

"Until the week I paid for is up."

Alberta nodded and rolled her drink between her palms, wrapping stubby fingers around the glass. "Not planning on staying any longer than that? I could offer you a special rate if you'd like another week."

It was tempting to say yes, to buy some time, but Jackson kept his mouth shut. What did Alberta want?

"I mean, you seem to like her well enough, and you two made a cozy little picture this morning."

"Is that a fact," he drawled. "You didn't look exactly charmed at the time."

Alberta's cheeks reddened, but she continued to smile. "I was just surprised that you allowed her to touch your weapon."

Jackson gave the woman a small, sly grin. "Catalina can touch my weapon any time she wants. Remember that, Alberta."

162

"So," Alberta ignored him. "What do you say? Another week?"

Jackson shook his head slowly. "No thanks. A week with any one woman is plenty long enough."

Alberta's features relaxed, and Jackson realized that he'd given her exactly the answer she wanted.

"I understand, Kid. We wouldn't want you getting too enamored of our Cat. That could cause all kinds of trouble."

Jackson nodded just once, and Alberta seemed satisfied with that silent response.

"You understand, Kid. She's prettier than most we get around here, and some men can get right addle-brained when they look at a fair face for a while. And a virgin to boot. That makes some men plumb crazy, like no one else should touch their woman. I can't tell you how many times I've had to toss some poor sap out of this place 'cause he developed romantic feelings for one of my girls. Particularly the new ones." Alberta took a deep breath and sighed. "I just wanted to make certain you weren't getting too attached."

Jackson maintained a calm front. "I never do."

Once Alberta was satisfied she moved on. Juanita gave him no more than a glance. She didn't even smile at him. Apparently she'd given up on making a buck from him this trip and was focusing her attentions elsewhere. The gambler who had bid on Catalina, at the moment.

He couldn't leave her here. Catalina wouldn't survive, and he couldn't shake the knowledge that she was his . . . his responsibility. He'd found her, he'd brought her here, and he'd bought her. She was his, damn her.

He turned his eyes to the stairs, and she was standing there. Dressed in the revealing gold and black outfit Alberta had provided, grinning as though this were all a joke, or child's play. As though none of it were real.

She kept her eyes on his face as she walked down the stairs, and though he knew he should look away, he couldn't. With every step her well-shaped calves swung out just enough for him to get a good look. Her full skirt swished with every swing of her hips, and her smile, that wide grin, faded just a little.

As she approached the table, Jackson kicked a chair out with his booted foot. Tonight she would not work the room. Tonight she would not sit on any miner's lap. Tonight she would sit with him, and he would look his fill.

And later he would send her to their room and he would continue to sit at this table and wait until early morning, when he could be certain she was asleep. Because even though he felt deep inside that she was his, he knew Catalina Lane was much too good for the likes of Kid Creede.

Chapter Eleven

Catalina paced there at the foot of the bed where she'd watched over Jackson. Where was he? He'd sent her to the room hours ago, all but ordered her out of the saloon. She'd changed quickly, certain he would be right behind her, and then she'd begun the long wait.

She wasn't adept at seduction, and that was a fact. He'd ignored her advances, ignored the sexy nightgown . . . ignored her. Even tonight, as they'd sat at the round table in the back of Alberta's saloon. Neither of them drank a drop of Alberta's whiskey, though filled glasses had been placed on their table. He didn't insist that she mingle, so she'd stayed there beside him, grateful for the protection of his company and . . . to be honest . . . the chance to spend a little more time close to him.

That was when she'd decided to try, one more time, to convince Jackson to make love to her. Catalina sighed and plopped down on the edge of the big bed. What was wrong with her that she had to work so hard to get a man to touch her?

Kim would know what to do, but that didn't do Catalina any good. Funny, but she didn't think of Kim as a person yet to be born, but as a friend in another place. Living her life as Catalina did her own, wondering what had become of her best friend and ex-roommate.

Men adored Kim. She always had admirers calling and sending flowers, leaving messages on the answering machine, even after they'd been unceremoniously dumped for some minor infraction. And the thing of it was, Catalina knew, even though she loved her friend like a sister, that Kim wasn't beautiful. She was cute, even pretty at times, but she wasn't beautiful. She had the difficult-to-define *it*, an air that attracted men no matter what she said or did. Catalina knew that whatever that air was, she didn't have it.

With a sigh, Catalina stretched out on the bed and threw her arms over her head. This was her last chance. Tomorrow she would be gone, and she might never again meet a man who made her feel the way Jackson did. It had taken her twenty-seven years—and an incredible journey—to find him. What if he was the one? The only one?

Jackson opened the door so quietly that he had entered the room before Catalina knew he was there. He looked startled when she lifted her head, and for a moment she thought he was going to leave again, step into the hall without a word and close that door on her.

But instead he closed and locked the door, keeping his back to her. "It's late," he grumbled. "You should be asleep."

"I'm not tired," Catalina said, sitting up and self-consciously righting her nightgown's low neckline.

"Neither am I." Jackson sat in the chair he normally placed beneath the doorknob, making every effort not to look in her direction.

"You're not going to sit up all night, are you?" The question sounded silly and juvenile and terribly transparent, and she knew it as soon as the words left her mouth.

Jackson didn't answer her, but thrust his legs out, leaned his head back, and closed his eyes. As though she wasn't even in the room. Invisible. Insignificant.

Catalina rose slowly and silently. Jackson must not have heard her, because he didn't move, didn't tell her to get back into bed. She took tiny steps, quiet ones on bare feet, until she stood behind him.

When she rested her hands on his shoulders Catalina thought Jackson would come straight up out of his chair. He all but jumped, and his skin twitched beneath her fingers. She didn't step back, or move her hands away from him, but instead dug her fingers into his muscle, kneading lightly, rubbing her thumbs against the back of his neck.

"You're very tense," she said softly, rotating her thumbs against rigid muscle.

"It's late," he grumbled. "Get to sleep."

"I told you I'm not tired." Catalina continued the massage, working her thumbs slowly up to the hairline and back down again. It wasn't doing any good. Jackson's muscles were just as tight as they'd been when she'd started. Maybe even tighter.

"Get to bed, Catalina," he ordered.

She leaned forward, placing her mouth close

to his shoulder. "Not alone."

She could feel it, the stilling breath he took, the cold control that washed over his whole body. "I told you, Catalina. I don't . . ."

"Don't say it," she snapped, pulling her hands away from his neck and shoulders. "I know quite well where you stand on sleeping with inexperienced women."

"Listen." Jackson didn't turn around to look at her, but leaned his head forward slightly and placed two fingers at his temples. "You don't have to do this just to convince me to take you away from Baxter. I already told you I'll take you with me when I go."

"That's not why . . . I'm glad, but that's not why I want you to make love to me."

Jackson didn't move, didn't answer.

Catalina walked quickly to the dresser and picked up one of the keys to the blue room. "If my virginity is really such an obstacle, perhaps I should have it taken care of. Shouldn't be too much trouble to find a man who would be willing to handle that chore. After all, this is a bordello. If there's no one left downstairs, I'll just go door-to-door, knocking until I find a customer who will be accommodating. Perhaps Harold Goodman is around. Alberta said he was real quick." The key wouldn't slip into the lock, and Catalina realized that her hands were trembling. The key scraped against the doorknob as she jabbed at the keyhole, missing and taking aim again.

Finally the key slid into the lock, but before Catalina could twist the key Jackson's hand was covering her wrist.

"Don't," he whispered silkily.

"Why the hell not?" She hadn't intended for her voice to tremble as her hands did, but her fear and her anger were clear, even to her own ears.

"You're shaking." His fingers caressed her wrist, and he moved his lips close to her ear. "You don't want to do this, Catalina." He placed a gentle pressure on her wrist, and the key slipped from the lock.

"I don't want to, but I will if I have to." Her voice was a bit stronger, but still she knew Jackson would question her resolve. She did. It was just a bluff, delivered in anger. She wouldn't have gotten three steps down the hallway.

Jackson took the key from her, and she let it slip from her fingers. When he turned her in his arms she pivoted with her head down. He was going to put her to bed and he was going to sit up in that damned chair all night.

"Why are you doing this to me, Catalina?" he whispered, his voice free of anger.

"Just forget it," Catalina mumbled. She had never been more embarrassed, felt more rejected, not even when Wilson had left her at the altar.

Jackson cupped her chin and forced her to look at him. His fingers brushed her face, and he pressed her back against the door. He was bringing his face to hers, parting his lips to kiss her, but he stopped a heartbeat away.

"Are you going to flip me onto my back this time?" he asked smoothly.

Catalina shook her head slightly.

"Will you tell me fairy tales about knights and princes and 1996?"

She shook her head again, a faint gesture.

Jackson kissed her then, brushed his lips against hers and wrapped his arms tightly around her. Catalina worked her arms around his neck and held him close, parting her lips as Jackson continued to kiss her, deeper and more completely with every passing heartbeat. His hands began to dance over her body, fingers brushing over her back, her arms, her hips, and with every touch, with every shared breath, Catalina was more certain that this was the man she'd waited for.

He lifted her in his arms and carried her to the bed, brushing his lips against her throat and, once, under her chin. Jackson gently set her on the bed and began to work the ties that held the nightgown closed across her breasts.

She wanted to tell him that he was her magic, the man she had dreamed of all her life. Most of all, she wanted to tell him that she loved him.

But she didn't dare. Tomorrow morning she would be gone. There was no other way.

Jackson ran his fingers over her nipples and cupped her breasts as he bent to kiss her again, and Catalina almost came off the bed, the pull was so powerful.

"I've waited too long for you, Catalina," he whispered as he undressed, never moving far from her. "It won't be the way I'd like for it to be . . . this first time."

When he took her in his arms and pressed his warm, naked body against hers, Catalina closed her eyes and tried to drink him in, to revel in his touch. How could he be so warm, and so hard? So calm while his heart beat as hard as hers? His breath was heavy and fast in her ear, and still it seemed he never lost control.

Jackson lay on top of her, pressing her into the mattress, kissing her deeply while he spread her thighs. His lips never left hers, even as he drove deeply into her, quickly, easily, with just a moment of pain. And then he was still, filling her body and soul, making her whole.

When he began to move again it was with slow deliberation, and each movement made her body quiver. He thrust his tongue deep within her mouth as he moved even faster, and Catalina lifted her hips to take him.

He shuddered and shook and held her tightly, and then his breathing returned almost to normal. Jackson rolled onto his side and brought her with him, so that her head rested in the crook of his shoulder. Perfectly, Catalina thought.

"Next time," he whispered into her ear, "will be better for you."

Catalina snuggled against him, but she couldn't chase away the chill. They wouldn't have another time. Still, for now there was nothing as satisfying as lying with Jackson.

"We could leave tonight," she whispered, "while it's still dark."

Jackson groaned, but just a little. "A few more days, Catalina, darlin'. A few more days." He was drifting off to sleep, mumbling something she couldn't quite understand. Once, she was almost positive she heard the word *mine*.

*   *   *

Mine. All mine. The same thought he'd fallen asleep with was with him when he opened his eyes. Catalina was curled against his side, her legs tangled with his, a less than perfectly satisfied expression on her face. He brushed a strand of hair away from her eyes so he could see her better. Never in his life had he felt possessive about a woman. Never. But when Catalina had stood trembling at the door and threatened to go to another man he had known what it felt like to want something so badly he ached deep inside.

She hadn't meant it, and he knew that. After a momentary flash of white-hot anger he had recognized and understood the truth. That she wouldn't allow another man to touch her. That she wanted him to be the man she had waited her whole life for.

She wouldn't regret it. For tonight, and maybe for a few days more, she was his. He didn't believe in forever, and thankfully Catalina hadn't spoken of love or asked for promises.

He ran his hand slowly down her side, over her hip. He'd never felt skin so smooth, never seen a shape so perfect. Of course, he'd never actually slept with a woman he'd bedded before, either. It seemed so . . . intimate.

Catalina stirred beneath his hand and cuddled against him even closer, pressing her face to his side. He didn't want her to regret being his for a short time. He wanted to watch her come apart in his arms, to experience the same pleasure he had.

His hand settled over her breast and lingered

there, his fingers brushing lightly over the silky skin, his thumb rocking against the nipple that responded immediately. Catalina stirred, and Jackson slid his hand lower, over a flat belly to rest between her thighs.

Her eyes opened slowly, fluttering as she turned her face to his.

Jackson gave her a smile that she returned sleepily.

When he lowered his head to take a taut nipple in his mouth she sucked in her breath and held it. He raised his lips to hers and kissed her, slow and fast and slow again, until she was on the edge of a new wonder.

Only then did he thrust into her, joining with her in a way that he knew—in a final lucid thought—was different from anything he had ever known. And he felt, at that moment, as though he had been as naive and untouched as Catalina, until he'd found her. Until she'd found him. Until she'd opened herself to him.

She lurched under him, throwing her head back and lifting her hips to take all of him. And then Jackson lost himself in the only pure and real beauty he had ever known.

Mine. All mine.

Catalina dressed quietly, slipping into the tan dress she'd worn the day Jackson had taken her with him to meet Doc Booker. She stepped into the black boots easily, silently, watching Jackson for some sign that he heard her.

She'd awakened to find that she'd slept too late, much later than she'd intended. She'd stayed awake half the night waiting for Jackson, and he'd managed to keep her awake for most of the remainder of it.

As much as she'd wanted that one night with Jackson, it only made it harder for her to leave.

Fully dressed, the wulfenite tucked into a deep pocket, Catalina stood over the bed. For the first time since she'd met him there was peace etched on Jackson's face. He didn't look as if he could come awake and aware in less than a heartbeat; he was deep asleep, his bearded face buried in a pillow.

If he opened his eyes and caught her there, she wouldn't be able to leave. He would take that decision away from her. For a moment she willed it, as hard as she could. For him to wake, to make her stay with him. To take her in his arms and make love to her as he had last night. With passion and power and beauty.

After a moment Catalina silently backed away from the bed. It was selfish and foolish and deadly for her to wish for Jackson to wake and hold her there. She was doing this for him, trying to give him a chance for survival. It was all she could do for him.

"Good-bye, Jackson," she mouthed the words as she stood by the door with the key in her hand. She didn't dare say a word aloud, or touch his shoulder, or kiss him. It was for the best. "I do love you."

She had hoped to find the ground floor deserted, but Alberta and her moose of a bartender were cleaning up from last night, and they both eyed her suspiciously as she came down the stairs. She couldn't allow either of them to accompany her, or to follow her. They had to *know* she was coming back.

"Where do you think you're going?" Alberta snapped as Catalina headed for the batwing doors.

Catalina spun and gave Alberta what she hoped was an impatient glance with no apprehension. "The Kid asked me to pick up a couple of things for him at the general store."

"Oh, really?" Alberta obviously didn't believe her. "Perhaps I should check with him."

Catalina smiled. "Go right ahead. But I warn you, he's trying to get a little extra sleep this morning, and he can be quite a bear when he's disturbed."

Alberta hesitated. In spite of her bravado, she was still a little afraid of Kid Creede. "Milo." She turned to the silent bartender. "Go with her."

"Well," Catalina stepped forward, a single step toward Alberta. "If he's going to be watching me, you can watch the Kid. I won't be gone long, and you can tell that bitch Juanita that if I find her anywhere near my room when I get back, I'll snatch her bald-headed."

Alberta's smirk only made her look older and less attractive, but the satisfaction was evident on her face and in her relaxed stance. "I'll pass that warning along, if necessary."

Milo followed her out the door, but he no longer seemed suspicious of her motives. He and Alberta fully expected her to hurry with her chore and rush back to Kid Creede before Juanita could get her claws into him.

The bartender dogged her steps through the general store, and Catalina picked up odds and ends. Canned goods, tobacco, a clean shirt. Goodness knows Jackson could use a new shirt. She chose a white one, in spite of his apparent penchant for black. Window dressing, she'd decided, like the hair and the beard and the attitude he wore like that flapping duster.

She waited until there was another customer at the counter, and then she stepped forward. From there she could see Alberta's, and she cocked her head so she could see through the window and to the second-and third-floor balconies, deserted at this time of day.

"I knew it!" she spat, and then she turned to dump her purchases in Milo's arms. "I see that tramp on my balcony." She glanced back and ducked down to see the building more clearly. "Now she's gone inside! I'll kill her; I swear I will. That . . . that . . ." She looked at the storekeeper and the customer who had turned their heads to stare, wide-eyed, at her. "That hussy."

She spun away and stalked for the door. "Have those purchases tallied up and put on the Kid's bill," she called over her shoulder. "I'll be right back."

A quick glance over her shoulder revealed a confused Milo standing there with the goods in his hands. Confused, but not worried. He wouldn't drop the purchases and run after her.

Catalina was out the door and down the boardwalk in less than a minute. There was an alleyway that ran between the general store and a small cafe, and she ducked in there before anyone could see her.

She didn't have a lot of time. Milo would have the storekeeper tally her purchases, and then he would no doubt deliver them to her room. He'd wake up Jackson, and then they would both know that she was missing. She'd better be gone by the time Jackson and Milo got together.

Like it or not, she was going to have to steal a horse. She'd always heard that was a hanging offense in the West, but there was nothing to be done for it. She had to get out of town in a hurry, and get as far away from Baxter as possible. Back to the place where Jackson had found her? Could she return to 1996? Did she really want to?

Catalina fingered the wulfenite that was tucked into the deep pocket. She wasn't certain it was necessary for the journey back . . . wasn't even certain she could return. But it had been a part of the magic that had brought her to 1896; of that she was certain.

Standing in the alley, she looked across the street and to the balcony of her room at Alberta's bordello. Jackson slept on, unaware that she was leaving. Would he be angry or relieved? She had a strong suspicion that he would consider himself well rid of her. All she could do now was pray that he'd get out of Baxter, and fast.

Was it possible to change that one fact? Would her presence and disappearance change circumstances just enough to save him? She was afraid to think too hard on that question. There was still a strong possibility that Jackson would die on this street.

Catalina ran down the alleyway, away from Alberta's. There was no time to wonder if she was doing the right thing or not. It was all she could do.

She cut through the overgrown weeds that grew at the back of the general store, and passed two other buildings before she cut through another alley to the main street again. This particular building appeared to be abandoned, but there was a decent-looking horse, saddled and ready to steal, hitched to a post out front.

The tether wrapped around the post gave her a bit of trouble, and she had to take an extra minute to untangle the knot she made. She tried not to think of the trip ahead, if she could control the horse, if she could find her way back to the doorway that had brought her here, if Jackson would follow her. She concentrated on one thing at a time. Unknotting the leather strap. Easing the horse with a few softly spoken words. Stepping gingerly into the stirrup. She was almost home free when a hand flew forward and grasped the saddlehorn.

Harold Goodman stared up at her, not even a hint of anger in his boyish face. "Thievery, Catalina?"

She looked down into his face and tried to smile. "Of course not. I was just . . . trying it out."

He wasn't convinced, and Catalina wasn't surprised. Her voice was weak and hesitant, and she squealed as Goodman pulled her from the horse. He caught her before she hit the ground and held her tight, wrapping his arms around her, pinning her arms to her sides.

"I can't let you go, Catalina. You might just try . . . whatever it was you did the other night at Alberta's."

"What if I promise not to?" she offered weakly. Goodman was holding his face close to hers . . . too close . . . and he continued to smile like an idiot.

He shook his head. "I don't trust you." He was squeezing her so tight, Catalina started to see stars. She couldn't take a decent breath, and she was forced to stare into Harold Goodman's face. He had pale skin, for a man who supposedly spent his days in the sun, and flat brown eyes, and a poor excuse for a mustache growing above his thin upper lip. She found herself staring at that growth.

"Lookin' for a kiss?" he asked softly.

"No," Catalina said breathlessly. "Wondering if that's supposed to be a mustache, or if you just forgot to wash your face this morning."

Not smart. She knew that as soon as the words left her mouth, but she couldn't stop them.

Goodman's smile faded. The man had such a sensitive ego! "We'll just see what the sheriff says about you trying to steal my horse."

"I wasn't going to steal . . ."

"Of course, I might be willing to forget the incident, if you'll take me back to Alberta's and give me a free sample of what I'll be purchasing next week."

Catalina brought the heel of her boot down on top of his foot, but all he did was laugh and return the attack, stomping on her foot with his own heavy boot.

"Let me go," she warned chillingly. "You'll be sorry. Kid Creede will make you sorry, if you don't let me go right this minute."

Harold was unimpressed. "I won't have to worry about Kid Creede much longer, and neither will you, sweetie. As a matter of fact, you've made things right easy for me. I was afraid the bastard was going to hole up in that whorehouse all week, but I think I know how to draw him out."

Catalina quit struggling. "What do you mean?"

Harold's weak smile was back. "Were you running away from him? Did he hurt you? You don't have to run."

He cut his eyes to the deserted building. A window was raised, and Catalina saw movement there. A cowboy peeked out and then settled himself at the open window. Across the street, on the roof of the sheriff's office, the sun flashed on metal . . . a rifle or a six-shooter?

The ambush. She was too late.

"If you're thinking that he'll come after me, you're sadly mistaken," Catalina said calmly. "He really likes Juanita better than me. Probably most of the other girls, too. I guess I'm just not his type."

He laughed at her, lightly, unconcerned. "Make up your mind, Catalina. Should I be shaking in my boots? Or am I wasting my time? I don't think I'm wasting my time, and I'm not afraid."

Goodman clasped her even tighter, locking his arms around her and squeezing with all his might. If he kept this up, she was going to pass out.

The pressure lessened, just a little, and Catalina took a deep breath.

"That's right," Goodman said softly. "Scream at the top of your lungs, sweetie."

Catalina refused to scream. She refused to be the bait that lured Jackson to his death.

"Come on." Goodman grew impatient, jerking her around so that she could see the balcony where, hopefully, Jackson still slept. "A nice, ear-splitting scream."

Catalina looked into Goodman's face. God, how she hated him! Because Jackson refused to murder an innocent old man, because he had refused Goodman's job offer, he was to be killed. Maybe she couldn't change history. Maybe she would—after all—have to watch Jackson die. It would break her heart, in a way so painful it hurt just to think of it. Maybe she would have to watch, but she was damned if she'd play any part in it.

She tried to break free, but it was no use. Goodman wasn't going to budge. Her arms were useless, pinned at her sides, and the lack of air was making her weak. Finally she stopped struggling and looked Harold Goodman in the eye, mustering all the strength she had left.

"Kiss my ass."

Chapter Twelve

Jackson opened his eyes when the sliver of sun hit his face. How long had he slept? Certainly no more than two or three hours.

But he never slept that deep, that good. And it was all because of Catalina. He wanted her again, half asleep, warm and soft and breathless. He wanted to watch her lose control again. Most of all, in spite of all his reservations, he wanted to claim her as his own again.

As his vision cleared, he reached out for her. For a moment he thought the rumpled coverlet at the edge of the bed hid a sleeping Catalina, but the moment his hand touched the cold sheet he knew the bed was empty. And he knew, as he came fully awake and sat up, that she wasn't in the room.

Catalina could find all sorts of trouble left on her own.

She did love the balcony, so he checked there first, dressing as he crossed the room. He knew it was deserted even before he parted the drapes. He would have heard her, would have known she was there. Jackson blinked hard against the bright morning sun, and then turned his eyes to the street below.

It didn't take long to find her. She always drew a crowd, Catalina Lane did.

Jackson placed both hands on the railing and leaned forward, watching. It appeared that Harold Goodman was holding Catalina, and a good dozen townspeople had gathered around them to watch whatever was going on. She didn't seem to be struggling, and for a split second Jackson wondered if he should interfere at all. She could handle herself.

But then Catalina's leg swung out, and she tried to kick Harold. He could hear Harold's echoing laughter, and then the coward kicked Catalina with a booted foot. He could see her leg give way and then quickly straighten again.

He stepped into his boots as he walked to the door and was buckling his gunbelt as he flew down the stairs, giving no thought at all to his actions.

"Kid," Alberta called as he stalked across the cleared floor of the saloon and toward the batwing doors, "I've got a message here from Harold Goodman. He wants to meet with you as soon as . . ."

Jackson turned his head slightly but didn't slow his stride. Alberta was waving a small folded sheet of paper in front of her bosom, offering it to him.

"I'm going to see Harold right now," he said, and Alberta must have heard something she didn't like in his voice, because her smile faded and the hand that offered Harold's note dropped slowly.

He walked down the middle of the street, his

eyes on Harold's back. All he could see of Catalina was her skirt, billowing out behind the man
who held her. She barely moved at all.

In the past fifteen years his actions had rarely
been colored by anger, but he couldn't deny the
fury that rose within him now. Harold was going
to pay.

Someone must have warned Harold, because
the man spun quickly, still holding Catalina prisoner in his arms. Harold smiled . . . an odd reaction for a man who must certainly know that
he'd made a grave mistake.

Harold spun Catalina around, twisting her
arms behind her back until she winced. She
struggled briefly, and then she lifted her face to
Jackson and was suddenly still. Those golden
eyes grew wide, and her face was blanched of all
color. She parted her lips but said nothing. Harold clamped a hand over her mouth.

The scuffle resumed, as Catalina attempted to
break the hold Harold had on her wrists. She
twisted and pulled, and once tossed her head
back into Harold's nose. The man yelped but
didn't release her.

And then she bit his hand. Harold's hand flew
away from her mouth, and Catalina pulled away
from him and screamed.

Jackson felt the first bullet as he heard the explosion of the rifle. His right shoulder, he
thought almost calmly. Not fatal, not even serious. Before he could draw his weapons a second
shot exploded into his side. More serious, maybe
even deadly.

A third shot found its target, and Jackson fell

to the ground. Catalina had been right all along.
Ambushed on the street in Baxter.

Catalina rushed forward, ignoring the bullets
that continued to fly. Jackson hadn't even drawn
his six-shooters, and still they continued to fire.
Four, five bullets in that still body. Near-misses
exploded in the dirt near his head and legs. The
firing stopped when Catalina was standing over
Jackson.

It was all her fault. She was the reason Kid
Creede had died. Catalina dropped to her knees
and rolled Jackson carefully from his side to his
back. She laid two fingers at his throat, fully expecting to find no heartbeat. But it was there,
faint and irregular, and Jackson opened his eyes.

"Lie still," Catalina whispered. "Help will be
here soon." Surely one of the people who had
watched would fetch a doctor for Jackson.

He looked calm, resigned, with no hint of
panic in his eyes. "You were right all along," he
whispered weakly. "Ambushed in Baxter. How
did you . . ." His voice trailed away.

"Don't talk. You need to save your strength."

Jackson shook his head slightly. "Too late." His
bright eyes caught and held hers. "I want you to
take my horse and get out of Baxter. Now." Jackson's voice faded, and he closed his eyes.

"Jackson," Catalina whispered desperately.
"Wake up. You can still recover. We can change
history. The book said a dozen times, and you
were only shot five." Shot only five times; one
bullet was enough to kill any man, even Kid

Creede. "Please, Jackson. I didn't come all this way just to lose you."

But Jackson didn't answer. He lay there perfectly still as Catalina brushed her hands over his face and neck.

Her hands trailed down his neck to his chest, and over the warm blood that seeped from his wounds. It was the feel of his blood on her hands that made her think clearly.

Catalina lifted her head and looked around her. No one had moved. They all stood well away from the injured man, their faces solemn but unmoved.

"Someone get the doctor," Catalina snapped, and still no one moved. "Hurry!"

A tall man at the edge of the crowd fidgeted. "We ain't got no doctor no more."

No doctor. She would have to tend him herself, and she knew nothing but the basics. If only she'd spent more time in the medical section of the library and less in the history section, she'd know what to do.

"Don't worry, Jackson," she whispered. "This time things will be different."

But he didn't hear her, and Catalina couldn't dismiss her nagging doubt. It didn't matter that she loved Jackson. What if history couldn't be changed, no matter how hard she wished it?

She took a deep breath and closed her eyes. *Push back the panic*, she told herself silently. *Jackson will certainly die if you panic.*

Still kneeling beside Jackson, Catalina lifted her eyes to the crowd that stayed well back. "I'll need some help getting him inside." There was a small tremor in her voice, but other than that she sounded calm and in control. "Preferably some place other than Alberta's. Some place closer. The less we move him, the better off he'll be."

No one moved. Their stony faces showed no horror at what had happened, no compassion at all.

"Come on." She raised her voice. "You can't just leave him here."

It came to her then, the way it had been . . . was supposed to be. The people of Baxter would allow Jackson to bleed to death in the street, alone to the end.

"I just need someone to help me carry him inside. Back to Alberta's, if there's no other choice."

"Nope." Alberta's coarse voice rose from the silent crowd. "I don't want any war in my establishment."

One by one the crowd turned and walked away. Alberta nodded curtly to Catalina. "Come on, Cat."

Catalina shook her head. "I'll never step foot in your place again."

Alberta smiled. "You've got no other place to go, Cat. There's not a respectable family in town who would house one of my girls."

Juanita posed next to Alberta, a practiced pout on her full lips. And then both women turned and walked away. They had claimed to care for Jackson, for Kid Creede, but they'd leave him to die in the street without even a backward glance.

Even the sheriff turned away.

"You!" Catalina yelled at his stiff back, and the reluctant lawman slowly spun around.

"You have to arrest Harold Goodman and those men who shot the Kid," Catalina insisted.

"Looked like a fair fight to me," the sheriff said lazily.

"A fair fight?" Catalina almost jumped to her feet but stopped herself short. "He didn't even draw his guns. You call that a fair fight?"

The sheriff sighed and turned away, unwilling to spend his energy to argue with her.

"At least help me get him inside!" Catalina shouted as the sheriff entered his office and slammed the door shut.

Behind her, Catalina heard Goodman's low chuckle. "No one's going to cry over the death of a killer like Kid Creede. One less varmint to worry about, as far as most folks are concerned."

Catalina looked over her shoulder as Goodman mounted the horse she had been set to steal. He looked down at her and tipped his hat.

"I'll see you," he said smoothly, "later this week."

He rode away, taking with him the cowardly men who had shot Jackson from their high and hidden posts.

Left alone on the street, Catalina turned back to Jackson. He was unconscious . . . dying . . . and no one would help her.

She slid the knife Jackson kept inside his boot from its sheath and cut a strip of material from the hem of her skirt.

"First things first," she said calmly to the unconscious man beside her. "We'll have to get the bleeding stopped."

Catalina wrapped the strip tightly around the

wound in Jackson's arm. One step at a time, she reminded herself coolly. Once his wounds were bound she could drag him into that abandoned building. It would hurt him, she was certain, but she had to get him off the street. Later she would worry about water and food, and fresh bandages.

She cut another long strip from the skirt and bandaged an ugly-looking wound on his thigh. No exit wound on this one, she noted with a pounding heart as she tied the makeshift bandage tight enough to slow the bleeding.

The rattle of an approaching vehicle didn't register until it was almost upon them, and Catalina looked up to find the team of horses all but in her face. The driver would run them both over without a second thought, but Catalina refused to move. The horses veered, and the buckboard passed Catalina and an unconscious Jackson before coming to a stop in the middle of the street.

Doc Booker hopped down and strode to her with a sour look on his face.

"Come to get a good look?" Catalina snapped. "Want to watch Kid Creede bleed to death? Well, come on down. Run your fingers through the blood on his skin, wipe it off on a hanky and save it for your grandchildren."

The old man stopped, his dusty boots almost touching Jackson's leg. "Got no grandchildren," he said in a low, no-nonsense voice.

Catalina turned her attention back to Jackson and tried to ignore the old man, but Doc Booker dropped down, Jackson's motionless body between them, and began to study the wounds.

"Doc . . ." Catalina said in a low voice. "You're

189

a doctor." It was too much to hope for.

The old man shook his head slowly. "Nope. Not anymore, anyways."

But he continued to examine Jackson as if he knew exactly what he was doing.

"He's not going to make it," Booker said gravely.

"Not if he's left in the street like this." Catalina tried to catch and hold the old man's eyes. "If you used to be a doctor, you can help."

Booker was shaking his head slowly. "It's been thirty years since I've seen anything like this."

"I can't just let him die," she said softly.

She could see the warring emotions in the old man's eyes and remembered the fear that had been there when he'd first seen Jackson.

"He's a killer," the old man said, somber and unflinching.

She couldn't argue with that. Jackson wouldn't have argued with it, either. "I love him," she whispered, and she saw the old man's defenses fall. "I have to try."

"He did warn me about Harold," Booker conceded, and Catalina knew she'd have his help. "It won't do any good, I warn you. He's still going to die. But if it will make you feel better to watch over him until that happens, I reckon I can help."

Doc Booker grabbed a rough-looking blanket and spread it across the bed of his wagon. Purchases from the general store were shoved aside, stacked along the edge of the buckboard.

"It's a good long ways to my place," he warned. "The Kid may not make it."

"He'll make it," Catalina said assuredly, feeling—for the first time—that it might be true.

The buckboard bounced, and Catalina leaned over Jackson to keep his body still. Doc Booker had tried to convince her to ride up front with him, and she could see in his face that he expected Jackson to be dead by the time they reached his ranch. But Catalina had insisted on riding with Jackson.

She continued to cut strips of fabric from her skirt and her petticoat, making fat packs and bandaging them tightly to stop the flow of blood. Fortunately, none of his wounds bled badly. No arteries nicked, no gushing wounds to drain Jackson too quickly. Just a slow and deadly seeping of his life's blood.

Five shots had found their mark. The history book had said an even dozen. Had that information been incorrect, or had her presence ended the gunfire more quickly? She knew now exactly how Jackson had died—or how he was supposed to have died—and that knowledge chilled her. Abandoned on the street to bleed to death.

"Where are we?" Jackson's eyes were narrow slits that opened and closed and opened again with obvious effort.

"You're awake." Catalina leaned over, blocking the sun from his face, and his eyes opened a little wider. "Don't move," she warned. "You've been . . ." What would he remember? ". . . hurt."

"Shot five times," he whispered. "I'd call that hurt."

"Don't be sarcastic, Jackson. Not now." Catalina bit her bottom lip as she studied his face. He was so pale, and there were dark circles under his eyes and hollows in his cheeks that hadn't been there before.

"You'll be all right," she tried to reassure him.

"Where are we?" he repeated his earlier question.

"Doc Booker is taking us to his ranch. He used to be a doctor, so he'll have no trouble patching you up." She tried to sound confident, but there was doubt in her voice. What if Doc Booker was right? What if they couldn't save Jackson?

Jackson laid a hand over hers, the hand that was resting lightly on his chest. "Don't go back to Baxter. Get Doc Booker to take you to Tucson. My money's back at Alberta's, but these Colts will get you a little cash, if you sell them when you get to Tucson."

He squeezed her hand weakly and took a shallow breath. "Change your name if you plan to stay in Arizona Territory. Better yet, head east. Texas is nice. If you go far enough east it's green, and there are a couple of good-sized towns there. Maybe they need a librarian."

"You can take me there," Catalina whispered. "As soon as you're recovered."

"I'm not . . ." Jackson began.

Catalina pressed two fingers over his lips. "Don't say it. You're going to be just fine."

Her fingers slid away from his lips, over the soft black beard that covered the lower half of his face. No antibiotics. No blood transfusions. No intravenous tubes to feed him and keep his body nourished if he couldn't eat. No anesthesia to knock him out so the bullet in his thigh could be removed.

"Promise me," Catalina whispered urgently as Jackson began to close his eyes again.

"I don't . . ."

"Promise me that you won't die."

He opened his eyes fully and stared at her. "I can't do that, darlin'."

"I won't let you rest until you promise me. I want your word that you won't give up and die."

Jackson drew the hand he held to his lips and lightly kissed her palm. His lips were too cool. "You'll do all right without me."

"I won't . . ."

"It's time," Jackson said simply. "And it's been a long time comin'. I'm glad I met you before I got shot, Catalina Lane. You know, when I first met you I thought you were loco." His voice was fading.

"I know."

Jackson's eyes drifted shut, and Catalina placed her face close to his. "No. Don't you pass out until you promise me. Jackson?"

"I can't."

Catalina was laying almost on top of him, covering his chest, trying to warm his chilled body. He shouldn't be so cold.

"Jackson Cady," she whispered, her mouth close to his. "You can't leave me. I came all this way to find you, and I won't allow you to die."

His eyes remained closed, and he said nothing.

"I love you, Jackson," she mumbled, almost afraid to say the words aloud. In the past few years—as she'd put aside her belief in magic—she had dismissed a thousand times the romantic love that made fools of perfectly intelligent women. She rested her lips on his, a brief brush of her mouth against his. "I love you," she said more clearly.

Jackson said nothing, didn't move, and Catalina began to believe that she had waited too long to tell him how she felt.

"All right," Jackson breathed softly. "I promise."

He could feel every rut in the road, every turn of the wheel. Each bullet had burned a path as it had entered his body, but now he could sense nothing where the wounds should be. That was more frightening than being shot . . . not being able to feel the pain.

Catalina's hand lay on his chest, and his hand covered hers. He could feel that, at least. Her warm, soft skin over his heart.

She loved him. He hadn't wanted that, at least he hadn't thought he wanted it. But at the moment it was something to hold on to. She loved him. It was impossible; more than he had ever imagined for himself. Catalina Lane was pretty and smart and pure, and still she had given him her body and her heart. It was more than he deserved.

Why would she love him? It made no sense, but he decided to let the nagging question go and just believe.

For Catalina he could change his life. Everything she'd said to him . . . was it only yesterday?

. . . was true. It was a big country. He could change his name, move far away, and live a normal life.

A normal life, he chided himself. He didn't even know what a normal life was. What could he do? How would he support himself and Catalina? How could he forget what he was?

Catalina could help him . . . help him forget, teach him what a normal life was like. Show him what it was like to meet a person and not see fear in their eyes.

For years he'd dreamed of gold. Of striking it rich. Gus had started that . . . spending every waking minute talking about finding gold, and how great their lives would be once they had it. Even after Gus's death, and after giving up mining for good, he'd continued to dream of gold. It haunted him, more nightmare than dream, and sometimes when he woke he could still see it, shining and yellow and bright.

He'd dreamed of gold again last night, when he'd fallen asleep with Catalina in his arms. This time it had been no nightmare, but a quiet dream that came with a feeling of peace and happiness he hadn't known since Gus's death sixteen years earlier.

The gold he had dreamed of last night was no hard ore men killed and died for. It wasn't worth a lot of money . . . and still it was the most valuable treasure in the world.

It was the gold in Catalina's eyes that had filled his dreams. Flecks of gold in amber more precious than any motherlode. Hard and flashing, soft and filled with tears. Condemning and for-

195

giving. He'd seen it all there.

And love, too. He'd tried to deny it, but he'd seen love in those eyes. Catalina's eyes. The most precious gold he'd ever seen, would ever see.

He saw them now, even with his eyes tightly closed. Her scent surrounded him; her breathing above him was fast and irregular, her hand beneath his trembled. If he'd had the strength he would have opened his eyes for another look at that gold, but he didn't. He pictured those eyes in his mind, and tried to take in their strength.

He would need all that strength if he was to keep his promise.

There wasn't much to Doc Booker's ranch, and Catalina had a hard time imagining why Harold Goodman felt he had to have this place. The house was a small, crude building of adobe brick and wood, and a few plants in what appeared to be a garden struggled to survive. She saw less than a dozen head of cattle, and a handful of chickens. It looked more like a poor farm than a ranch.

In the distance, beyond the small house, was the towering red rock she'd been drawn to that day. It seemed so long ago, but it had just been a few days. Somewhere on the other side of that rock was a doorway that would take her back to 1996, and all that she had left behind.

Jackson roused himself just long enough to be of some help as she and Doc all but carried him inside. With one arm over her shoulder and one over Doc's, Jackson was able to shuffle slowly into the house. There was a large room with a kitchen in one corner and a bed in the other. A fireplace, a table and a couple of chairs, and a couple of trunks finished out the room.

There was a closed door at the back of the room, and she thought it might be a bedroom. It made no difference. The bed in the corner of the main room was closer, and Jackson was getting heavy.

With Booker's help she lowered Jackson to the bed, and then Jackson passed out again, crossways on the bed, his booted feet still on the floor.

Booker stepped away from the bed and pulled back the curtains from both windows to allow sunlight to brighten the room.

"Boiled water," Catalina said, her eyes remaining on Jackson. "Clean bandages. Whiskey." Her voice was low, as much for herself as for Booker. "Fluids. Water, tea, broth. Sugar water."

She pulled off Jackson's boots and slowly straightened his body, until he lay lengthways on the big bed. The thick bandages she'd applied in the buckboard were already stained with blood.

"Here," Booker said brusquely, shoving a bundle at her.

Catalina took the folded soft material and drew Jackson's knife to cut strips for new bandages.

"No!" Booker stopped her with his sharp command, his hand over hers. "I thought you might want to change. These belonged to my wife. She passed on five years ago, but I couldn't bring myself to get rid of her things."

"I'm fine, really." She tried to hand the clothing back to the old man, but he refused to take them. Catalina looked down at what was left of her dress. The petticoat and the skirt were gone, and what was left ended in tatters well above her knees. Scandalous, to Doc Booker.

"All right." Catalina gathered the skirt and blouse to her chest. "Will you start boiling the water and gather some clean bandages while I change?"

Booker shook his head, letting Catalina know that he thought her efforts were wasted. But she could be stubborn when she had to be.

"And then you'll have to take that bullet out of his thigh."

Booker was shaking his head again before she was finished delivering that order.

"I can't do it!" Catalina insisted. "And it has to be done."

"I told you," Booker said darkly. "It's been thirty years."

It came to Catalina, what she should have realized the first time he'd told her how long it had been since he'd been a doctor.

"The Civil War," she whispered.

"An unholy, uncivil war, the War Between the States," he said in a low voice. "I removed more than my share of balls and bullets. Lost more than my share of young men. I have no wish to go through that again."

"But you were a young man yourself."

Booker shook his head. "I was in my thirties. Some of the soldiers I saw weren't even young men; they were children, fifteen and sixteen years old. Shot, like your friend. Sometimes, when I thought all would be well, they'd take a turn for the worst in the night and be dead by morning. A few lived, but so many more didn't."

"But . . . we know more now," Catalina insisted. "We'll sterilize everything: the instruments you use on Jackson; the wounds themselves, your hands and mine."

"I haven't followed the medical profession in thirty years, young lady."

"I have," she said. "Sort of." What did she really know? Nothing. But she and Booker together . . .

Booker turned his back on her. "Get into some decent clothes. You may be accustomed to gallivanting around that bawdy house half dressed, but this is a Christian household and you will not prance around here indecently exposed." He stepped to the side and pointed to the closed door. "You can change in Victoria's room."

Catalina opened the door and stepped into a room that had the smell of disuse. It was clean but smelled a little musty, as if the single window hadn't been opened in years. Five years, probably.

She removed the ruined dress quickly and threw the remnants on a narrow bed covered with lacy pillows. "If this is truly a Christian household, you'll help me," Catalina shouted.

"I am helping you!" the old man answered, raising his voice to be heard from beyond the heavy door.

"You'll get that bullet out of Jackson's leg!"

She heard a deep snort, of disgust or resignation or, perhaps, both.

"It's not too terribly deep, I don't think, and it appears that the other four bullets passed straight through. A couple are really no more than scratches."

"I've seen men die from wounds that were no more than scratches."

"Not this time," Catalina shouted. "I'll handle everything else, if you'll just remove the bullet. Jackson won't die of an infection, if we can just keep the wounds clean." She hoped that was true.

Booker was silent for a long while as Catalina struggled into the high-necked blouse and calico skirt. Nothing about being a woman in the nineteenth century was easy! Tiny buttons, and too damn many of them, and she didn't dare show herself until they were all fastened.

Catalina finally stepped from the small feminine bedroom to find Booker standing over the patient he didn't want.

"Jackson," he said softly. "Is that his real name?"

"Yes." Catalina stepped to his side. "Jackson Cady. All you know of him is Kid Creede's reputation, and that means you don't know him at all. You know the myth, but you don't know the man."

Booker turned away from her and set water to boil on the stove. Catalina still didn't know if she would have his assistance or not.

The bandages came off slowly, starting with the least-threatening scratch in his side. Catalina doused her hands in the whiskey Booker had placed on the bedside table, and cleaned the deep scratch with a rag dipped in boiled water. Jackson flinched but didn't open his eyes. When she poured the whiskey over the furrow he flinched once and then was still. Through it all, he hadn't made a sound.

If he could just stay unconscious until she was done . . . Each wound got the same treatment, and was rebandaged with the clean white cotton Booker handed her. Catalina kept her eyes on the patient, never looking up at the old man who provided her with all that she requested.

Finally she had to deal with the leg. She cut away the material surrounding the wound and cleaned it as thoroughly as the others. This would be the bullet that killed him, if she couldn't handle the job. The bullet had to come out, and the wound had to be completely cleaned and sterilized.

There was so much blood, and his skin was so cold. When would the fever come, if she wasn't successful? Tonight? Tomorrow? Next week? Her hands hovered over the wound, and she clenched them tightly to stop the shaking.

"Move aside, young lady," Booker ordered gruffly, and Catalina looked up to see him standing over her with a battered and scarred black physician's bag in his hands.

Chapter Thirteen

Doc Booker had lit two lamps and set them near the bed, one on a small table at the head and another on a chest near the foot. Their light cast strange shadows whenever Catalina leaned forward to check on Jackson, to see if there wasn't some small movement she couldn't detect from her station in a hard-backed chair at his bedside.

The surgery had gone fairly quickly, but it had taken all of Catalina's courage to assist Doc Booker. She never could have done what needed to be done alone. Never.

But that had been hours earlier, while there had still been light streaming through the windows. It had been dark for quite some time now, and the room was dim. But the light from the lamps revealed to her all too clearly how pale Jackson was and, in spite of her wishful thinking, each time she leaned forward she realized that he hadn't moved at all.

"You're going to be just fine," she whispered, bending over him once again. "And I'll be right here, for as long as it takes."

Doc Booker's shadow fell across Jackson's face, and she moved back slightly as the old man slouched over the bed.

"Is
"N

's forehead,
the pulse at
the brief ex-

ke it," Booker said

that. Not yet."

ive times, miss. There's nothing
. . ."

to him, Jackson," Catalina inter-
g forward and easing Booker away
n. "You're going to wake up and
going to be just fine."

hear you. . . ."

e can," Catalina insisted. "There have
dies done. People have remembered
loved ones' voices while in a coma, or
s while they were under anesthesia, when
hould have been completely out of it. Some
of the brain, or the heart, or the soul, is lis-
ng, and I won't have you telling Jackson any
s about dying."

"Studies?" Doc backed away from her.

Catalina looked up at him briefly. "Aisle three,
midsection, second shelf from the top."

Doc Booker settled himself in a chair on the
other side of the room, well away from her and
her . . . their patient. He obviously didn't believe
her. What would he think if she told him about
penicillin, heart transplants, working artificial
limbs? Brain surgery, heart surgery, life support?
If Jackson was lying in the Indian Springs Hos-

pital there would be little doubt about his survival. But here . . .

"When you're able you can take me to East Texas, just like you said this morning. I've never been there, except to drive through on the interstate once or twice. Grandma Lane had a sister in Georgia, and I drove her over for a visit. She hated to fly. Said it just wasn't natural. And after the crash . . . well, there was no way she'd set foot in an airplane." Catalina looked down at the rough wood floor beneath her feet, and at the low-burning lamp near Jackson's head. Grandma Lane would be born in another fifteen years.

She'd never understood her grandmother's aversion to anything modern. Grandma Lane had never driven over forty miles an hour, and she hadn't trusted microwave ovens any more than she'd trusted airplanes. Granny had nearly hyperventilated when she'd seen her only granddaughter's first miniskirt. But she'd been born into this world, and now Catalina understood that skepticism. So many changes, so fast.

"Maybe they will need a librarian in East Texas. And you, Jackson . . . what will you do?"

Catalina reached forward and smoothed the hair away from his face. There it was, that widow's peak, and that stark and narrow streak of white at one temple. His skin was cool, for now.

"I wish I could take you back with me. In 1996 there is no Kid Creede. No one looking to beat a man with a reputation, no one looking for a hired gun to settle a land dispute. I'd love to show you everything that's changed, take you to the movies

"Is he comin' around?"

"No," Catalina said softly.

Booker laid his palm on Jackson's forehead, and then placed two fingers against the pulse at his throat. He frowned throughout the brief examination.

"He's not going to make it," Booker said gruffly.

"You can't know that. Not yet."

"He was shot five times, miss. There's nothing anyone can do. . . ."

"Don't listen to him, Jackson," Catalina interrupted, leaning forward and easing Booker away from Jackson. "You're going to wake up and everything's going to be just fine."

"He can't hear you. . . ."

"Yes, he can," Catalina insisted. "There have been studies done. People have remembered hearing loved ones' voices while in a coma, or doctors while they were under anesthesia, when they should have been completely out of it. Some part of the brain, or the heart, or the soul, is listening, and I won't have you telling Jackson any lies about dying."

"Studies?" Doc backed away from her.

Catalina looked up at him briefly. "Aisle three, midsection, second shelf from the top."

Doc Booker settled himself in a chair on the other side of the room, well away from her and her . . . their patient. He obviously didn't believe her. What would he think if she told him about penicillin, heart transplants, working artificial limbs? Brain surgery, heart surgery, life support? If Jackson was lying in the Indian Springs Hospital there would be little doubt about his survival. But here . . .

"When you're able you can take me to East Texas, just like you said this morning. I've never been there, except to drive through on the interstate once or twice. Grandma Lane had a sister in Georgia, and I drove her over for a visit. She hated to fly. Said it just wasn't natural. And after the crash . . . well, there was no way she'd set foot in an airplane." Catalina looked down at the rough wood floor beneath her feet, and at the low-burning lamp near Jackson's head. Grandma Lane would be born in another fifteen years.

She'd never understood her grandmother's aversion to anything modern. Grandma Lane had never driven over forty miles an hour, and she hadn't trusted microwave ovens any more than she'd trusted airplanes. Granny had nearly hyperventilated when she'd seen her only granddaughter's first miniskirt. But she'd been born into this world, and now Catalina understood that skepticism. So many changes, so fast.

"Maybe they will need a librarian in East Texas. And you, Jackson . . . what will you do?"

Catalina reached forward and smoothed the hair away from his face. There it was, that widow's peak, and that stark and narrow streak of white at one temple. His skin was cool, for now.

"I wish I could take you back with me. In 1996 there is no Kid Creede. No one looking to beat a man with a reputation, no one looking for a hired gun to settle a land dispute. I'd love to show you everything that's changed, take you to the movies and for a ride in my Mustang."

Catalina lowered her voice. "We put a man on the moon, Jackson. You can get from New York to California in a matter of hours, not days or weeks. You can cross the ocean in the air. Of course, you're probably like Grandma Lane. I don't suppose I could get you into an airplane."

She laid her hand over his heart. It was still beating, though not as strongly as it should be. "I'd give everything I owned for a ten-day supply of antibiotics, right now."

She began to tell him, in a hushed voice, all the wonders of the world. They hadn't seemed wonders to her before, but now, to walk into a simple supermarket or a pharmacy she had taken for granted would be a blessing.

She told him all about the library where she'd worked, and about her friend Kim, and growing up with her grandmother. Grandma Lane, she called her when she spoke of her. But she'd been Granny to Catalina all her life. Plain old Granny, she'd insisted, and even Catalina's close friends had called her that.

"Granny would have liked you," Catalina divulged, "but she would have held you down and cut your hair, and she would have harangued you until you shaved off that beard."

She tried to imagine what Jackson would look like with short hair and no beard. She laid her hands over the lower half of his face, and then she slid her hands upward and smoothed his hair away from his face. Handsome still, but not so intimidating.

"You should get some sleep," Doc Booker suggested gruffly from his perch in the far corner of the room.

Catalina twisted her head to look at the old man who had likely saved Jackson's life. "I can't."

"I'll sit with him," he offered reluctantly. "He won't be left alone."

Still, Catalina shook her head. "I can't leave him. I said I wouldn't."

She turned back to Jackson, ignoring the grunts Doc Booker made as he rose to his feet and shuffled across the floor.

"Is he an old friend?" Doc asked from directly behind her. "I heard that he brought you into town and left you at Alberta's, and then, well . . ."

"Bid on me like I was a side of beef?" Catalina finished curtly.

"Something like that," Doc mumbled.

Catalina sighed deeply. "I've known Jackson for less than a week." It seemed like so much longer, as if she'd known him forever. "In that time he's saved me from dying of thirst in the desert, saved me from Harold Goodman, saved my virtue." She looked over her shoulder and up at the man who stared down at her with a frown creasing his forehead. "And I fell in love with him. Maybe because he's saved me so often. Maybe . . . just because he's the right man for me. Do you believe in love, Dr. Booker?"

"Just Doc," he barked. "I'm no doctor. No more."

"You are. I saw you take that bullet out of his thigh like a real pro. And you didn't answer my question. Do you believe in love?"

Doc hesitated. "Yes," he said reluctantly.

Catalina turned back to Jackson, willing him to move, to wake and speak to her. "A week ago I didn't."

The fever came early in the morning. She had prepared herself, or had tried to, certain that it would come. The fever wasn't terribly high, but Jackson's skin was warm to her touch, and his breathing changed slightly. Doc Booker shook his head in resignation, seeing this as the beginning of the end, but Catalina took a different stand.

"As long as his temperature doesn't get too high, it's okay. The fever is fighting the infection."

Doc Booker continued to shake his head, but Catalina was determined to ignore his pessimism.

She cooled Jackson's skin with a damp cloth, and had Doc Booker hold the patient's head so she could spoon sugar water down his throat. It was while she was trying to force just one more spoonful into his mouth that he opened his eyes slightly and glared at her.

"Go away," he muttered in a low voice, staring straight at her.

Catalina smiled and lifted the spoon to his lips again. "You are the most stubborn, wonderful man in the world, Jackson Cady."

He swallowed the sugar water and made a face. "Thunderation, what is this?"

Catalina told him, and tried to spoon another bit into his mouth.

Jackson shook his head. "I'm not takin' that. Just leave me alone."

Catalina stood slowly, set the cup and spoon on the seat of her chair and gingerly climbed onto the bed. She didn't look at Doc Booker, not even when the old man gasped as she straddled their uncooperative patient, one knee on either side of his waist. Then she lifted the cup and offered Jackson another spoonful.

"It's for your own good," she said sensibly, spooning the sweet water over his tongue.

Jackson swallowed, glaring up at her. "Who's Granny?" he asked, a confused frown on his face.

"My Grandma Lane," Catalina said. "She raised me."

Jackson nodded. "I remember. You told me. I dreamed that she wanted to . . . cut my hair."

"And shave your beard," Catalina added smugly.

Jackson took another spoonful without protest. "How did you know?"

Catalina shrugged her shoulders. "Lucky guess. One more spoonful."

He accepted it sullenly, tiredly, and Doc Booker lowered Jackson's head to the pillow.

Catalina eased off the bed, careful not to jar the bed or touch any of Jackson's bandaged wounds. For the moment he was lucid, but she was afraid the fever was only the beginning. If she was right, the worst was yet to come.

Jackson closed his eyes. "Now, go away."

She lowered herself into the chair by Jackson's bed, smoothing her wrinkled skirt and pushing her hair away from her face.

"Never," she whispered.

She was afraid to leave his side, even when Doc

Booker volunteered—in his own grouchy way—to take her place. In her heart she knew no one would care for Jackson as she did.

So she didn't sleep. She was an intelligent woman who knew that her mere presence wouldn't make Jackson any stronger, that her watchfulness wouldn't keep him alive. Still, she couldn't sleep. When she began to doze she forced her eyes open.

She memorized every line in his face. Crow's feet, lit by the lamp by his head. The furrow between his eyes. Jackson had frowned too much, in the past. She aimed to change that. For the most part he was perfect. There was a harshness about him that kept him from being truly beautiful, but he was close to flawless. That nose was just a bit too long, but it was straight and strong. She had never cared for men with little stubby noses, she told herself as she leaned over Jackson once again.

His face was close to perfect, but she knew all too well that his body was scarred. More now than before. He had been marked by his violent life, branded forever for the choices he'd made.

He'd more than paid for the life he'd led until this point.

"You need your sleep," Doc said gruffly. Catalina nearly jumped out of her chair. She hadn't even heard him rise from his pallet on the opposite side of the room and cross to the bed.

"When Jackson wakes up," she said. "That's when I'll sleep."

He started to argue with her, as he had often in the past days. She knew those arguments well, knew them logically, as well as Doc did.

But her heart, her heart knew different.

The dreams were vivid and real and filled with strange pictures he didn't understand. People flying, arms outstretched, high in the air. Moving pictures the size of a barn he had to crane his head to see. Other images, too odd to decipher.

The only constant in those dreams was Catalina, and when he woke she was always there. Washing his face, talking to him in whispered tones, spooning that awful sweet water into his mouth. What he really wanted was coffee, but when he'd managed to ask for it Catalina had refused to allow him even a single cup. Said the coffee would dehydrate him, or some such nonsense, and then she said something really strange. Aisle four, just around the corner, bottom shelf.

He began to wish for the numbness that had followed the ambush. Every muscle ached, and he could feel the path each bullet had taken after striking his body. At least it seemed that he could.

When he opened his eyes and saw Catalina clearly for the first time since all this had begun something inside him broke. He would've believed it to be his heart, if he'd had one.

There were dark circles under her eyes, and for once she wasn't smiling. Her eyes were closed, but he knew she wasn't asleep. The mouth was too tense, and her hands were clasped tightly in her lap. The room was dark, but for the light of a single lamp near the bed, and he could hear

Doc Booker breathing, the deep, rattling near-snore of a man asleep on the other side of the room.

"Catalina," he whispered, and her eyes flew open.

"Jackson? What is it? What's wrong?" She jumped up and held her palm against his forehead, and then she let out a long sigh. "The fever's broken. Thank heavens. I'd begun to think . . ." Her voice broke.

"That I wouldn't keep my promise?" he finished for her.

She sagged down, sitting carefully on the edge of the bed. "For a while. You had me scared, Jackson."

It was still there, the fear in her eyes.

"I don't make many promises, but I do keep 'em."

She tried to smile, a weak effort, and Jackson slid his hand across the top of the bed to hers. Her fingers were chilled, and they trembled slightly as they twined through his.

"Lie down," he whispered, shifting his body slowly and painfully against the wall, giving her room to lie beside him.

Catalina shook her head. "I can't. You need your rest, and I might fall asleep and bump into you and then . . ."

"How long since you slept?"

Catalina looked down at their hands. "Four days. But I did doze in the chair a few times."

"Four days?"

"I was afraid to fall asleep. Afraid you . . . afraid I'd wake up and you'd be gone. Especially

211

the past couple of days. You wouldn't wake up and talk to me, not even to ask for coffee or to tell me to go away."

"We'll talk all day tomorrow, if you like," he said, tugging on her hand. "But tonight, you sleep."

She stretched out beside him, staying on the edge of the bed and continuing to hold his hand. "I am rather tired."

"I can see that," he whispered.

"I'll be very still," Catalina promised, closing her eyes.

Even if he could have easily reached the lamp, he wouldn't have put it out. It cast soft light over Catalina's face, and he was content just to watch her. She fell asleep almost immediately, her lips parting slightly and her grip on his hand relaxed.

He forgot his pain, for a while, staring at her face, holding her soft and strong hand. He had told her to go away, but she'd stayed at his side, hadn't given up on him. Had insisted that he recover. Had told him that she loved him.

For the first time since Gus had died, Jackson could look to the future and see something bright. Bright because Catalina was there.

Catalina opened her eyes reluctantly, expecting—for a split second—to see her digital clock and the clear telephone Kim had given her for Christmas by the bed. Instead, her fuzzy vision focused on the chair she'd spent the past four days sleeping in, waiting for Jackson to wake up, and she bolted straight up in the bed.

Jackson was sleeping, peacefully it seemed,

and she remembered that he had been lucid for a moment last night. She touched his forehead and found his skin normal. Not cold, not hot. Perfect.

Jackson opened his eyes slowly and pinned that pale blue gaze on her face.

"Good morning, gorgeous," Catalina said sleepily, sliding her hand away from his face.

Jackson said nothing, but stared at her steadily. He was still pale, but not deathly white.

Catalina sat on the edge of the bed, facing away from Jackson. He was going to be fine. And now what? Doc Booker was already up and gone, and late-morning light poured through the windows. She'd needed that sleep, and she hadn't even dreamed, or realized that she slept next to Jackson.

She could feel and hear Jackson shifting his weight, moving slowly back to the center of the bed. For four days all she'd thought about was saving him. Nothing else.

Now that it appeared she was successful, another thought occurred to her.

She'd changed history. And she didn't dare try to convince Jackson that her story about coming from the future was true. There was no way to convince him. No real proof. He'd only accuse her of being loco again.

Could she take him with her through the doorway? And if she did, if it was possible for them to travel together, would they go forward or back? Through her blouse, she fingered the hard wulfenite she'd suspended from a leather thong she'd found in Victoria Booker's bedroom. Together, would they change history again?

"Maybe I didn't." Catalina stood, but still she didn't turn to face Jackson.

"Maybe you didn't what?"

What if she was wrong about what Jackson wanted? Maybe, deep down, he really was more Kid Creede than Jackson Cady. Maybe he didn't want a new life. There was only one way to find out.

She pivoted and looked down at the bed. The notorious Kid Creede was as helpless as a baby, bandaged and weak. "What if Jackson Cady survives, and Kid Creede doesn't?"

"We're one and the same, darlin'," Jackson said without hesitation.

Catalina shook her head slightly. "They all saw you shot. No one expects you to survive. If Doc Booker tells them that you . . . that you didn't make it . . . we could leave here and have a fresh start somewhere else."

"*We*, Catalina?"

She couldn't answer, so she nodded slowly.

"It can't be that simple." Jackson stared at the ceiling, avoiding her gaze.

"It is." Catalina bit her bottom lip. "Even if you decide to leave here alone, it can be done. An empty grave with your name on it, an article in a few of the larger newspapers, and there is no more Kid Creede."

"It's who I am."

"No. I don't believe that. Maybe once that was true, but not now." She wanted so desperately for him to agree, but she still wasn't certain that he would.

"Too many people know this face. Wanted posters. Even a dime novel with a fair likeness on the cover. Dropping the name Kid Creede isn't going to change that."

Catalina smiled. "That's true. But if we shave your beard and cut your hair short, and get rid of all that black clothing . . . no one will recognize you."

Jackson closed his eyes and shook his head. "I wish it was possible, but it's not. You can't fool people like that. I'll still be exactly who I've always been."

Catalina wanted to scream at him, or beg him, but she remained silent. Maybe he was right. Maybe she couldn't pull it off. Maybe he didn't want to leave Kid Creede behind. Maybe he simply didn't want her.

"Let me try," she whispered. "You don't have to take me with you, if you don't want to. I can find my way home on my own, if I have to."

"Back to Indian Springs?" he whispered, as though it was impossible to say the words aloud.

Catalina shrugged her shoulders. "I don't know. I guess so."

"Don't go back there," Jackson said quickly.

Catalina didn't breathe. She held her breath and wondered if she'd heard him right. If she could stay with Jackson, she didn't want to go back. There was nothing to go back to.

Jackson rolled onto his side and worked his way into a sitting position, his back against the wall. It was an obvious effort, and he ignored her weak protests and offers of help. The sheet fell to his waist. There was nothing on his chest and arms but white bandages and a sprinkling of crisp black hair. Black hair tipped with chestnut waved over his shoulders, and he glared at Catalina with those piercing blue eyes that had caught her attention the first time she'd seen them.

"Stay with me," he whispered, and for the first time since she'd met him there was trepidation in his voice. Did he think she would say no? Catalina wondered if he remembered that she'd told him she loved him. He'd been out of it, but he might have heard her.

"I want to stay," Catalina whispered. "With you." She stood by the side of the bed with her hands clasped tightly. God, this was hard! The words stuck in her throat, and she felt like a little girl, afraid and uncertain. She looked at the hem of her calico skirt. "I love you," she whispered.

She didn't look up, but she heard Jackson moving on the bed. Why didn't he say something? Then his hand was grasping hers, and he tugged her gently toward him.

"Come on, Catalina," he said breathlessly. "You're making this difficult."

Catalina placed one knee on the bed, still unable to look at Jackson. "Sit here," he ordered gruffly, and she sat beside him, her back against the wall, her tired body leaning against his good side.

"Look at me," he ordered gruffly, and Catalina lifted her face to his. "And tell me again."

A smile grew slowly on Catalina's face. He wasn't angry, and he wasn't agitated. There was a spark of warmth in his eyes and a softening of his hard lips that she'd rarely seen.

"You made me fall in love with you," she whispered. "I don't know how, and I don't know why, but it's true."

"I don't understand how one woman could change my life so fast." There was a hint of childlike wonder in Jackson's voice.

Catalina snuggled easily against Jackson's side. "It's going to work out perfectly, isn't it?"

"If you say so," Jackson conceded.

"And you'll let me cut your hair and shave your beard?" She reached up and rested her palm against one cheek. She'd gotten accustomed to that bearded face in a very short time.

"Darlin'," Jackson said lightly, "if you'll kiss me, I'm yours to do with as you please."

Catalina scooted up onto her knees and knelt beside him. He could still barely move, so she laid her lips over his gently and gave him a tender kiss. She rested her palms against his neck, her thumbs brushing his bearded jaw.

"I love you," she said as she pulled slowly away. It got easier, she decided. Especially knowing that he cared about her. Even if he didn't love her. Yet. At least he wasn't horrified that she'd fallen in love with him.

"Catalina . . . I . . ." Jackson's voice was gruff, uncertain. "I'm not very good at this sort of thing."

"What sort of thing is that?"

"Marry me," he whispered.

Catalina smiled and gave him one more slow and gentle kiss before she backed away from him and off the bed.

"Yes."

Chapter Fourteen

The advantage of such a small house, Catalina decided, was the absolute necessity of organization. It took her no time at all to find Doc's razor and a pair of scissors.

Jackson was frighteningly cooperative, leaning back and allowing her to cut away. She started with his hair, because she figured that would be easiest. Thick strands of softly curling hair fell away, taking all the sun-lightened strands and leaving only stark black. His hair had once waved over his shoulders; now it curled softly at the nape of his neck.

There was a cowlick at his widow's peak, and that hair had a will of its own. The streak of white she had seen at Alberta's, as he'd pushed the mass away from his face, was visible at one temple. It was thin, small, a streak of lightning across a black sky.

His right shoulder was tightly bound, so Catalina had to shave him as well. He didn't move a muscle, and those bright eyes never closed or left her face. Trust was something new for Jackson, she was certain. It was probably a big step for him to allow a woman to hold a razor to his throat.

219

She was slow and painfully careful, scraping away the soap and the black beard, aware, with every passing second, that this transformation was much deeper than the obvious physical changes—much more than the shedding of his beard and the shortening of his hair.

The skin she revealed was a shade lighter than the rest of Jackson's face, and she uncovered a surprising pair of deep dimples.

When she was finished Catalina sat back and surveyed her work. If not for the eyes, she wouldn't have recognized him herself.

Jackson ran his mobile hand over his clean-shaven face and the shortened hair at the back of his neck. He appeared—for the first time since she'd offered this idea—to be skeptical.

Catalina returned the scissors and the shaving implements to their proper places, and then rejoined Jackson with a small hand mirror. It was silver-backed, and definitely a woman's. Doc's late wife's?

Catalina handed the mirror to Jackson and waited for his reaction. He turned his face first one way and then the other, but he didn't smile. He didn't *exactly* frown, either.

"Well," Catalina snapped impatiently. "What do you think?"

Jackson lowered the mirror slowly. "What do *I* think? What difference does it make what I think? What do *you* think?"

Catalina sat on the edge of the bed and took the mirror from his hand. "I think you're beautiful."

Jackson snorted.

"I'll miss the beard, but I love the dimples." Catalina smiled and leaned in slightly. "No wonder you grew that beard. It's difficult to look formidable with dimples like that, isn't it?"

Jackson ignored the comment. "Do I look . . . different enough to suit you?"

Catalina nodded once. It was true. No one would recognize him like this. They could go anywhere, start fresh, leave Kid Creede behind.

Doc Booker threw open the door and stomped in, his eyes on the floor. He didn't approve of all that had gone on . . . in his house or before . . . and he certainly wouldn't have forgotten or forgiven rising that morning and finding her sleeping in the same bed with Jackson. Shocking.

"Doc?" Catalina called softly to the old man.

He lifted his head and glanced sourly toward the bed. His hard gaze lit on Catalina and then on Jackson. His eyes grew large, then narrowed, and then he stepped toward the bed.

"What the heck?" he muttered, staring down at Jackson. "Kid?" Doc looked his patient up and down, disbelief and more than a little suspicion etched on his face.

Catalina stood. "Doc Booker, I'd like you to meet Jackson Cady. My fiancé."

Consternation. That was the only word for the expression on Doc's face.

They would need Doc Booker's help if this was going to work. Catalina explained her plan to him quickly, before he could think to question her. There was a moment of dead silence when she was done.

Finally Doc lifted his eyes from Jackson to her. "Fiancé?"

Catalina nodded and smiled.

"No more killing? No more . . . Kid Creede?" For this question he turned his attention back to Jackson. Jackson shook his head slowly.

"And you expect everyone will just take your word that he's dead?" Doc asked Catalina skeptically. He was squinting at Jackson, looking—she assumed—for some sign of the outlaw he knew was there.

"Mine," she answered softly, "and yours."

Catalina tugged with one finger at the choking collar of the black dress for what seemed like the thousandth time since they'd left the ranch. This was another of Mrs. Booker's dresses, a black muslin mourning dress with a high collar and long sleeves that puffed high at the shoulders. Her hair was pulled back into a simple bun, at Doc's insistence, and she clutched a lace-trimmed hanky in one hand. She'd been instructed to dab at her eyes with that handkerchief at regular intervals.

"I'm a little nervous," Catalina confessed when Baxter was in sight. They passed a gnarled old tree, a sentinel at the edge of town.

"You should be very nervous," Doc said darkly. "If we don't do this right, we could all three end up dead."

She hadn't wanted to leave Jackson alone, even for half a day. He was still weak, and Doc had assured her that he would be for some time. If he was found . . . if Harold Goodman decided to

go to the ranch while Doc Booker was in town
. . . Jackson would be defenseless.

Doc parked his buckboard in the same place
she and Jackson had found him a week earlier.
It was near the church, and they walked directly
to the white steepled building that stood apart
from the rest of the town. There was already a
crowd out front, and everyone turned to stare at
her and Doc. All conversation stopped.

Catalina expected that at any moment they
would stoop to pick up handfuls of rocks and
stone her. There wasn't a smiling face in the
crowd. Not a forgiving one, either. That woman
. . . Millicent, was it? . . . stepped forward. She
stood in the middle of the pathway, directly in
front of the wide front door of the church.

"Mrs. Brown," Doc said solemnly, a greeting as
well as a touch of challenge in his voice as he
nodded his head in the direction of the disap-
proving woman.

Millicent Brown didn't move. She alone stood
on the pathway, the crowd around her suppor-
tive of her action but separate from it.

"You're not bringing that woman into God's
house?" It was more an order than a question.

Catalina put her hand on Doc's arm, and he
patted it consolingly. They had expected some
opposition. "The young woman has come to pray
for the soul of her lost friend. Surely you
wouldn't deny her that comfort."

Millicent didn't move, but crossed her arms defiantly. "Kid Creede had no soul. The world's a
better place without him. He's burning in hell,
and he'll burn there for all eternity."

"Move aside, Millicent," Doc ordered harshly.

"Yes, Millicent," a soft voice added, and a plain woman who was dressed in black, much as Catalina was, stepped forward. "Where is your Christian charity? We all know that Doc Booker is a God-fearing man with a stern but good heart. If he can support Miss Lane in this difficult time, surely we all can do the same."

Doc nodded in her direction. "Thank you, Mrs. Dunston."

Catalina thought for a moment that Mrs. Dunston was going to blush.

Millicent Brown never would have stepped aside, but for the quiet order of the preacher, who had appeared at the open door. Catalina kept her hand on Doc Booker's arm as they walked into the church, and she could feel the hate, the burning eyes that were certainly fastened on her back. The hairs on the back of her neck stood up, but she never faltered, never let her fear show. She kept step with Doc Booker, her head held high, her spine ramrod straight.

As they proceeded down the aisle, the preacher smiled at her, a small, sad smile for one whose soul had certainly been lost. She could hear the congregation behind her, entering the church. She didn't turn to glance over her shoulder, though she was tempted to see if the only person who had openly sided with Doc—that soft-voiced Mrs. Dunston—was right behind them.

"Did I hear that the . . . ummm . . . the gentleman died?" the preacher asked as Doc saw Catalina seated on the front pew.

It was Doc who answered. He was, he'd admitted, a terrible liar, so the story he told held as much truth as possible.

"Yes," Doc said gravely. "He held on longer than I'd thought he would. Kid Creede passed on yesterday, and I buried him out at the ranch."

The preacher nodded solemnly.

"Miss Lane will need our help," Doc continued. "This past week has made her see the light. She's a new woman, and she's leaving behind the life she once led. There are some," he said meaningfully, "who will not want her to lead the life of a good, Christian woman."

Catalina bravely glanced behind her. The second pew was filled, and the one behind that as well, and on the opposite side of the aisle churchgoers settled themselves, straightening fancy bonnets and smoothing skirts, tugging at string ties and straining against tight collars. Mrs. Dunston sat in the front pew across the aisle, very pointedly not looking their way. She studied her own hands with apparent great interest.

But no one spoke. They were all listening raptly. And they all, evidently, knew that Doc was speaking about Alberta. The woman who thought of Catalina as her *property*, to be bought and sold.

Evidently, the church's war with Alberta was stronger than their condemnation of her. If she was to be an ally in that battle, then she was forgiven . . . at least by some. She could see that in their softening faces. Even Millicent Brown seemed less hostile. A little.

Catalina heard nothing of the service. She stood when Doc stood, and bowed her head when he did, and muttered amen a beat behind those around her. Her mind was on Jackson. At the moment he was unprotected . . . as if her presence would save him if Harold Goodman put in an appearance at the ranch. He'd stayed away all week; certainly he wouldn't go there now. But Catalina couldn't shake her fears.

Later she would most likely have to face Alberta. The madam certainly knew by now that Catalina was in town. Catalina could only hope that Doc was right . . . that the woman would relent when faced with the entire congregation of the Baxter Baptist Church.

Catalina kept her head down as Doc led her from the crowded church after the sermon. She nodded silently to the consoling preacher, who shook Doc's hand and then hers as they left the building. Catalina searched the crowd for the intriguing Mrs. Dunston, but the woman was nowhere to be found. She kept her eyes on the ground as Doc Booker led her down the street toward the sheriff's office. Doc insisted that this was necessary, that it would end things once and for all, but Catalina wasn't so sure.

The sheriff was skeptical, but Catalina said nothing, allowing Doc to do all the talking. He told the sheriff of Kid Creede's lingering death, and that on his deathbed the Kid had left all he owned to Catalina Lane.

He did it unwillingly, but the sheriff collected Jackson's horse from the livery, and his saddle as well. He suggested that Catalina collect their things from Alberta's, but she adamantly refused. She wouldn't walk into that place again.

The sheriff gave in, faced with her obvious fear, and sent a deputy to fetch her personal belongings, and Jackson's, from Alberta's.

Easy, Catalina thought as she left the sheriff's office clutching a bundle that contained Jackson's change of clothes, his duster, and her wedding dress and moccasins. Much too easy.

Alberta was waiting for them, standing in the street with Milo at her side.

"Cat," she said sharply, crossing her arms over her ample bosom, "you took your time, but I knew you'd be back."

"I'm not back," Catalina said, facing Alberta bravely. "I'm never coming back."

Alberta raised her eyebrows in an amused expression of mock disbelief. "You work for me . . ."

"No more," Catalina interrupted.

Several church members joined Catalina and Doc on the boardwalk, and Alberta seemed just to notice. Her eyes scanned the crowd and her smug smile faded.

"You can't just leave."

"I can, and I will."

Juanita came running down the street, an unusually long skirt held aloft in both hands. "Is it true?" she asked breathlessly, her eyes on Catalina's face. "Is the Kid dead?"

Catalina nodded. Juanita's face fell, and she dropped her skirt so that it touched the dirt. "Tarnation," she muttered. "I'll never get to San Francisco."

There were no tears, not even feigned sadness. Catalina wanted to scratch the hussy's eyes out, but in a way she was relieved. She didn't want any other woman in love with Jackson . . . not even if that woman believed him dead. He was hers, and hers alone.

"We buried him yesterday." Another of Doc's half-truths, spoken by Catalina. They'd buried his torn and bloody clothes and marked the grave with a crude wooden marker. Kid Creede was truly dead, but she had Jackson. She would always have Jackson.

"You're not going to allow her to stay at your ranch, are you, Doc?" An unidentified voice from the church crowd rang out.

"Of course not," Doc said righteously. "That wouldn't be proper. She'll be staying with me temporarily, until my nephew arrives from Virginia. He'll take her to live with my sister, Mary Katherine."

"Your nephew?" the same voice asked, and Catalina identified it. A small man standing in the back, all but hiding behind Millicent Brown. She'd seen him before . . . in Alberta's.

Doc nodded. "Yes. My nephew, Jackson Cady."

"So," Catalina breathed, looking away from Doc and out over the endless landscape, "what's with Mrs. Dunston?"

Doc harumphed, something he was very good at. "What do you mean, what's with her? She's Reverend Preston's sister, and she's just recently come to live with him."

"She's got a major crush on you, you know." Catalina turned her head to the old man just in time to see him blush.

"Ridiculous notion," he snapped. "She's much too young for me, and she's been a widow for only eight months."

"Counting, are we?"

"No," he snapped at her again. "We're not."

"You needn't be cranky," Catalina pulled at the collar of her mourning dress again. "I'm just trying to make conversation. It's quite a long trip, and I've been worried about Jackson."

When the house came into view Catalina had to grip the wagon seat to keep herself from leaping to the ground. The horsedrawn conveyance moved much too slowly, particularly at a time like this.

Catalina jumped from the buckboard before it had come to a complete stop, and she ran toward the house. It was late afternoon . . . Jackson had been alone in the house all day. She'd seen him close to death for so long, it was impossible to remain calm. A part of her knew she would find him waiting, resting safely in the bed where he belonged, but until she saw him she wouldn't relax.

She threw the door open and turned toward the bed where Jackson was supposed to be. But the wide bed in that corner of the main room was rumpled and empty.

He couldn't be gone. Catalina ran to the closed door at the back of the room and threw it open. Victoria Booker's small room was as quiet and deserted as the rest of the house. She hurried through the main room, trying to push down the panic that welled up inside her. All this time . . . while she'd been telling herself that her worries were for nothing . . . something had been happening.

Catalina had never been given to real panic before, but she'd certainly experienced her share of that undesirable emotion in this past week.

She circled the house, checking the outhouse first. There was a chamber pot under the bed, but Jackson had as much distaste for that object as she did. He'd be a fool to try to walk to the privy alone, but that didn't mean he wouldn't try. But even that space was empty.

Jackson wasn't strong enough to have gotten very far on foot. "I never should have left him here alone," she muttered as she rounded the house.

Before she could reenter the house, Doc Booker came out of the barn, supporting an obviously weak Jackson with one less than steady arm. Jackson stood a full head taller than the doctor, and they looked as if they might topple at any moment.

"Look what I found in the barn," Doc Booker called shakily as Catalina ran toward them.

"What were you doing in the barn?" Catalina asked, her voice shaking as much as Doc's, but for a different reason. She'd never leave Jackson again, even for half a day.

"Harold Goodman and a couple of his hands rode out this way. I heard them coming and snuck out the window and hid in the barn." His voice was full of obvious self-disgust. Running and hiding were new to Jackson. Kid Creede would have crouched in a window with both pistols and plenty of ammunition.

But it would have ruined their plan.

"I was so worried . . ." Catalina began.

"I heard the buckboard," Jackson said, leaning into her as she slipped her arm around his waist. "But I couldn't get up."

Catalina shook her head. "Earlier today, while we were in Baxter . . . Goodman wasn't there, and I was afraid he might find you here. And then Millicent Brown said you were burning in hell, and that made me so mad I couldn't say a word. Not a single word. I was so worried the whole time we were gone that something might happen and I wouldn't be here."

"It's a good thing you weren't here," Jackson said darkly.

"Why?"

"Even after Goodman found the grave, he still searched the house and sent a hand to look in the barn."

"He didn't see you?"

"I was under a goddamn pile of straw."

Doc Booker chuckled, an effort for him as he supported so much of Jackson's weight. "New experience for you?"

Jackson just grunted.

"They were looking for you," Jackson said as Catalina reached out and opened the door. "He knew Doc would be in town on Sunday, but I reckon he figured you wouldn't be."

Jackson got heavier and heavier as they approached the corner. He didn't speak again until they had lowered him gently to the bed, and Doc was checking his bandages to see if he'd reopened any wounds.

"Tell me something, Doc?" Jackson asked breathlessly as the old man bent over his thigh. "Why, if Harold wants this place so bad, doesn't he just shoot you or burn you out? Hell, it should be easy enough, with no one here but you."

"And you should know," Doc added curtly.

"And I should know," Jackson confirmed in a low voice.

Doc was happy with what he found. No fresh bleeding in spite of Jackson's extra activity. "Few years back, there was a fever made its way through his daddy's ranch." Doc glared down at Jackson. "It's still his daddy's ranch, in my eyes. That kid never did a lick of work in his life. Harold was just a boy, and somehow the fever passed him by. But his mama, and his daddy, and a good many of the hands and their families had it."

Doc stood and walked away from the bed, and busied himself at the stove, making coffee. "Ben Goodman was one of the few men in these parts who knew that I had been a real doctor, once. He asked me for my help, and I did what I could. Maybe I saved a few lives, maybe they were just stronger than the others and would have made it anyway. In any case, Ben felt as if he owed me a debt, and so did many of his men. Some of them are still there. Harold would probably get rid of them, if he could run that place by himself. But he can't." Doc suddenly sounded tired. Deeply tired. "They keep me alive. Harold would have killed me himself as soon as his daddy died, if it hadn't been for them."

Jackson closed his eyes and nodded his head. "At least that makes some sort of sense. But there's one other thing that makes no sense, Doc. Why does Harold want this place? Nothing personal, but it ain't much to look at, and what I saw of the land this afternoon . . . well, let's just say I'm confused."

"It's not the ranch he wants," Doc said half-heartedly, refusing to look at them. There was a long pause, and Catalina waited patiently for the man to continue. Finally he turned from the stove and stared first at her and then at Jackson. Doc took a deep sigh, a sigh almost of surrender.

"It's not the ranch," he repeated. "It's the gold."

"Gold?" Jackson repeated, finding the strength to sit up.

Booker nodded his head. "Harold's had quite a bit of success mining his daddy's property. He had some fancy dude from back East come out and take a look around, and this dude told Harold that the motherlode was most likely on my side of the property line."

"Have you ever checked it out yourself?" Jackson asked.

Doc Booker shook his head slightly. "I'm no miner. I don't need gold, and I don't want it. Everything I need is right here, and this is where I'll stay until the day I die. I swear, gold has made fools of more men. . . ." He glanced over his shoulder suspiciously. "Aren't you going to ask me exactly where this gold is? Will I have you to worry about, as well as Harold Goodman?"

Jackson smiled. Catalina started to defend him, but he laid a hand on her arm and she was silent. It was his dream, what he'd waited for all his life. Gold . . . enough to make all his dreams come true.

"You've never even considered mining it yourself?"

Doc shook his head. "Don't want it, don't need it. Does that surprise you?"

Jackson shook his head, and he continued to smile. "Not at all."

"Well?" the old man snapped.

Jackson took his eyes off the old man and stared at Catalina. She knew. She understood. She was the best thing that had ever happened to him, and he didn't need anything else. Didn't want anything else.

His initial reaction, when he'd looked out the front window and seen riders headed for the Booker ranch, had been to check his guns and prepare to die. He'd done it a hundred times.

But he couldn't let them know he was alive, and he didn't want to die. He had, for the first time in his life, something to live for.

He lifted one hand, and Catalina took it. "Well, Doc," he said easily, "I hate to disappoint you. A week ago I would have done my best to scare that property out of you. I might even would've shot you for it, though I would have tried not to kill you."

"Mighty kind of you," Doc said sarcastically.

"But I don't expect to be around long enough to do any mining. We're headed to East Texas, as soon as I'm able to travel."

He couldn't say the words, but Jackson knew he already had his treasure. He'd found it in the desert, and he hadn't even had to dig for it. It was just standing there, waiting for him. He liked dreaming of a gold that was warm instead of cold, a treasure that filled him with peace, not insanity. A gold worth any sacrifice.

Catalina leaned forward slightly. "As if you could scare anything out of anyone with those dimples."

Doc Booker shook his head in apparent wonder. "Just when I think I have everything figured out . . ."

Chapter Fifteen

Catalina leaned over the bed, placing her face close to Jackson's. It broke her heart to see him so pale, so weak. It just wasn't right.

He had dismissed Doc's gold without another word, even though she knew it was what he had always wanted. Would she be enough to make him leave behind everything he knew, everything he'd always lived for?

She had no doubts about herself, no qualms about leaving behind the conveniences of her time. That was all they were: conveniences, not necessities. All she needed was Jackson. Catalina smiled to herself. A naive and sickeningly romantic notion, that love was all she needed. It was the stuff of romance novels and country songs, but it was true.

There was nothing in the future—her past—to return to. She would miss Kim, and sometimes she wondered what her old roommate thought about the disappearance. If only there was some way to let Kim know that she was safe, and happy. Happier than she'd ever been.

Without warning, without a change in his breathing or his expression, Jackson opened his eyes. God, that gaze shot right through her. She was defenseless against it.

"How do you feel?" she whispered.

"Not great," he confessed. "Not too bad, considering. I must say, you're a diligent nurse, watching me so closely as I sleep." He smiled, taking the bite out of his words.

"Am I bothering you?"

"No." Jackson slid a hand from under the covers and found hers. "If you want, you can slide into this bed with me and keep me warm and watch me all you want."

"You're chilled?" Catalina grasped his hand and leaned forward to lay her lips on his forehead. No fever that she could detect.

Jackson took a deep breath, and she could hear the subtle exasperation. He wasn't a man to be babied, but for God's sake, what did he expect her to do? Sit back and calmly wait to see if infection set in and killed him?

But he said nothing. Jackson drew his fingers from hers and wrapped his arm around her, holding her close. "I'm not chilled. I have no fever. The wounds are healing nicely, thanks to you and Doc Booker." Surprisingly, his voice was kind. "Just because a man wishes for a woman to warm his bed, that doesn't mean he's dying."

"I should hope not."

Catalina rested her head against his shoulder, easily, so as not to jar anything that shouldn't be moved. "I don't mean to smother you, Jackson."

"You're not," she could almost hear a hint of humor in his voice. "You're quite light against my chest, as a matter of fact."

Catalina lifted her head to see if he was joking

with her. He wasn't. "Not that kind of smother-ing. Watching over you too closely. Babying you. Worrying too much. I can't help it, Jackson. I came . . . a very long way to find you, and I don't want to let you go."

"I'm not going anywhere." He ran his hand along her back. "Even if I don't know what you see in a scoundrel like me."

"A scoundrel?" she asked, teasingly, but Jack-son's smile faded.

"You know what I am, Catalina; what I've al-ways been."

"I know I love you," she whispered. "And that's enough for me. That's all I need, Jackson."

He pulled her head back to his shoulder, but not before she saw the spark of bewilderment in his eyes.

He healed, a little every day, and the infection Catalina had been so afraid of never appeared. The color came back to his face, to his lips, and slowly his strength returned as well.

No matter how sternly she ordered Jackson to stay in bed, he began to refuse, and Catalina couldn't help but feel an almost ecstatic rush of relief when he sat up so easily and scowled at her and ran his fingers through his newly shortened hair. He was becoming restless, but it was still too early to think of travel.

Any thoughts she'd ever had of finding her way back disappeared. This was where she belonged. Some cosmic mistake had been made when she was born—a hundred years too late. She felt more at home in Doc Booker's cabin than she ever had in Indian Springs, or anywhere else but Grandma Lane's house.

Catalina stirred a bubbling pot of beans and bacon. Reluctantly, Doc was teaching her to cook. She told him she'd come from a wealthy family where she'd been kept from such menial duties, explaining away her ineptitude. The lie made more sense than the truth: that she could cook an entire meal in a microwave, or roast a hen she'd bought—plucked and cleaned—at the grocery store, and that, in all honesty, she rarely cooked, thanks to fast food.

She wiped her hands on the apron that covered the dress Doc had given her, one of several that fit her almost perfectly. They were all plain, high-necked and long-sleeved, and this one was a pretty calico, tiny flowers on a pale blue background.

"Smells good."

Catalina turned slowly and faced the bed. Jackson was sitting on the edge, his hands on the mattress beside him, an almost solemn expression on his face.

"It'll be ready soon," Catalina promised with a little smile. "You really should lie down until it's time to eat."

Jackson ignored her and stood slowly. "I've done plenty enough lying down."

Catalina's heart leapt into her throat. Weak as he still was, there was a power in Jackson that took her breath away, even without the persona of Kid Creede that she was so certain had been deliberate. The black clothing, but for the pair of pants he wore, had been replaced. He wore a plain white shirt—the one she had grabbed at the general store and left in Milo's hands.

He shaved himself every morning now, and Catalina always watched him out of the corner of her eye as she pretended to mend one of Doc's old shirts, or one of the dresses that had belonged to his wife. Twice she had stabbed her thumb, painfully, as she tried to do both.

The cabin seemed smaller when Jackson was standing; the room seemed to close in on her. Catalina shook her head and smiled. "It's only been three weeks."

Three weeks. He should have died, but he stood before her healthy and growing stronger, watching her with those pale blue eyes that saw everything. A second chance; how many people ever really get a second chance?

Jackson took a step toward her, limping, favoring the leg from which Doc Booker had removed the bullet. He'd been moving around a little since that day Harold Goodman had come calling, that Sunday Jackson had hidden in the barn. They hadn't seen Goodman or any of his men since, and Catalina wondered what the man was up to. She was certain he hadn't given up so easily, and the quiet days were like the calm before the storm.

"How do you feel?" Catalina asked softly. Each step Jackson took was obviously an effort, yet he continued walking toward her.

"Better," he said smoothly, and Catalina knew it was the truth. The smile grew on his face as he neared her.

Catalina didn't move as Jackson came to her.

"I see I was right," he said as he stopped before her, so close she could feel his body heat, could smell the soap he used and the lingering scent of cigar smoke. She still hadn't been able to convince him that smoking those things was bad for him, but she would. Eventually.

"Right about what?" Catalina had to lift her chin to look directly into Jackson's face.

"When I woke up and saw you here I was certain you'd somehow gotten prettier while I slept." Jackson lowered his face, until his lips were almost on hers. "I thought that was impossible."

He laid his lips on hers, and Catalina wrapped her arms around his waist. It was everything she'd always heard a truly great kiss was supposed to be but had never quite believed. Her knees went weak, her stomach jumped, and she could feel the beat of her heart all through her body, a growing, pulsing beat that drove away everything else.

Jackson wrapped one arm around her and pulled her close, deepening the kiss. Catalina felt jolted, as if there were electricity coursing through her every vein, sparking every nerve. She pressed her hands against Jackson's back, held her chest against his. Her entire body ached, but it was a delicious ache.

She would have sunk to the floor if he hadn't supported her with his good arm.

He thrust his tongue into her mouth, and Catalina followed his lead. She could feel and hear the moan that escaped his lips, and answered with one of her own.

A small cry burst from her mouth when Jackson pulled away from her, but he didn't leave her, didn't loosen his hold on her. He trailed his lips down the side of her neck, and she threw her head back, baring her throat for him. Fire. She was on fire. Bolts of lightning surged through her body, wild and bright.

He brought his lips to hers again, firm and demanding, and Catalina felt and heard another groan deep in her throat. She wanted Jackson, and she wanted him now. Here. On the floor beneath their feet. The bed was too damn far away. Miles away.

"Dang blast it!"

Doc slammed the door.

Catalina pulled her lips away from Jackson, but he didn't release her and she didn't slide her hands away from his back. Doc was glaring at the two of them as if they'd committed a great sin . . . and perhaps in his eyes they had. She'd been so caught up in that kiss, she hadn't even heard the squeaky door open.

"I see you're feeling better," Doc said, directing his glare at Jackson. There was no kindness in his words, no caring physician's relief that his patient was healing so nicely. There was just a biting condemnation that Catalina was becoming much too accustomed to.

"Yep," Jackson said, releasing Catalina slowly. She wasn't ready to leave his arms, not by a long shot. She could still feel his lips on hers, his hand at her back, the deep ache he'd started with a simple kiss. Simple? There had been nothing simple about it.

"Good." Doc gave them a grin that made Catalina wary. It wasn't a friendly smile. It was calculating and vindictive. "Starting tomorrow you can help me out around the place."

He removed his hat and hung it on a peg by the door, and shucked off his thin jacket.

"Jackson can't possibly . . ." she began.

Booker tilted his chin and raised his eyebrows. There was an expression of suspicion and disbelief and harsh judgment on the old man's face. It was just a kiss, Catalina thought angrily; and then she reminded herself of where she was. Of *when* she was.

"Do you really think he's ready?" she asked, her voice calmer, more reasonable than just moments earlier.

"Looks like it to me," Doc mumbled.

Catalina was ready to argue, but Jackson placed a stilling hand on her arm. "He's right. I need to get busy, get out of this house, and I might could be some help."

Doc practically snorted. Disbelief? Derision? Catalina ignored him and turned her attention to Jackson.

"It's too soon. If you're not able to travel, I don't see how you expect to be able to . . . to do whatever it is Doc does all day. You should be resting," she insisted.

Jackson stepped away from her, and Catalina looked up into his face. His lips were still flushed from their kiss, and his eyes were unusually bright. "The Doc's right," he said softly. "I'll get my strength back faster if I make myself useful."

"Besides," Doc said harshly, "it don't look right, the two of you alone in this house all day. I can't let my place go to seed just to chaperone you two."

"I don't care how it looks," Catalina snapped. "Besides, who's around to see?"

Doc lifted a stubborn chin. "It don't matter if I never get another visitor, it still don't look right. Sometimes the Reverend Preston stops by, and I wouldn't want him to think there's anything untoward going on here, in my house."

Doc Booker grinned, and Catalina dreaded whatever was coming. She didn't like the gleam in his eyes. Not at all. "As a matter of fact," he said, an unnatural lightness in his voice, "I think it might be a grand idea for the Kid . . . I mean, Jackson and me to move out to the barn. A couple of pallets, a few blankets . . ."

"No," Catalina objected. "I have my own room." She pointed, without turning her head, to the closed door at the back of the room. The late Victoria Booker's room, complete with lace curtains and pillows and a narrow bed. "It gets much too cold at night for Jackson to be sleeping in the barn."

"I have plenty of blankets," Doc assured her. "And if the Kid . . ."

"Jackson," Catalina snapped, correcting the old man before he had a chance to correct himself.

Doc smiled, a more genuine smile this time. "If Jackson gets cold and lonely, he can snuggle up to his horse. At least until after the wedding."

Catalina was furious, but Jackson laughed. "You're right, Doc. Until I can travel, it would be best if I slept in the barn."

She turned an exasperated face to him. "Really, Jackson, that's not necessary."

He took her hand, holding her fingers gingerly, and gave her a smile that was much too serene. "Yes," he whispered, and his voice was low and for her alone, "it is very necessary."

There was a moment of strained silence in the small room. If Jackson was working with Doc all day long, and sleeping in the barn at night, she would never see him. And it could be weeks before he was ready to travel any great distance. In spite of his protests, his returning color, his wicked smile, he was still weak.

"I don't like it," she said softly.

"There's a solution," Doc said smugly, offering no more, even when Catalina stared at him and waited.

Finally she spoke, and her words were harsh. "And what would that solution be?"

"We could make a trip to Baxter, and let the Reverend Preston get you two properly wed."

Catalina could feel the blood rush from her face, and knew she faced the two men pale, white as the proverbial ghost. "No," she said softly. "Jackson can't go back to Baxter. Ever."

Doc frowned. "No one there would recognize him, and I've told everyone about my nephew Jackson. We could just tell everyone that the two of you were smitten at first sight, and decided . . ."

"No," Catalina said again, and this time her voice was stronger. She couldn't shake the feeling that history couldn't really be changed, that somehow, if Jackson returned to Baxter, he would die on the street as he was fated. Shot, a dozen times. Ambushed.

Jackson held one palm against her cheek, a comforting gesture but tentative at best. "Catalina?" He whispered her name, and only then did she meet his questioning gaze.

"Promise me you won't ever go back to Baxter," she insisted softly.

Jackson hesitated, and rocked his thumb across her cheek, a mindless caress as he searched her eyes.

"Promise me, Jackson."

"All right," he whispered. "If it's that important to you . . ."

"It is," she said, the words expelled with her sigh of relief.

Jackson shifted slightly as his body rebelled against the hard pallet. True, he spent most nights on the ground, or at least it seemed that way. On the trail, camping away from town. Except for a few places, like Alberta's, he made a point of resting far from town, away from people. He'd never had a real home, that he could remember. Had never wanted one, until now.

Truth was, it wasn't the hard ground that bothered him. It was knowing that Catalina was sleeping so close by, and that he couldn't touch her. Not yet.

He could close his eyes and remember so clearly what she had felt like, that one night they'd been lovers. When he'd known that he wanted her but had not yet realized that he loved her. When he'd lost himself as never before, given and taken more than ever before. When he had, in his heart and soul, claimed Catalina for his own.

Doc Booker snored unevenly, snorting on occasion and then falling into a soft rumble. Jackson knew that he and the Doc had nothing in common. The old man was righteous and pious and judgmental, the kind of man Jackson had despised all his life. He and the doctor-turned-rancher had nothing to bring them together . . . except for one shared realization.

Catalina was special. He couldn't treat her like one of Alberta's girls. She should have what she always wanted, her special wedding night. She deserved that. She deserved everything.

She was the only good thing that had ever happened to him, the only decent person he'd taken into his life. She could make him forget what he was . . . what he'd been.

So he tried to forget that he hurt with wanting her, that he'd seen her own need in those whiskey eyes. He tried to forget by wondering what it would be like to have a real home. To sleep in a bed every night with his wife, to have children, to live with love instead of fear.

Doc groaned and rose unsteadily, weaving on his feet before he headed for the barn door that was cracked slightly open. Moonlight spilled in as the old man opened the door quietly.

Moments later Doc Booker was back, closing the door as easily as he had opened it.

"Everything all right?" Jackson asked softly.

The old man, no more than a shadow in the dark barn, jumped when Jackson spoke.

"I thought you were asleep." Doc whispered hoarsely.

"I've slept too much in the past three weeks."

Doc Booker settled himself on his pallet, but he didn't lie down. He faced Jackson, sitting awkwardly on the temporary bed. "I'm up and down all night now. What I wouldn't give for just one long, uninterrupted night of sleep."

"Did you check on Catalina?"

Doc Booker chuckled, low and almost friendly. "No; I checked on the privy. Miss Catalina's fine, I assure you. Locked up tight."

"Locked in, huh?"

"Yep. I made her bolt the door, and I checked it the first time I was up."

Jackson just grunted, a noncommittal rumble that meant nothing.

Doc laughed again, a little louder this time. "So when's the wedding?"

Jackson rolled up into a sitting position and faced the Doc. It didn't look as if either of them was going to get any more sleep tonight.

"Not until we leave here. You heard her . . . she's terrified of what might happen if I go back into Baxter."

"No one there will recognize you, now."

Jackson believed that was probably true, but he didn't want to tell the old man about Catalina's earlier claims—that she had traveled back in time a hundred years. That he was supposed to die in Baxter.

"I made a promise. I told her I wouldn't go back, so we'll have to wait until I can travel."

Doc Booker was silent. "That shouldn't be too

much longer. You're healing nicely, for a man I was certain was dead."

They sat there, the silence between them companionable for once, and Jackson wondered what he should say next. He'd never thanked the Doc for saving his life . . . that was the sort of nicety he was unaccustomed to.

"I'm going to town tomorrow," Doc said cautiously. "I need some supplies, and you could use some new duds. I'd loan you some of mine, but the pants would be a mite short, and you look to me of an age to have been out of knickers for quite some time. Miss Catalina and I have discussed it, and I think I know what she wants."

"Takin' her with you?" Jackson asked casually.

"Nope. It would be best if she stays here. Alberta has been mighty quiet, but I don't trust that woman. The only reason she hasn't come out here and tried to take Catalina is that she's afraid of going to war with the Baptists. Nope, goin' to church on Sunday is all that's safe for Miss Catalina, and even then I have to listen to her caterwaul about leaving you here alone, and I worry that we might meet up with someone on the way back."

"I'll be able to travel soon," Jackson assured the old man . . . and himself. "Catalina and I need to get away from here."

"You're not ready just yet, son," Doc said gruffly. "It's a miracle you're alive; don't rush it."

"It is a miracle," Jackson said softly, and he wasn't speaking of his recovery, but of finding Catalina when he'd lost all hope.

Somehow Doc knew exactly what he meant.

"She deserves better than the likes of you," he said without rancor.

"Yep," Jackson agreed. "That she does. Have you ever seen a woman more..." Jackson searched for the right words to describe Catalina. Beautiful, certainly, but more than that. Luminous, when she smiled and when she wept and broke his heart. Unexpected, tossing him and Harold Goodman to the ground with apparent ease. Strong, demanding that he live when he'd already given up. "Amazing," he finally said.

Doc answered with a thoughtful murmur, and Jackson stretched back on his hard pallet. Morning would soon be upon them, warming sun and bright light. While Doc was gone he could steal another kiss...

No, he couldn't. With Doc away from the ranch, there would be nothing and no one to stop them from taking what they both wanted. He wanted to wait... for Catalina's sake... but he could only stand so much.

Catalina rolled slowly from the bed, straining her ears as she listened to the quiet house. It seemed so empty without Jackson in it. When she opened the door and peeked into the main room it chilled her heart to see the empty bed.

Gray morning light lit the room, but the sun wasn't yet up. Time to fix breakfast for Jackson and Doc and herself, a big meal to carry them through the busy morning.

Doc had taught her, with little evidence of patience, how to cook. He hadn't complained, but she had a feeling Doc Booker would be glad to be rid of them as soon as Jackson was able to travel. They had disrupted his quiet life, and at times he seemed awfully impatient.

She was impatient herself. Anxious to be far away from Baxter. Anxious to be alone with Jackson again. He still moved carefully and slowly, but she could see that he improved every day.

He had not been pleased to hear that Doc had told the townspeople about his nephew Jackson Cady, who was coming to fetch her. The old guy had even gone to the telegraph office, sent a strangely worded message to his sister—who evidently was real—to make the story believable.

If anyone were to stop by, Jackson's presence here would be explained. Catalina didn't want anyone from Baxter stopping by, no matter how changed Jackson's appearance was. She tried to assure him—and herself—that no one would recognize him, but she knew if she looked into those pale blue eyes she would know. Would anyone else? Had anyone else been so captivated by those eyes that they would recognize them anywhere, no matter what other changes there had been?

Without the guns, the duster, the black shirt, he did look remarkably different. Going through Doc's discarded things, she had found a pair of spectacles. They had been his wife's, he'd explained, as Catalina had perched them on her nose. Much too strong. They made her head swim and her eyes water.

She'd set them aside and uttered a passing thought to Jackson that if anyone were to stop by he could wear them to further disguise himself. He was not, to put it lightly, particularly taken with the idea.

She didn't want to see anyone from Baxter ever again. The Sunday visits were bad enough. Doc insisted, and Jackson assured her that it was necessary. But Catalina kept staring at the spot, there on the street, where Jackson had been shot and left to die, and she saw it again and again in her mind. Heard the explosions, saw the blood, saw Jackson fall.

Catalina stayed close to Doc during those visits, and always remained silent. The Baptists had forgiven her, but they hadn't forgotten what she'd been. What they'd believed her to be. She caught some of the men staring at her with entirely too much interest in their eyes, and the women were still wary of her. It was easiest to stay shyly at Doc's side, to pray silently, and to leave town as quickly as possible.

The only saving grace was Helen Dunston, the Reverend Preston's widowed sister. It was so plain to see that the woman was taken with Doc. Well, plain to her, but evidently not so plain to Doc Booker. Another stubborn man. Catalina had tried to tell him a hundred times that Mrs. Dunston was sweet on him, but he just blushed and blustered, shrugging off her certainty and nearly jumping out of the buckboard—even as it crept down the road—when she'd suggested that he court the widow.

Much too soon, he grumbled. And he was old enough to be her father, by a long shot. When she'd told him that she didn't think Helen Dunston cared how old he was he'd turned a lovely shade of pink.

Harold Goodman kept his distance. He wasn't a churchgoer, and he hadn't made another visit to Doc's ranch since that first Sunday. The man was a weasel. It was almost unbearable, the waiting. Catalina was certain Goodman had something up his sleeve. A man like that didn't take kindly to losing. He was too petty to simply let it go.

If they were lucky, she and Jackson would be far away from this place before he tried anything again. But what about Doc? Granted, she couldn't claim to be much in the way of protection for the old man, and even Jackson couldn't help much, at this point. But he shouldn't have to face Harold Goodman and whatever gunman he brought in alone.

Catalina went to the window that faced the barn, drawn there. The barn door swung open and Jackson stepped outside with a cautious step, limping slightly. He stopped just outside the door and stared away from the cabin, toward the red rock that had drawn her to this place. He was perfectly still, powerful and beautiful and graceful.

He hadn't asked her again where she'd come from.

Catalina knew he didn't believe her story, didn't believe the truth, and she couldn't blame him. Until it had happened to her, she wouldn't have believed it either. It didn't matter. It was a surprise to her to realize that, but it was true.

Their life together was a gift, a treasure that

Linda Jones

shouldn't have been found. It didn't matter how she had gotten here, only that she was here now.

Her stomach growled, and she felt a wave of nausea wash over her. Of late, nineteenth-century food had not been agreeing with her. She rubbed a hand distractedly over her belly.

If Jackson didn't ask, she wouldn't mention again where she'd come from. If he could accept her as she was, now, and put away the past, she could put away all she knew as well.

The wind gusted, and a soft breeze lifted Jackson's newly shortened hair away from his face, and still he didn't move.

Catalina knew then that they would have to go far away from this place, far away from any place Kid Creede had ever been. Anyone who knew the Kid would recognize him now, stoic and strong. Pensive and . . . deadly. There was still a look of death about him. He'd seen too much to put it all behind him.

What held his attention so fully? Did he see ghosts in the distance? Or did he look to the future?

Chapter Sixteen

Catalina loaded the table with biscuits and honey, pan-fried ham, and scrambled eggs. She had finally learned to prepare coffee the way Jackson and Doc liked it—strong enough to peel paint—and both men drank entirely too much of the thick, dark brew.

She weakened her own cup with at least as much milk as coffee, and dumped in a heaping spoonful of sugar. It was the only way to make the stuff palatable.

Jackson seemed inordinately fond of his eggs this morning. He had given them all of his attention, hardly glancing her way. It was very unlike him. She knew he wasn't shy by any means, and he certainly wasn't afraid of her. So why wouldn't he look at her?

Finally Catalina got her wish, and Jackson lifted his head to look at her with narrowed eyes. He smiled, just a little, and Catalina put away all her doubts.

"Doc's going to town today," he said, breaking a biscuit in half.

"Oh," Catalina turned to Doc, tearing her eyes away from Jackson. "What's the occasion?" He hadn't mentioned taking her with him, and that would mean an entire day with Jackson. Alone, miles from everyone.

"We need supplies. I used a month's allotment of flour teaching you to make a decent biscuit." He raised a biscuit to his mouth and took a big bite. "It was worth it, too."

That last addition to his statement forced Catalina to forgive the first part.

"Well, you must give Helen Dunston my best wishes while you're in town," Catalina said innocently, keeping her eyes wide and the smile that threatened from her face. "Surely you will be stopping in to say hello to your friend Reverend Preston."

Doc grunted and finished his biscuit without a word.

Something was bothering Jackson. There was a little furrow between his eyes that she had never seen before, and a muscle twitched at his jaw. Perhaps sleeping in the barn had not agreed with him.

She didn't have long to wonder what was troubling him. He lifted his head and waved a biscuit at Doc. "You shouldn't travel unarmed."

Doc shook his head. "I haven't carried a weapon in thirty years, and I'm not going to start now."

"There's a rifle hanging over the front door," Jackson pointed out. "A muzzle-loader," he muttered, disgusted, "but better than nothing. I could fix it for you. Take it apart and clean it up and put it back together again. It would be better than nothing."

"No," Doc said sternly.

Jackson sighed, that weary sigh she had heard so often in their first days together. "Take one of my Colts." It was an order, issued to a man who didn't take orders from anyone. "Catalina, where are they?"

She couldn't answer for a moment, and Jackson turned his hard face to her. There was an impatience in his eyes and in the set of his mouth that she didn't like at all.

"I packed them away, with the rest of your old things."

"Unpack them. Give one to Doc, and keep one with you at all times."

"No," Doc snapped, and her own negative response followed.

Jackson leveled a stern gaze on her. "You don't know what you're dealing with, but I do. There's nothing wrong with protecting yourself."

Catalina stood and turned her back on the men at the table. She busied herself, unnecessarily, at the stove. "Perhaps it wouldn't be a bad idea for Doc to carry something for protection, but it is his decision to make. Harold Goodman wants him dead. He doesn't exactly want to *kill* me."

It was evidently the wrong thing to say. She heard the scrape of chair legs against the floor and turned to face a fuming Jackson. Had it been too much to hope for, that he could completely abandon the violence that had ruled his life to this point? It was his answer to everything, to every problem.

"I saw what bullets did to you, Jackson," she said softly. "No matter what, I could never do that to another human being. If I held a gun on

257

Linda Jones

Harold Goodman or anyone else, I wouldn't be able to fire it. I would remember what guns had done to you, and I wouldn't see anything else."

There was a subtle softening of his eyes and the mouth that could be so harsh. He was trying to understand.

He tilted his head and glanced down at Doc. "I suppose you feel the same way."

"Well, sort of," Doc admitted. "I've seen more than my share of bloodshed."

When he turned his eyes to Catalina again she could see the fight that was going on there . . . if he could have forced her to wear a weapon on her hip at all times, he would. But he was trying to understand.

"I just don't want anything to happen to you," he admitted, and it was a confession, of sorts, that he cared for her. He sighed again, with as much disgust as before. "Harold Goodman doesn't have the morals that make you two refuse to protect yourselves. He may be too cowardly to do the deed himself, but he has no reservations about having Doc killed. And you, Catalina . . . I know you think that you can take care of yourself . . ."

"I've been doing it for a long time."

Jackson was silent, and she knew that he was far from satisfied. With a filthy curse muttered just under his breath, he spun on his heel and stalked out of the room.

Jackson had managed to spend the entire morning in the barn. Catalina scrubbed the table with more energy than was necessary, putting all

258

of her strength—and all of her frustration—into long strokes.

He was avoiding her, and doing it so obviously that she couldn't fool herself into thinking it was anything other than deliberate. Was he still angry with her because she refused to carry a gun? She knew he didn't understand. Did he regret asking her to marry him? Had his proposal been nothing more than the desperation of a man who had thought himself dying? Now that he was certain to recover, was he finding it much too hard to leave Kid Creede behind? She had seen the harshness in his eyes that morning, the chill. How far would he carry this? Would he, like Wilson, leave her at the altar, or would she wake one morning and find him gone—long before wedding plans could even be made?

She glanced up as the door opened but didn't stop scrubbing the table that sat in the center of the room. Jackson stood in the doorway, hesitating, reluctant to enter the little house.

Doc was in town and wouldn't be back for several hours. The morning was gone. Wasted. They could have had some time alone, but Jackson had kept his distance.

"Come on in," Catalina looked down at the tabletop and scrubbed even harder. "I won't bite."

Jackson stepped into the room and closed the door softly behind him. His movements were graceful as always, but slow—careful.

"Are you all right?" Catalina set the rag with which she had managed to scrub every surface in the house on the shining table and straightened slowly. Jackson's face was pale, his lips the same pasty color as his cheeks, his eyes narrowed.

"I think I did too much," he said as he walked to a chair Catalina pulled away from the table.

She couldn't remain angry at him when he looked like that . . . almost as pale as he had been the day he'd been shot. "I'll fix you some tea. Maybe that will . . ."

"Is there any coffee left?" he interrupted her. She knew by now that Jackson hated tea, but Grandma Lane had sworn by a cup of sweet tea for what ailed you.

"It's cold. I could heat it up, but tea would really be better for . . ."

"Heat up the coffee," he ordered shortly.

Catalina turned away from him and did as he asked. As he demanded. He did have regrets. She could see them in his narrowed eyes, could feel those regrets in the new awkwardness between them.

She didn't look at him as she heated the coffee and then poured a single cup of the thick black brew.

"When do you think you'll be well enough to travel?" she asked, as casually as she could manage.

"Not soon enough," Jackson grumbled, and Catalina knew then that she'd been right all along. He wanted to leave her behind. As he'd healed, he'd changed his mind about her, about marriage and love and that new life. When had he decided? After that searing kiss? Or after their argument just that morning?

In either case, he had evidently decided to stay

away from her, so it would go no further. So the break would be easy.

Catalina didn't look at him as she set the tin cup on the table. She kept her eyes on the floor. If she looked at him and saw the truth in his eyes . . . that he didn't love her the way she loved him . . . she would cry like a baby. And that wouldn't do. Not at all. That would send Jackson running from the house, from Doc Booker's ranch.

"Catalina?" His voice was soft, unsure, a whispered question that hung between them. "Are you all right?"

She did lift her head then, and looked Jackson squarely in the eye. What she saw there wasn't indifference or uncertainty. A little worry, a little pain. And he did love her.

A smile crept across her face. "You're already beginning to look a little better than you did when you came through that door."

He pulled his eyes away from her and reached for the coffee.

Catalina placed a chair next to Jackson's and sat beside him, her skirt brushing his legs, her thigh next to his. Jackson all but groaned, loosing a deep grumble as she touched her hand to his leg.

"You've been avoiding me all morning," she accused softly.

"Yes, I have," he admitted curtly. "And a lot of good it's done me."

"Are you still angry with me?"

"I can't stay mad at you for very long," he said, as if he didn't understand. "Even when you're stubborn and pigheaded and wrong."

"I'm pigheaded?" Her fingers danced on his thigh.

Jackson didn't answer but to make a noncommittal sound in his throat. Something between a sigh and one of Doc's harumphs.

"Why are you avoiding me?"

Jackson turned and stared down at her face, narrowing his pale blue eyes. "You always ask *why*. You are the nosiest woman I've ever met."

"Thank you." Catalina drummed her fingers against Jackson's hard thigh.

"It wasn't a compliment, Catalina." Jackson grabbed her hand and placed it almost harshly on her own lap. "Don't you understand what I'm trying to do?"

"No." Catalina placed her hand back on his thigh. "What are you trying to do?"

Jackson took her hand and removed it from his leg, but he didn't drop it in her lap as he had done before. He held it, lacing his fingers through hers.

"I'm trying to give you what you want." He sighed. "And it's not easy."

"What I want?"

"Your magic." Jackson moved his thumb against the palm of her hand, rocking it gently back and forth. "You deserve your magic, your wedding night. I know there was that one night at Alberta's, but . . . things were different then."

Catalina wanted to throw her arms around his neck. "You're my magic, Jackson. All the magic I'll ever need. Yes, I waited for the right man, and I found you. A ceremony won't make me love you more."

"I want you to have everything you've ever

wanted." Jackson raised her hand to his lips.

"I do," Catalina assured him. "I have you."

Jackson's smiles were rare, but he gave her a brilliant one now. Dimples and crinkled eyes, he took her breath away, stole her heart with that smile.

"I've never done anything . . . right before. It's not easy."

"I don't want to wait," Catalina insisted softly. "You're still not able to travel, and we can't be married in Baxter. I won't be married in Baxter."

Jackson leaned over and gave her a quick kiss. "Soon," he promised. "We'll be able to leave in a few days, and we'll go to Tucson before we head to Texas. We can be married there, and stay in a nice hotel for a few days. I passed a hotel there a couple of times that looked right fancy. Four stories high, and there were little men out front in funny red uniforms carrying baggage and opening the door for everybody that went into the lobby."

"A honeymoon," Catalina whispered.

"Yes," Jackson whispered back. "So get the hell away from me . . . please."

Catalina slid from her chair and away from Jackson. "When can we leave?"

"Just a few more days," he promised

"Sit right there," Catalina ordered sweetly. "I'll fix you something to eat, and a cup of tea, whether you want it or not. You need it to get your strength back as quickly as possible."

Catalina fairly danced around the room. He did love her. He was her magic.

She saw the dust and went to the window. A

rider. She said nothing to Jackson. It was just a visitor for Doc, and she would tell them that he wasn't home. In spite of Doc's cover story about his *nephew*, Catalina didn't want Jackson facing anyone. It was too dangerous.

It would be simple enough to intercept the rider outside, while Jackson drank his coffee and rested. He didn't even have to know that anyone was there, if she met the rider far enough away from the house.

"I need to fetch a bucket of water from the well." Catalina spun toward the door.

"I'll get it." Jackson stood slowly.

"No." She gave him a bright smile. "You stay put and rest. You're still a little pale."

He nodded and sat back down, and Catalina stepped lightly through the door.

Jackson drummed his fingers impatiently on the table. She'd only been gone a minute, but his gut instinct told him something wasn't right. His gut instinct had saved his life more than once.

He moved to the window and for a moment held his breath. And wished that this time his gut instinct had been wrong.

Catalina stood with her back to him, a hand lifted to shield her eyes from the sun, as Harold Goodman dismounted. Why had she run all that way to meet Harold?

His old suspicious nature grabbed him by the throat, and his stomach did a sick, nervous flip that was a new experience for him. When he'd trusted no one he'd never been disappointed. He trusted Catalina with his heart and soul, and this hint of doubt chilled him to the bone.

How many times had Catalina told him that he would be ambushed in Baxter? Too many to dismiss, but he had dismissed it anyway. Now he couldn't. How had she known? Did she know Harold Goodman better than she'd let on?

Was Catalina just another player in this game to get Doc Booker's ranch and the rich ore that waited idly on it?

He didn't want to believe it was true, but she was talking earnestly to Ben Goodman's spineless kid as he watched from the window. And she hadn't said a word to him about seeing Harold approach . . . about seeing anyone approach.

Jackson's initial instinct was to rush out that door and confront them both, but he'd never been given to impulsive behavior. His latest impulsive act had gotten him shot . . . five times. Catalina had been there. In trouble, or so he had believed at the time. Had that been an act, too?

He buttoned the white shirt he wore to the top, all but choking himself. His hair he slicked straight back with both hands. And then he saw them: those wire-rimmed spectacles Catalina had decided would be a good addition to his disguise. Hell, he had nothing else, so he placed them on his nose.

The room swam, even when he pushed the spectacles down and peered over the top rim. Doc's beloved wife must have been almost blind.

He tripped stepping out of the door and so took small steps as he shuffled across the yard. There could be no limp, so he forced himself to walk steadily and evenly. Harold saw him coming, but

Catalina was still talking, and all her attention was on the man she faced.

His foot caught on something and Jackson stumbled forward, catching himself at the last moment and glancing over his shoulder and over the top of the spectacles to see what had tripped him up. A rock. Not too big, but evidently big enough. When he glanced around he saw Harold grin widely. At least the boy didn't seem to know who he was.

"You must be Doc's nephew from Virginia," Harold said, barely suppressing his laughter.

Catalina's head snapped around, and her whiskey eyes were wide and almost terrified. Was she afraid of what he would do to her? Had she been caught red-handed?

"Yes," she said before Jackson could speak. "This is Mr. Cady. Unfortunately he can't speak right now. He came down with a terrible cold on the trip and lost his voice completely," she said, speaking so quickly her words ran together. "Laryngitis," she clarified. "A terrible case."

Harold Goodman looked Jackson up and down, openly sizing him up. "That's too bad. I have a few questions I'd like to ask Mr. Cady. I didn't even know Doc had any family."

Was he afraid the existence of a nephew would ruin his plans? At least it didn't appear that Catalina had told Harold that Kid Creede was still alive . . . that Jackson Cady and Kid Creede were one and the same.

"What are you doing out here?" Catalina turned her back on Goodman and gave Jackson a censuring glare, eyebrows raised and lips

266

pursed. "You should be resting. I'll be in shortly to make that tea I promised you."

Jackson peered at her over the rim of the late Mrs. Booker's spectacles. What the hell was she up to?

"I hate tea," he answered in a rasping whisper, and Catalina rolled her eyes.

"Don't speak. It will only make things worse."

Jackson ignored her and turned his gaze to Harold. "What do you want?" he croaked.

Harold kept his eyes on Catalina. "I saw Doc on his way to town this morning. The road passes right by the ranch. I thought this would be a good time to call on Miss Lane. To see that she hasn't changed her mind about working in Baxter." He glanced to Jackson then, a mischievous sparkle in his eyes. "Did she tell you that she used to work in town?"

Jackson shook his head.

It seemed that Harold was trying to decide just how much to tell Doc Booker's nephew . . . that Catalina had done a turn in Alberta's bordello? That she had rarely been seen in a dress as prim as the one she wore now? Jackson made sure his expression gave away nothing; no anticipation or interest of any kind.

Harold evidently abandoned his game, deciding not to share what he knew. "I didn't know you had arrived, Mr. Cady, though of course I had heard you were coming." He turned his eyes back to Catalina, dismissing Jackson.

"He arrived just yesterday," Catalina explained quickly.

"So you haven't had time to tell him about your

short but exciting time in Baxter. Short, but sweet, isn't that right, Catalina," Harold teased, his mean streak evident in his voice and the hard set of his beady eyes.

He sounded so superior, so smug, that Jackson wanted to pound the man into the ground. But he stood perfectly still, pretending innocence. Catalina wrung her hands and glanced from Harold to Jackson and back again.

Harold turned his back on them and stepped into the stirrup. He jumped into the saddle and looked down at Catalina. "I just wanted to let you know that I have another friend coming to Baxter. He'll be here soon. You won't want to be here on this ranch when he arrives."

"Why can't you just leave Doc alone?" Catalina asked, shading her eyes with her hand as she turned her face up to Harold. "You have enough. You don't need this place."

Harold just smiled. "Darlin', a man never has enough. If Doc's smart, he'll go back to Virginia with you and clumsy Cady here." Harold nodded to Jackson, and his eyes lingered. "You look mighty familiar. Have you been this way before?"

Jackson shook his head slowly.

"There is a bit of a family resemblance," Catalina said quickly. "It's the shape of the mouth, I think, and the cheekbones. Just like Doc's."

Harold tipped his hat to her and grinned. "A friendly word of warnin', darlin'. You don't want to be here much longer. Come on back to Alberta's. She'll be happy to have you, and I promise to make it worth your while."

Catalina took a single angry step toward Harold's horse, but Jackson reached out and calmly pulled her back, a stilling hand on her arm. Best to allow Harold to ride away, for now. But his time would come. Jackson had already decided that.

Catalina watched Harold Goodman's back until she was certain he was really leaving. He was like a snake, and she knew that a snake could strike without warning. But he rode away slowly, not even glancing back, and she turned to Jackson with every intention of chastising him for leaving the house. Goodman might have recognized him, even with the changes he'd made in his appearance, and the too small glasses on his nose.

But she didn't say a word. Jackson was furious. She'd never seen him really angry before, she realized, as the fury blazed in his eyes. He slipped off the glasses and folded down the earpieces slowly.

"Do you have something to tell me, Catalina?" he asked in that silky voice that was as much Kid Creede as the black duster and the six-shooters.

"No. But you should have stayed in the house."

"Why?" Jackson slipped the glasses into his breast pocket, calmly and almost serenely, every movement smooth. "Did you have something to say to Harold Goodman that you didn't want me to hear?"

Catalina took a single step away from him. "Of course not. I didn't realize until I was halfway here that it was Goodman on the horse. I thought it was just a visitor for Doc, and I wanted to keep him away from the house, so he wouldn't see you."

Jackson didn't move, didn't speak. In fact, as far as she could tell, he wasn't even breathing.

"Don't look at me like that."

"You warned me, more than once, that I would be ambushed in Baxter," he said coldly. "How did you know that, Catalina?"

"I told you, but you didn't believe me." Her voice was small, shaky.

"That you came here from 1996?" he asked smoothly. "Hell no. I don't believe you. How well do you know Harold Goodman?"

Catalina started to defend herself but instead took another step back.

"Come on, Catalina," he pressed. "You've never been at a loss for words before. How long has this been set up?"

Catalina's heart sank. She could actually feel it: a weight in her chest that made her physically ill. It had been too much to hope for, that Jackson could change. That he could trust her, and leave Kid Creede on the Baxter street. She was facing Kid Creede right now.

"I've never lied to you, Jackson. I love you. If I was in on some sort of . . . plot with Harold Goodman, why would I have bothered to save your life?"

He was shaking his head slowly. "I don't know. You're a woman; maybe you went soft on him. How the hell am I supposed to know what you're thinking?"

"How can you believe . . . how can you even consider the possibility that I am somehow involved with that weasel Harold Goodman? That

I would betray you? That I would betray *anyone?*" She shook her head. Had he lived with betrayal so long that it was the first explanation . . . the only explanation . . . that came to him?

"Do you think the worst of everyone you know, Jackson, or only me?"

He said nothing but continued to watch her with narrowed eyes that bored into her soul and hurt her heart.

Catalina unbuttoned the first four buttons of the green calico she wore. Jackson said nothing, didn't move at all. Even his eyes remained lifeless. She took the leather thong between her fingers and lifted the wulfenite so that it lay in her hand.

"As far as I can tell, this is what brought me here." The truth, all of it. "An old Indian gave it to me. He said that all things were possible, if I'd only open my heart and my mind. I was walking toward that rock." She turned and faced the grouping of red rocks in the distance and started walking forward. "That big one, in the center. I was fascinated by that rock, and I was thinking about history, and men, and wishing for a different life." That was exactly what she had wished for. Exactly what she'd gotten.

"Damn it, Catalina." At least there was anger in his voice; that was better than no emotion at all. "All I want is the truth."

"All I've ever told you is the truth!" she shouted, spinning to face him and continuing to walk backward . . . toward the rocks. "You don't think I know how hard it is to understand? To believe?" She grasped the wulfenite tightly.

"It's just a rock," Jackson said, trying to sound reasonable. "A very pretty rock." He pointed to the wulfenite she clutched. A tip of the yellow-gold peeked out from between her fingers. "But just a rock. If you . . . You can tell me anything. I can forgive you," he said gruffly.

Catalina almost smiled, but it would have been bitter and ugly, so she didn't. How *noble* of him. He could forgive her for betraying him, for being a party to the ambush that had very nearly taken his life. But would he ever forget? If he truly believed her to be capable of betrayal, of deceit, then he could never truly love her.

She spun around so she wouldn't have to look into his face, and she continued to walk, taking long, angry strides away from Doc Booker's ranch. Jackson was behind her, keeping pace while keeping his distance. "In 1996," she began calmly, "Indian Springs is located right over there." She pointed past the grouping of tall red rocks. "I work in the library on Independence Avenue, right in the middle of downtown, and I drive my Mustang there five days a week. I have Sundays and Mondays off. My Mustang, by the way, is not a horse, but a car. An automobile. A horseless carriage." She glanced over her shoulder. Jackson was close, matching her step-for-step in spite of the limp that slowed him.

"I share an apartment with my friend Kim, or at least I did before the disastrous wedding that never took place."

Catalina stopped and stared at the red rocks in the distance. They were no farther away than they'd been that day when she'd grasped the wulfenite and been caught in that sandstorm . . . and been carried here. Would Kim wonder where she was? Of course she would. Would anyone else? Not likely. At least, not for long. Since Grandma Lane had passed away, all those years ago, Catalina hadn't been really close to anyone but Kim and Wilson, and even then . . . it was nothing like the connection she felt to Jackson. A man who believed her to be capable of the worst sort of treachery.

She hadn't thought about what she'd left behind, not since that first day or two. The Indian Springs library, and the nonfiction section where she'd spent so many afternoons—work done for the day, nothing to do but read and dust endless rows of old and new books.

She would miss that place, and Kim, and her Mustang.

The dirt at her feet danced, swirling delicately in whirlwinds that rose suddenly to all but engulf her. It was the same as before. Her breath was literally stolen away, and she began to feel as if she were floating.

"Catalina!" Jackson's voice called to her, but it was so far away . . . so distant. As though there was a thick wall between them.

She could go back. Here and now. If that was what she really wanted. Catalina closed her eyes tightly against the dirt, and all she saw was Jackson. Approaching her that first day, a somber picture on his horse. Standing in the doorway of Alberta's parlor, casual as you please as he bid on her. Leaning over to kiss her. Making love to her.

Catalina heard him call her name again, and it was further away than before. Faded. Faint. She could hear something else, too.

The unmistakable hum of a big truck, an eighteen-wheeler, close by. A car, wheels singing against asphalt.

She dropped the wulfenite that was still clutched in her hand, and thrust that hand out to the side. She tried to block out the hum of the truck, and Kim's face, and her memories of Indian Springs, and to see only Jackson. Only Jackson.

His hand was on hers, his fingers on her wrist—warm. Strong. *Real*.

And then it was over. The windstorm died. The highway sounds were gone as suddenly as they'd come, and Catalina fell backward, jerked from the ground and into Jackson's arms. They both fell back. Jackson landed in the dirt, and Catalina remained on top of him, too scared to move. His arms went around her, tight, powerful arms.

"Catalina," he whispered reverently.

Chapter Seventeen

Catalina leaned her head back against Jackson's shoulder and closed her eyes. She was still a little dizzy, shaken, afraid. Jackson's arms were tight around her waist, his breathing near her ear ragged and deep.

"Catalina," he murmured once again.

They stayed there on the ground, silent, still but for the rise and fall of their chests as they breathed deeply for several long minutes. The sun beat down on her face, but Catalina felt a deep chill that the sun couldn't chase away. She'd almost left this place. She'd almost left Jackson.

Jackson sat up without easing the grip that comforted her, and Catalina rested between his spread legs. Jackson Cady, a man she would have described as fearless only moments before, was shaking, a deep tremble she felt in his arms and the chest on which she rested her head. Catalina lifted her face and looked into his eyes, pale blue eyes that glittered like ice.

"You pulled me back," she whispered.

Jackson nodded his head slightly. "You were . . ." He swallowed, and the arms around her tightened. "Fading. The dirt came up around you, and then you started to . . . to go. But the

275

hand, the hand you raised was real, and I took it, and I held on, and I pulled. Catalina," he whispered her name. "Promise me you won't do that again."

Catalina shifted, scooting around and placing both her legs over one of Jackson's thighs. This way she could look easily into his face.

"Do you believe me now?" The chill that had gripped her was gone, chased away by her first glance at Jackson's face.

"I believe," he said softly, "but I don't understand how it's possible."

Catalina took the thong that held the wulfenite around her neck and lifted the crystal. She didn't dare touch it, but she studied the play of light on the yellow surface.

"I can't be certain, but I think this is a kind of key. An old Indian gave it to me, and . . . I told you what he said. When I came here I was thinking about the past . . . about *now*, and I got caught up in a sandstorm. Just now I was thinking about Kim and the library, and I was holding the wulfenite just like before, and it started to happen again."

She turned her head to the red rocks in the distance. "I'm almost certain those rocks have something to do with this. I was about the same distance away the first time, but I was on the other side." A frown stole over her face. "What if it's not a doorway, but a huge circle around those rocks? A . . . a hole. It's almost like stepping into a hole, and then floating instead of dropping."

"I want you to stay away from this place," Jackson said hoarsely. "And throw away that damned yellow rock."

"No." Catalina pulled her hand away when he tried to grab it. "This is what brought me to you, Jackson. I told you I traveled a long way to find love. To find you."

Catalina slipped from between his legs, but Jackson kept his hand on her arm, almost as if he were afraid to let her go. She lifted the leather thong over her head and put the wulfenite in the dirt.

She reached into Jackson's boot and withdrew his knife. He moved slowly to kneel beside her, and his hand slipped down to her wrist.

Catalina turned the wulfenite over again and again, searching for a weak spot. It was there, a thinner section near the center of the stone. She laid the tip of the knife in a hollow between two crystals that seemed to have grown together, and wiggled the tip of the knife to force it deep within the crevice.

Jackson's hand remained on her wrist as she raised it and brought it down on the hilt of the knife. There was a brief spark, a flash of light so bright and so quick it could have been the sun reflecting on the metal surface of the knife, and the wulfenite on the ground broke easily in two.

She lifted the piece of the crystal that was still attached to the leather thong and placed it around Jackson's neck. "A piece of what brought me to you."

He pulled her against him, at last releasing her wrist as he threw his arms around her.

When his grip loosened a bit, Catalina lifted

her face to him. He kissed her, a soft, lingering kiss that made Catalina melt in his arms. His heat surrounded her like a protective cocoon; his arms held her gently. And when he pulled his mouth away from hers it was with a low moan of regret.

"We've got to get away from this place and get married," he grumbled. "Soon."

Catalina perched on her knees between his spread legs and wrapped her arms around his neck. "We don't have to wait," she whispered.

"You said . . ." Jackson began.

"I said I love you. I said I traveled a hundred years to find you. Married? I feel more than married to you. I feel a part of you. Two halves of the same soul." She kissed him briefly to try to ease his obvious distress. "Do you believe in the existence of the soul?"

"Yes."

With one arm hooked around Jackson's neck, Catalina leaned over and scooped up the half of the wulfenite that still lay in the dirt.

"Two halves of the same stone," she said, holding the golden crystal on her palm. "One incomplete without the other. Just as I am incomplete without you."

Catalina placed a palm against Jackson's cheek. "Make love to me."

His lips met hers, kissing her softly, parting to claim her mouth as he had claimed her heart. Fully, without reservation, deep and soul-searing. Catalina tipped her head back and pressed her chest against his. The stone she had placed around his neck was caught between them, and it seemed that the crystal was warm, throbbing, alive, trapped between two pounding hearts.

Catalina wound her hands around Jackson's neck, twisting her fingers through his hair. She felt as if she were glowing, as certainly as the wulfenite had blazed with the sun on its surface.

She was falling backwards, slowly, Jackson's hands at her back. His lips left hers and trailed down her throat to the hollow at the base of her neck. He lingered there, maddeningly.

Jackson pulled away from her and rose slowly, never taking his hands from her. He lifted her from the ground gently, as if she might break, but he never loosed his grip. Did he think she would disappear again if he wasn't there to hold her in the nineteenth century?

"I will never leave you," Catalina said, looking up into pale eyes that were still a little dazed.

"Is that a promise?"

Catalina smiled. "A promise, a vow, a sworn oath."

Jackson kissed her again, as tenderly as before, and still the caress was filled with passion, the same longing that was tearing her apart. She felt, at that moment, a desire so intense it was painful. She pulled her lips away from his but kept her face close, so close she could almost feel the beat of his heart in the lips near hers.

"Are you going to make me ask again?" she whispered.

"No." Jackson kissed her, a quick and tender meeting of their lips, and then again and again. "Ahh, Catalina."

She loved the way he whispered her name, silk and velvet.

"You wrest promises from me and then you demand that I break them." There was more than a little humor in his soft voice.

"I never made you promise not to . . ."

He silenced her with another maddening kiss, and then he turned, his arm firmly around her waist, toward the little house. His step was slow, his hold on her secure. She knew what he was feeling—the fear of coming so close to separation, to a division so complete, so final, that nothing could repair it, and she slipped her arm around his waist as well.

Catalina led him to the narrow bed she'd been sleeping in, rather than the larger bed in the main room. Jackson didn't mind. He'd come too close to death in that big bed, too close to losing his chance for a lifetime with Catalina.

This was a woman's room, filled with lace and frills and the things a woman needs. Mirrors and brushes, ribbons and hairpins, all spread across the top of a polished dresser. Lace curtains, a white bedspread dotted with pillows—yellow and blue, with delicate embroidered flowers and birds, splashes of bright colors against the pale.

Catalina closed the door and placed her half of the crystal on the dresser with her other things. Jackson noticed that she was looking all around the room, avoiding his gaze. Nervous. He smiled. He was pretty damned nervous himself.

He placed his hands on her shoulders and turned her gently to face him. Catalina lifted her face to him, and Jackson lowered his head to kiss her—just a kiss—with his hands resting on her shoulders and her hands hanging at her sides—they kissed.

He'd almost lost her. Nothing had ever tasted so sweet, felt so right, and he couldn't forget how close he'd come to watching the only person he'd ever loved disappear before his eyes.

She pressed her body closer to his, and he felt the pressure of the golden stone against his chest, a reminder of the magic that had brought Catalina to him.

Her fingers worked at the buttons of his shirt, slowly, surely, her lips never faltering, and Jackson allowed his hands to slip down from her shoulders to brush lightly over her breasts. Catalina's breathing changed, quickened, and she made a whispery noise against his mouth. Not a moan, not a whimper, not a sigh. Or maybe all three.

The buttons of her calico dress slipped easily through his hands, baring the swell of her breast and a lacy chemise. He lowered his head to touch his lips to her throat. His mouth lingered there, tasting her, feeling the rapid beating of her heart. Without lifting his head he slipped the sleeves from her arms and lowered his head to taste the silky skin above her thin chemise. He kissed that skin as tenderly as he had her neck, and Catalina wrapped her fingers through his hair, holding him against her.

She couldn't hold him tight enough. The desire he had always felt for Catalina grew, until he was certain it would consume him, burn him from the inside out. It *was* like a fire, hot and uncontrollable.

He turned his attention to her arms, kissing the inner crook of her elbow, brushing his lips over her wrist, the palms of her hand. Catalina grabbed the open front of his shirt and slid it over his shoulders, and he shrugged it off.

They continued slowly, unfastening buttons and ties and buckles, tasting newly exposed skin, bringing their lips together when the drive to do so was so strong neither of them could fight it. Catalina spoke only once, to complain weakly that women in the nineteenth century wore entirely too many clothes.

As he laid Catalina on the narrow bed and placed himself above her, the stone she had hung around his neck swung forward between them. With a wistful smile, she reached up to slip it over his neck and placed it on the bedside table.

When she brought her hands back to him she traced his face with her fingers, and wrapped her hands around his head to pull his lips to her. He kissed her, and her hands explored his body: light, feathery touches that drove him past reason, past rational thought.

He tasted her, her lips and her neck, her breasts, her rosy nipples, and Catalina lifted her hips and guided him inside her. He thrust deep, lost in the rhythm and the power of passion. He moved and Catalina rocked with him. Her hands danced over his body, and when he buried himself deep inside her once more she grabbed him, holding on for dear life as the spasms rocked her.

He joined her, claiming her the only way he knew how.

Jackson rested his head against her shoulder and was completely still. Catalina's breathing was hard and ragged, and only gradually did it slow, return to near normal. When he lifted his head to look down at her she smiled at him, a satisfied and almost sly grin that forced him to smile back.

"I do love you," she whispered breathlessly.

He couldn't speak, so he kissed her.

Catalina all but purred, a long, slow murmur from deep in her throat. "When will Doc be home?"

"Not for another couple of hours at least."

"Goodness only knows when we'll be alone again." She ran her hand down his side, fluttering over a healing wound. "But I don't suppose I should ask too much of you," she said coyly. "You're not completely recuperated."

He raised his eyebrows. "Is that a challenge?"

"Certainly not."

"Because it sounded a little like a challenge."

Catalina shook her head slowly from side to side, and her whiskey eyes sparkled. "I wouldn't be so juvenile as to dare you . . ."

Jackson covered her mouth with his. Heaven help him, he wanted her as much as he had before.

He braced himself up on one elbow and looked down at Catalina. He couldn't let her sleep for very long, but he couldn't bear to disturb anything so beautifully peaceful.

Her lips were red and swollen, her cheeks flushed, and her hair spilled around her like a cloud spun from gold. He wanted to bury himself in her again, but it was too soon for her. She'd been a virgin when he'd bedded her in Baxter, and he wasn't certain how it was with a woman so inexperienced. He had worried about her that second time, but she had come to him without a qualm, had offered herself to him and then taken from him as well.

She'd called his name just once, and then had shattered beneath him as he'd driven deep and hard. If he'd ever doubted her insistence that they were two halves of a complete soul, he didn't any longer.

That one night they'd had in Baxter had been extraordinary, and he'd known then that Catalina was different. He had wanted her so badly, more than he'd ever wanted anything.

But this was different. Stronger, more frightening. In Baxter he had bedded her because he wanted her. Today he had become a part of her because he loved her. Making love, she called it, and that suddenly made sense.

He touched a strand of hair that floated across the pillow and caressed it gently. His smile faded. He'd almost lost her in that whirlwind of dust. For a moment his heart had stopped, when he'd seen her fade away from him as if she'd never been real—never been more than a dream. The first real fear he'd ever known had hit him then, like a bolt of lightning, hard and deep.

Losing Catalina was the only thing he feared. The only thing he would ever fear.

A hundred years. Her story shouldn't have been believable. He'd never given her explanations of her past, of her knowledge, more than a passing thought. But he couldn't deny what he'd seen with his own eyes.

Her eyes fluttered open and fastened on his face, gold sparks dancing merrily in that radiant face. "I fell asleep," she muttered contentedly.

"Yes, you did." Since she was already awake he gave in to the temptation to touch her, to trail his fingers across her breasts and down her flat belly. It was a lazy motion, a mark of possession. And joy. Just to touch her skin, to see her smile.

"I guess we should get dressed." Catalina didn't make a move, didn't even twitch a muscle, as Jackson continued to trail his fingers over her body. "When will Doc be back, do you suppose?"

"Soon," Jackson answered lazily. "Much too soon."

Catalina sat up slowly, rolling her bare shoulders. "If I hobble around the place with a huge smile on my face, do you think he'll guess what happened while he was gone?"

"I really don't care." He leaned forward and planted a quick kiss on her swollen lips.

"He'll be shocked," Catalina said. "And he did save your life. And this is his house."

"Regrets?" he asked, trailing a finger across her soft cheek and under her chin.

Her grin was so wide, he knew she was right. Doc would certainly know what had happened if she looked at him like that.

"None," she assured him.

He gathered her clothing for her and helped

285

her dress as slowly as he had undressed her. Only then did he reluctantly put his own clothes back on.

When he looked up, after his trousers had been properly fastened, Catalina was frowning at him.

"Did you really think I was somehow involved with Harold Goodman's plot to kill you?"

Jackson lifted his eyebrows slightly. "I thought you had forgotten about that."

She was shaking her head slowly.

"Not really," he admitted. "But when I looked out the window and saw you talking to him, away from the house, and you hadn't said a word about seeing him approach . . ."

"I explained that," Catalina said, but she stood and leaned close, and there was no anger in her eyes. "I was trying to keep him away from you. I guess I think everyone sees you as I do. You do look different, but I swear, Jackson, if you dyed your hair white and had plastic surgery, I'd still know those eyes."

"Plastic surgery?"

"Never mind."

Catalina grabbed the wulfenite she had placed on the bedside table and slipped it around his neck once again. "Goodness, Doc will be back soon and there's no dinner cooking, and I didn't finish the mending I started this morning, and . . ." She stopped suddenly and spun around to face him. "Jackson, what are we going to do about Doc Booker?"

He shook his head slowly.

"If he stays here, he'll be killed for certain. You

heard Goodman. He's hired another gun to come in and take care of Doc. If we leave him here alone . . ."

"What do you mean *if*?"

"Maybe we could convince him to come with us, to Texas." She said it so easily, it was as if the idea had just sprung into her mind. But Jackson had the feeling that Catalina had been cooking this one up for a while. Maybe since Harold had threatened the old man; maybe while she'd been lying beside him, pretending to sleep.

"I don't think he'll go." It was the truth. Pure stubbornness had kept the old man here this long, stubbornness and a love for the place he called his own.

Catalina turned away from him, and he saw the dejected slump of her shoulders. "I'll worry about him," she said quietly. "He's a cranky old guy, but he saved your life, and he helped me get Alberta off my back."

Jackson shook his head again, though Catalina couldn't see. There wasn't anything he wouldn't do for her.

"We can ask him," he finally agreed. "I can be quite persuasive, when I have to be."

Catalina spun on him, a bright liveliness in her every move. "I know," she whispered.

Catalina all but ran around the table, setting tin plates and flatware haphazardly in their approximate places. Jackson had spotted Doc's wagon from the window, approaching at a slow but steady pace.

Jackson seemed unconcerned, moving slowly, flashing her small smiles whenever she looked his way. The biscuits were almost done, and the stew—a concoction she had tossed together using dried meat and canned goods—was bubbling on the stove. It would just have to do.

She could hear Doc, now, his wagon wheels in the dirt, his hoarse voice calling to the horses. She checked the front of her dress to make absolutely certain all the buttons were properly fastened, and when she lifted her head she saw Jackson step into her room.

"Get out of there," she hissed. If Doc stepped into the house and Jackson came out of her bedroom . . . well, they'd certainly be tossed out, and Jackson wasn't quite ready to travel. Soon, he said. Soon.

Jackson came out swinging the piece of wulfenite she had left on the dresser, only now it was suspended from a length of white ribbon, knotted at the middle. He wore his piece against his skin. She could see the small lump it made beneath his shirt.

Without a word, he slipped the beribboned wulfenite around her neck, being careful not to muss her recently repaired hairstyle. The stone rested between her breasts, and he covered it with his hand. His smile faded, and he looked almost uncertain, hesitant. Scared? Was that fear mixed with indecision in those pale blue eyes?

He opened his mouth as if to speak, and then he closed it again, bending forward to kiss her lightly, no more than a faint brush of his lips against hers.

"I love you," he whispered harshly, awkwardly, and then he stepped away from her . . . just as Doc threw open the door.

Chapter Eighteen

"Nope," Doc Booker said firmly again. "I'm not running away from anybody. Especially not a little snotnose like Harold Goodman."

Jackson had said little, and Catalina threw him an imploring glance. He sighed and set his spoon aside, resting both elbows on the table. "Harold Goodman may be a snot-nosed brat, but he's a dangerous one. He damn near killed me."

"If it's my time to die, then so be it," Doc said angrily. He turned tired eyes to Catalina. "You're getting to be quite the cook. This is delicious stew."

"You're trying to change the subject."

"Yep."

Catalina picked at her bowl of stew. Suddenly it made her stomach turn. Just the smell. It was as if she could identify every ingredient by the odor, and not one of them was pleasant. The meat was especially strong, and that onion . . . She pushed the bowl away and tried a sip of milk, wondered exactly *when* refrigerators were going to be invented.

"I didn't mean to upset you," Doc said kindly. "It means more to me than you can know, that you're concerned for my welfare. I appreciate it, but I think you're going to have your hands full taking care of *this* one." He nodded in Jackson's direction.

Catalina stared down at the folded hands resting in her lap. All right, so she couldn't change the world. She'd saved Jackson. Maybe that was the only interference she was allowed.

"We would love to have you come with us," she tried one more time. "If you change your mind . . ."

"Thank you," he interrupted her gruffly, "but I'm too old to be leaving behind everything I know. You two, now that's different. I admire what you're doing. It takes courage to start over. Courage I don't have."

Catalina lifted her head and stared at Jackson. "We'll be leaving soon," she said, resigned to leaving Doc behind. "Probably next week."

"I figured that," Doc rumbled.

"Jackson's growing stronger every day," she continued. "He could probably travel now, if he had to."

"Probably."

"We owe you so much," Catalina said, and even though she wanted her voice to be strong, it wavered. "We'll never forget you."

"I'm not dead yet," Doc barked, but there was a spark of tenderness in his eyes.

Catalina felt as if she was back in school—that very strict all girls' school in Spring Hill—and she was breaking the rules.

Jackson was right beside her, the fingers of one hand twined through hers, a basket loaded with

291

biscuits and ham and a horribly tough little cake swinging from the other.

Doc was all the way on the opposite side of his little ranch for the afternoon, mending a section of fence where the posts had rotted through and fallen. Jackson had tried to help, but Doc had sent him back to the house, declaring him unfit for any sort of ranching duties.

So Catalina had packed them a picnic, and had insisted that they explore a little. There was little leisure time, and she never had enough time alone with Jackson.

He barely limped at all any more, except at the end of the day, when he was very tired, and he didn't have any trouble keeping up with her as she plunged forward.

They almost stumbled into the little creek, it was so narrow and shallow. It certainly wasn't suitable for bathing or swimming or washing clothes, though she was tempted to lie in the middle of it and let the water wash over her. At last, a glimpse at water that she hadn't had to pump.

The trees at the edge of the water cast inviting shade, and appeared to be much healthier than the struggling excuses she had seen near Doc's house.

"Here," she said certainly, spinning on Jackson and giving him a smile.

"Finally," he muttered, but he returned her smile and set their lunch on the ground. "Do you think we're still in Arizona Territory?"

"Grouch," she accused.

"Tireless wench," he answered.

"Wench?" She moved closer to Jackson, all but settling her chin on his chest. "I don't know if I like that or not."

"It's better than grouch."

Jackson sat on the ground in the cool shade and pulled her with him, wrapping his arms around her waist and placing her easily beside him. He seemed content, at the moment, and she knew Jackson well enough to realize that real peace was rare for him, and perhaps would always be.

"I do apologize," she said formally. "You have a wonderfully cheerful disposition, my dear."

"And you," he answered as she turned to kiss the much too tempting side of his neck, "are still tireless."

He made love to her there on the ground, without haste, his every move languid, managing—without removing a single stitch of clothing—to touch her everywhere. By the time he entered her she was ready to scream for him. It seemed that every nerve in her body was screaming. She cried out his name as the orgasm tore through her on endless waves and the cry was ripped from deep within her. She had never expected this. Had never known that it was possible for love—physical love—to make her feel as if she were falling apart. As if the molecules within her were rearranged, shredded, and reformed into something new and beautiful.

As if she had never lived before she'd found Jackson. Her love, her man, the other half of her soul.

She felt his own release, his own uncontrollable cry, and he locked his lips to hers, devouring her, possessing her more completely than she'd ever thought possible.

When she could breathe again, when she felt that she could speak, Catalina wrapped her fingers through Jackson's hair and lifted his head so that she could see his face. She could see that he was as amazed as she at the power they created when they came together, and was relieved—pleased—ecstatic—to know that he had never known that power with any other woman.

"Do you think it will always be this way between us?" she asked, whispering.

"I do," he answered, his voice as soft as hers.

"I never dreamed . . . I never knew . . ." How did you express yourself at such a time to a nineteenth-century man who thought only prostitutes showed their legs? A man who had once thought she was easy simply because she'd allowed him to see her bare from the knees down? "I love you," she said simply. "More than I ever thought was possible."

Jackson smiled, and then he buried his face against her neck and ran his hands down her sides, slowly, lazily, seductively. They were still joined, still dressed, for heaven's sake, with just a few pieces of clothing askew.

Catalina wrapped her hands around his neck and brought his lips to hers, and she could feel him grow again within her.

Jackson pulled his lips away from hers just briefly, to smile and whisper huskily, "Tireless wench."

* * *

They were eating when they saw the figure approaching from the opposite side of the creek, and Catalina's heart leapt into her throat. An Indian, certainly, just as she had imagined one would look in this time. Bare-chested, wearing buckskin pants and moccasins, long black hair braided, with feathers and beads. It wasn't until he was almost to the creek that she realized he was just a boy, twelve or thirteen. No more, certainly, though he was almost as tall as she was.

Jackson was tense, cursing about not having his Colts, even after he saw that it was only a child. Catalina smiled and laid a hand on Jackson's knee. Would he ever learn to trust strangers?

The Indian stopped before crossing the water, a question on his beautiful, peaceful face. Catalina rose and motioned the boy over, ignoring Jackson's whispered curse. He was tense, coiled, distrustful even of a child.

"Hello," Catalina called, wondering if the child spoke English. "Would you like something to eat?"

He smiled and nodded his acceptance as he stepped carelessly across the water. There was a sack slung over his shoulder, and he carried no weapons that Catalina could see. Up close he looked even younger, more serene, definitely harmless. Still, Jackson did not relax.

Catalina fished out a biscuit and a piece of ham and made a sandwich. There was half a canteen of water, and she handed that to the boy also. She and Jackson had eaten little, having spent their time on other activities. It was fortunate that the boy hadn't appeared fifteen minutes earlier.

He ate as if he was starved, and even accepted a piece of the horrible cake Catalina had made. Eventually even Jackson relaxed.

She waited until the child was finished eating before she attempted to speak to him.

"My name is Catalina, and this is Jackson."

The boy smiled, but Catalina had no idea if he understood her. He popped the last piece of cake into his mouth, brushed off the crumbs, and offered his hand to her. "Thank you. I was really hungry."

There was no hint of an accent, and his English was quite good.

"My name's Qaletaqa," he said casually. "It's nice to meet you."

"What are you doing way out here?" Jackson asked, his suspicion so clear, Catalina was afraid Qaletaqa would be insulted. But the Indian boy smiled warmly.

"Traveling. Seeing the world."

"By yourself?" Catalina asked, her voice sharper than she had intended.

Qaletaqa's smile faded, just a little, and his gaze was riveted on Catalina. "Yes," he said almost solemnly. "Alone."

Catalina felt a chill she couldn't explain away, a tingling at the back of her neck. "Do you travel far?" She could almost swear that she had looked into those eyes before.

The charming smile was back. "Very far."

She offered the boy more cake, but he declined politely. "I have traveled farther than I thought possible. I have seen corners of the world that no other man has ever seen. There are miracles all around us, you know, but most humans never even notice them. They refuse to open their hearts and their minds."

Catalina almost couldn't speak. When she did manage a sound her voice was no more than a whisper. "Open your heart and your mind and all things are possible."

Qaletaqa smiled brightly. "Yes. You understand."

"Yes. No, not really. Are you . . ." There were so many questions she wanted to ask. *Will we meet again in a hundred years? Are you the one who brought me here?*

"I must give you something in exchange for the wonderful food you have shared with me." Qaletaqa pulled the sack he carried over his shoulder to the front and placed it between his legs. "What would be suitable?" He opened the top of the sack and reached inside, not looking at all.

"It's not necessary . . ." Catalina began.

"You will insult me," he claimed with a smile.

His hand appeared from within the bag, clutching two lengths of leather, braided neatly and knotted at each end.

"These were braided from one length. I did the work myself. It symbolizes unity, oneness, harmony." He pulled the cords apart, and offered them, one in each hand, to Catalina and Jackson. "Surely you have something you might wish to suspend from these simple gifts, something to remember our brief encounter by."

Jackson took the length that was offered him,

and Catalina could only wonder if he felt any of the amazement she did at the moment. She wanted to ask the boy if he had a flannel shirt or two in his sack, but she didn't. It was preposterous. Bizarre. But she took the braided cord with a mumbled word of thanks.

Qaletaqa jumped to his feet, agile in that way only the very young are, and thanked Catalina for the food. "Even the cake," he added as he turned to cross the creek.

On the other side he spun to face them once again, and flashed that winning smile. "I think that perhaps we will meet again one day, Goldie."

He was gone before Catalina could find her tongue.

"I can't go to church," Catalina moaned pitifully. Jackson stood by the bed, his hand smoothing back her hair, his eyes worried. He'd bathed her face and brought her a toothbrush and baking soda and water to clean her mouth.

Catalina knew that if she threw up again, there would be nothing left inside her, no stomach at all. Still her insides revolted. The stomach flu; she'd been fighting it down for more than a week, ignoring the flutters in her stomach, the weakness that came over her at the end of the day. They were supposed to leave in a matter of days, and now this. What a time to get sick.

"I'm sorry," she said weakly.

Doc Booker stuck his head in the door, a frown on his face. Engaged or not, it was improper for Jackson to be by her bed.

"She's really sick," Jackson said, turning to

Doc. "Can't you give her anything?"

Catalina heard the real worry in Jackson's voice, and maybe Doc did, too, because he finally relented and came into the room to look down at her.

"She says it's the stomach flu," Jackson said, brushing his hand against her temple, softly, soothingly.

Doc harumphed.

"She was sick yesterday, too, and a couple of days last week."

Doc shucked off his good church jacket, a less than friendly scowl on his face. "Is that a fact."

Catalina couldn't understand why he was so angry that she wouldn't be attending church services with him this week. She'd been a faithful churchgoer during her stay at Doc's ranch.

He kicked Jackson out of the room, and Catalina almost smiled. Not many people could get away with that.

Doc laid a hand on her forehead, and listened to her pulse. He scowled throughout the examination, even when he pressed lightly on her abdomen. When he was done he bent over the bed, placing his face close to hers.

"Miss Catalina," he began formally, "I don't want you to take offense. Remember, I'm a doctor."

She nodded slightly, all that she could manage.

"When was the last time you had your monthly flow?"

Catalina closed her eyes. Not since she'd traveled back. She hadn't even thought of the time that had passed. Two months? She counted back and was certain that it had been at least that long.

She told Doc, her voice a whisper, how long it had been. She didn't whisper because she was embarrassed, as he apparently thought, but because she was shocked. It had to have happened their first night together.

Her child had been conceived in a whore-house.

Jackson's child.

She smiled brightly, almost forgetting how horrible she felt. "Morning sickness."

Doc nodded, disapproval clear in his eyes.

"I wonder what Jackson will think of this?" There had been so many changes in his life, so fast. How would he feel about this one?

"Is it his?" Doc asked gruffly, his voice low.

"Of course it is." Catalina pushed herself up on both elbows. She gave Doc Booker the indignant stare he deserved, and was rewarded with a small smile. He had come to like Jackson, after all.

"I reckon he'll be pleased."

Doc started to step away from the bed, and Catalina reached out to take his hand. "I want to tell him," she whispered.

The old man nodded and smiled again. Two smiles in such a short time; surely that was a record for the crotchety Doc.

Jackson was waiting right outside, and he stepped into the room as soon as Doc opened the bedroom door.

"Well?" He looked at Doc for a long moment, and then he turned to Catalina. She smiled at him, but it did nothing to ease the concern on his face.

"She won't be coming to church with me today, and I would recommend that she postpone any travel plans for a while."

Doc left with those slightly ominous words, and Jackson turned a worried frown to Catalina. "It's bad?"

Catalina patted the bed beside her, and Jackson lowered himself gently beside her. He was prepared for the worst, steeling himself for the news.

"It's not bad at all," Catalina said softly.

"But Doc said you couldn't travel."

Catalina lifted her hand in a wave of dismissal. "Old-fashioned thinking. I can do whatever I please."

The nausea was already fading, and Catalina sat up to face Jackson. She took one hand and twined her fingers through his. "I'm pregnant, Jackson. We're going to have a baby."

She'd thought he would be relieved, but he turned as white as the bedspread that covered her legs and clutched a bit too tightly at her fingers.

"A baby?"

Catalina nodded. "Conceived at Alberta's. Almost two months ago."

Jackson looked almost as pale as he had when she'd thought he was going to die, and his hands trembled just slightly. A fearless man, struck dumb by the very notion of a child.

After a few strained moments the shocked expression on his face faded, and he smiled—just a little. "A baby," he repeated. "That's . . . nice."

"Nice?" Catalina pulled her fingers away from his and sat up straight. "I'm going to bear your child. I'm going to be sick all the time, and get horrendously fat, and it will be worth every moment of pain and discomfort. Nice? Nice? Can't you do any better than that?"

His smile turned into a grin, and he leaned toward her. "How about *very* nice."

"If it's very nice, why did you turn white when I told you?" Catalina placed her hands on his hard shoulders and kissed him lightly in spite of her harsh words.

"Because it's also very scary," he whispered. "I don't know how to be a father."

"Of course you do."

"I don't even remember my own parents, much less how to care for a child, a helpless baby."

She could see it now, the trepidation in his eyes. "Do you really believe," she began huskily, "that any child of ours could be helpless?"

Jackson gave her a half grin, almost sheepish. "I don't suppose so."

"I'm feeling a little better," she said, resting her head against his shoulder.

"Are you?" He stroked her hair and held her tenderly, as if she might break. Catalina had a feeling that he was going to be stubborn about this, like Doc Booker, treating her as if she were ill for the next seven months.

"Pregnancy is a perfectly natural state for a woman my age," she said sensibly, trailing her lips across his throat.

He mumbled a reply, but it didn't sound as if he believed her.

He held her gingerly for a long while, and they listened as Doc's buckboard pulled away from the ranch. Jackson didn't move, only stroked her hair gently. Too gently. While there was certainly a lot to be said for nineteenth-century men, this apparent dread of pregnancy had all the possibilities of a real drawback.

"Jackson," she whispered, lifting her head from his shoulder to stare into his still pale face. "Kiss me."

He did, a kiss much too hesitant.

"I won't break," she prodded.

"But you're . . . we'll have to take it easy, right?"

"I am able to do anything an unpregnant woman can do." She emphasized the point by sliding her hand down his body and resting it between his legs, stroking him, feeling him grow hard beneath her fingers.

He didn't argue when she fell back onto the bed, bringing him with her.

"Anything?" he whispered.

"Do you realize, my darling Jackson, that this nightgown I'm wearing is much easier to remove than the dress I was wearing the last time we were alone in the house?"

"I certainly do." He ran his hands over the soft cotton that covered her body.

"And do you realize, Jackson my love, that I'm wearing absolutely nothing underneath?"

He lifted his head and looked her in the eye as he slid the long skirt of her nightgown up and brushed his fingers against her bare thigh.

"You're a wicked woman, Catalina Lane."

"Yes, I know," she said, deftly unfastening the buttons of his twill pants. "When are zippers going to be invented, anyway?" she asked, fumbling with the last button.

"What's a zipper?" Jackson buried his face against her neck, then drew away for a moment to push her nightgown over her breasts, over her head.

"Never mind."

Catalina lifted the curtain and stared into a black and moonless night. "He should've been home hours ago."

Jackson didn't seem to be concerned at all. He had listed for her several times a number of reasons why Doc hadn't returned. A broken wheel, a horse with a thrown shoe, a sick friend . . . but Catalina didn't quite buy any one of them.

"Well, he won't be coming in tonight," Jackson assured her, approaching from behind, taking her hand and allowing the curtain to fall into place. "It's too dark."

"We should look for him," Catalina insisted as Jackson settled his hands on her shoulders. "He might have had trouble on the road, or he might have gotten sick."

"It's too dark," Jackson said again. "If he doesn't show up bright and early in the morning, we'll search for him."

Catalina felt a cold fear touch her heart, turning her blood cold. "You can't go into Baxter." She whispered the words that spoke of her greatest fear. "The book . . ." She turned slowly and lifted her face to stare into pale blue eyes, eyes once icy that now were soft. Still and clear. "It said you would die on the street in Baxter. Shot a dozen times."

"But you saved me from that."

Catalina was shaking her head before he'd finished. "I can't be certain. I don't remember the date. I was always terrible with dates. What if I didn't change history at all? You can't possibly go into Baxter. If Doc doesn't show up tomorrow, early, I'll look for him."

Jackson narrowed his eyes. "No. You can't leave here by yourself. It's not safe."

Catalina chewed her lip. He was right, of course, but it seemed to her—she *knew*—that it would be much more dangerous for Jackson to travel to Baxter.

"Maybe he'll show up in the morning," she said halfheartedly.

"I'm sure he will." He was trying to console her, but Jackson sounded as unsettled as Catalina. It was true there were any number of reasons Doc might have had to spend the night in town, but Catalina was certain he would have broken his neck to get home and assure himself that she and Jackson weren't alone in his home overnight. It was simply too improper. Scandalous.

Jackson cupped her chin in his hand and lowered his lips to hers, softly brushing his mouth against hers. "I hate to see you with a worried frown on your face," he whispered. "Doc's spending the night in town, and we have the house to ourselves. That's nothing to frown about, Catalina."

She wrapped her arms around his waist and held him tight, filled with wonder that she had found him. There was a glowing warmth deep inside, a glow that stole away all her worries for a while, and it was as much a wonder to her as the journey she had made to find her one true love, her soul mate, the other half of herself.

He gave her a gentle kiss, his hands moving over her back almost tentatively, delicately, as if he was afraid she might break. She wanted to assure him that she wouldn't, that she could take whatever he offered her . . . soft or hard . . . fast or slow . . . she wanted everything Jackson had to give, and more.

"I've been doing some thinking," Jackson said, drawing just slightly away from her. "About the baby."

He sounded a little unsure, and Catalina held her breath.

"We talked one night about magic," he said softly, though they were all alone, miles from any other human being. "And I must admit I have a hard time accepting anything I can't see with my own eyes."

"Including magic?"

Jackson nodded. "But this . . ." He slid his hand down to rest on her still-flat stomach. "It's real magic. That you should come from so far away, and that I should find you in the middle of the desert, and that on our first night together we created something, *someone*. It was meant to be, this child. Our child. No matter what happens to me . . ."

Catalina reached up and laid a finger over Jackson's lips. "Nothing's going to happen to you," she insisted, but a deep chill stole away the glow that had warmed her.

Jackson smiled, a half grin, as he took her fingers and kissed them. "When we get to Texas we'll have a dozen more."

"A dozen? I don't think so. Maybe three."

Jackson backed her toward the wide bed in the corner of the room. "Only three?"

"We'll discuss it later."

Jackson undressed her as he practically danced her to the bed, his hands deft, his lips finding hers. Tonight she would sleep in his arms. Once Doc returned she would have to wait until they left the ranch and started their long journey to Texas. It wouldn't be much longer.

She gently fell back on the bed, and Jackson fell with her. "I love you, Catalina," he whispered hoarsely.

She kissed his skin, soft and warm and hard. "I love you, too." She wanted to look into his eyes and tell him even more. That he had proven to her that love really did exist, that the soul was stronger than time itself. But her body was aching for his, and for the moment *I love you, too* was enough. She had forever to tell him the rest.

He heard the hoofbeats coming closer; it took him only a few sleepy seconds to realize that it wasn't Doc's buckboard.

"Catalina." He gave her a gentle shove as he

rolled from the bed and began to dress quickly. She murmured and rolled away from him, onto her stomach, burying her face into the bed.

He called her name louder, and this time she lifted her head to look at him and gave him a sleepy smile. "Good morning," she mumbled before dropping her head to the bed again.

"Someone's coming," he snapped. "And it's not Doc."

Catalina came alive then, springing from the bed and searching the room for her clothes. She heard the riders, too, by now, and didn't have time to do more than slip into the dress she'd worn the day before and step into a pair of boots.

"How do you feel this morning?" he asked.

Catalina wrinkled her nose. "Not too bad. Nothing like yesterday."

He gave her what he hoped was a reassuring smile. "Good." Jackson wished for his gunbelt, but it had been packed away with everything else that reminded Catalina of Kid Creede. The riders were just outside the door now, and all he could do was grab the rifle that hung over the frame. The weapon hadn't been fired in years—it probably wasn't even loaded—and Jackson cursed under his breath as he threw open the front door and stepped outside, into the gray light of early morning.

Two men sat their horses before him. One was Harold Goodman, perched in his saddle like a man who owned the world. The other Jackson took a moment to recognize . . . and when he was certain he was right he swore under his breath again.

Joseph Wynkoop, an ugly sonofabitch. Jackson hadn't seen him in six years. They'd traveled together for a short while, before Jackson had discovered that Koop had no scruples at all.

If Harold had hired Koop to kill Doc, the old man was probably already dead.

Koop hung back while Harold urged his horse closer to Jackson.

"Mr. Cady," he said cheerfully, "I'm afraid I have some bad news for you. It seems your uncle has been in an accident. A fatal accident. It happened on his way out of town yesterday, just moments after he'd sold me this place. You will be leaving today, I presume?"

It was a command, one that Jackson was anxious to obey. He wanted Catalina away from this place. She would be safe in Texas.

At the same time, he knew he had to do something about Goodman. The kid had murdered an old man. For land. For gold. It wasn't right.

"We hadn't planned on leaving just yet," Jackson said evenly. "I suppose we'll have to stick around to see that my uncle receives a decent burial."

Catalina stepped out of the house, and he heard her sharp intake of breath. "He's dead? Doc's dead?"

"Yep." Harold Goodman leaned forward, grinning like a fool.

"Get back in the house, Catalina," Jackson ordered, but she ignored his command and stepped past him.

"You killed him, didn't you?"

Jackson didn't dare take his eyes off Harold,

but he could hear the tears in Catalina's voice.

"Nope," Harold assured her easily. "He did." He jerked a thumb over his shoulder to indicate Koop, waiting patiently to his rear.

Jackson knew he could take them both if he had his Colts. If Catalina would get out of the way. It made no difference. He didn't know if the weapon in his hands would even fire.

Catalina stepped forward, toward Harold's horse. "How could you have that nice old man killed? He never did anything to you. How many years did he have left? This place could have been yours eventually, you greedy bastard."

Jackson stepped forward and grabbed her sleeve, trying to pull her back, but she jerked her arm away without even looking at him.

"And you." She turned her attention to Koop, took one look at that tough face, and stepped back. She recognized that he was no green kid like Harold Goodman. Koop had the face of a man who killed without thinking, without regret. Regret? Jackson doubted Koop knew what that was, and he'd certainly never felt it.

"Inside, Catalina," Jackson ordered sharply.

Koop leaned forward in the saddle and grinned. "Well, hello, Kid," he said smoothly. "I thought that was you."

Harold's smile faded as he realized who he faced, and he reacted quickly. Too quickly. Catalina had turned to do as Jackson asked, or at least to return to his side. But Harold reached out and grabbed her by the hair, jerking her to his side. Koop pulled his pistol and pointed it at her head.

"Drop the rifle," Koop ordered softly, and Jackson did so without thinking. Catalina stood between the mounted men, motionless. Harold held a handful of her hair, pulling it much too hard, and Koop held the barrel of his weapon against her temple.

"Shoot him," Harold ordered.

Jackson waited for the blast of Koop's Colt, but there was a long moment of complete silence.

Koop didn't move the gun barrel away from Catalina's head.

"I said shoot him, dammit!"

Koop shook his head. "Can't do that. He's not armed."

"Doc Booker wasn't armed," Harold seethed. "That didn't stop you."

The hired gun shrugged his broad shoulders. "That was different. It was business. This is pleasure."

"Pick up that rifle." Harold ordered, nodding to the weapon on the ground.

Jackson ignored Harold and stared at Koop. "What do you want?"

"I want it all, and I want the world to see," Koop said, moving the gun barrel in small circles at Catalina's head, brushing her hair with its cold steel. "Is she yours?"

"No," Jackson said quickly. "Let her go."

Koop actually laughed. "I don't believe you, Kid. I thought you were a better liar than that."

The hired gunman turned to Harold. "Hand her up here, to me."

Harold was obviously taken aback. The tables had turned quickly, and Koop was now giving the orders. "I don't see—"

"Do it," Koop said calmly. "Or you're next. It would be a real pleasure to take care of your whinin' ass when I'm done with the Kid."

Harold did as he was told, all but jumping from his saddle to lift Catalina to Koop, setting her before the gunman. Koop snaked an arm around her waist, keeping the gun pointed at her head.

"Baxter. Three hours, Kid."

"If you touch her, if you hurt her, you'll wish for a quick death, Koop. I swear it."

Catalina's hair whipped around her face, caught by a cool, dancing breeze. She had said nothing, scared, shocked, uncertain, but Jackson saw the lucidity come back into her eyes.

"Stay away from Baxter," she insisted, her voice almost calm. "You know what will happen. You promised me." The last was a hoarse whisper. A plea, more than a reminder.

Jackson stared at Catalina's face, ignoring the two men who were taking her away from him. She was scared not for herself, but for him. He returned his eyes to Koop's face.

"Three hours," Jackson said in a velvety smooth voice that betrayed none of his emotions.

He stood there and watched them ride away, Koop and Harold Goodman and Catalina.

Jackson threw open the door to the little house, allowing the brightening sun to fill the room. He knew what he had to do.

He searched her room first, yanking drawers from the dresser, emptying the wardrobe that held the calico dresses Catalina had been wearing. He tried not to panic, knew he *could not* panic, but for God's sake he could *smell* her, could *feel* her in the fabric in his hands. All he found were pastels and fragile material. No black, no steel.

He finally found it all, minutes later. They had been the longest minutes of his life.

Catalina had packed all his old things in a chest at the end of the bed, mixed in with blankets and some of Mrs. Booker's old dresses. He threw it all on the bed and finally found what he was looking for in the bottom of the chest, under a faded blue gown with delicate lace and tiny pearls.

His silver spurs. The black clothing Catalina had so happily replaced. The black duster. His gunbelt, with two Colt Peacemakers still in their holsters.

A chill came over him as he put everything on the bed. He should have known it was too good to last.

Chapter Nineteen

Catalina struggled against the man who half dragged, half carried her into Alberta's place. The heels of her boots scraped across the boardwalk, and she did her best to elbow the man in his generous gut. All he did was chuckle under his breath.

Everything she'd done up to now, all her plans, were for nothing. She'd never felt so utterly helpless, so insignificant. Jackson was going to die on the street, just as the history book said.

The man Jackson had called Koop deposited her roughly in a chair at the back of the room. They had the saloon all to themselves, apparently.

"Sit there and be a good girl," he said in a gruff voice.

Catalina jumped to her feet, but Koop pushed her roughly back into the chair. Before she knew what was happening he had dropped a rope around her and was tying her to the chair. The rope bit into her arms as he tied it tightly at the back of the chair. That done, he tied her ankles to the chair legs, ignoring the feeble kicks she planted on his arms and his chest. Catalina looked up, tightly bound, and there was Alberta, a smug smile on her face.

"He won't come," Catalina said without a tremor in her voice. She felt that shaking deep down, though.

Koop wasn't buying it. "He'll come, all right. The Kid always had a strange sense of justice." He sat beside her and leaned back as if he didn't have a care in the world, his arms crossed over a broad chest, that gut all but distended.

"It's called a conscience," Catalina snapped.

Alberta didn't sit, but walked around the table, swinging her wide hips. "Don't listen to her," the madam cooed. "The Kid will be here. He had a soft spot for her all along. Caused me nothing but trouble."

Koop only grinned. "Well, it will be his downfall. That and his . . . conscience." He peered at Catalina knowingly. "The whole town will be watching, and my reputation will be made. The man who shot Kid Creede."

Catalina licked her lips. It wasn't right, that she should come all this way . . . only to have to watch Jackson die.

"He'll kill you," she said, but this time the tremor was in her voice.

Koop laughed. "One minute you tell me he's not coming, and the next you say he's going to kill me. Make up your mind, woman."

Koop reached out and brushed the back of his hand along her cheek. Catalina tried not to tremble, not to give in to the nausea that gripped her when he touched her. "If you're so certain he'll kill me, how about a little bet? If I win, I get a tumble."

Catalina tried to back away from his hand, but there was nowhere to go. "If you win," she promised, believing every word, "I'll kill you myself."

He didn't laugh at that, and he finally withdrew his hand.

Milo appeared, stepping behind the bar to polish the wood surface, to arrange bottles and glasses for the crowd yet to come. Alberta was never far away from the table and the gunman who intended to kill Jackson, and her eyes were bright as she placed a single glass of whiskey in front of Koop. Catalina could almost feel the excitement radiating off the madam, the blood lust she barely held in check, and she hated Alberta more at that moment than she ever had.

Koop quickly drained the glass, and Alberta was there to refill it. Catalina hoped, for a moment, that he might get drunk. That would give Jackson an edge. But Koop only sipped at the second glass, and watched Catalina over the rim. He had beady eyes, a muddy brown with no life, no soul.

"How could you murder a defenseless old man?" Catalina asked finally, her anger overriding her good sense.

"For six hundred dollars," he said calmly. "It was nothing personal," he assured her with a smile that told her he really thought that should make a difference. "Now, with the Kid, it's right personal."

"Why?"

Koop looked almost pensive, narrowing his eyes and leaning forward slightly.

He slowly raised his right hand and pushed

back the filthy cuff. Catalina saw the scar before he ran a thick finger over it.

"He shot me. And then he left me to fend for myself, bleedin' all over the place."

"I'm sure he had a good reason. Did you draw on him first?" Catalina knew before the question was out of her mouth that that wasn't what had happened. Jackson shot to kill. He had told her that, and told her why.

Koop snorted. "You think the Kid is better than me? That he wouldn't draw on me first?"

Catalina had no doubts about her answer. "I *know* he's a better man than you. If he shot you, he had a good reason. And if he hit your hand, that's what he was aiming for."

"He shot me from behind," Koop said defensively. "I was only doin' my job, darlin'. Hell, the same thing he does for a livin'."

"Jackson's nothing like you," Catalina whispered.

"Jackson, is it?"

Catalina refused to answer.

"I met the Kid a few years back. We were both traveling through Colorado. I knew him, by reputation, and of course he had heard of me." Koop had an inflated opinion of himself. Catalina could see that in his confident smile, and the sparkle that appeared briefly in his eyes. "We stopped in this little town north of Denver, and that's where we got offered the job. The Kid turned it down flat, but I needed the money, so I took it on. The old farmer came to town, and I took him out right there."

Catalina couldn't help but compare that incident to the job Jackson had been offered here in Baxter.

"And Jackson shot you?"

"Not until I killed the woman. That farmer's wife. Hell, she was caterwauling something awful."

And he would kill her, once Jackson was dead. Catalina knew that now. Koop had no soul, no conscience, and there was no one in Baxter who would help her.

She gave him a confident smile, even as her insides churned and her head pounded. "He won't be aiming for your hand today. Do you prefer to be killed with a shot to the head or to the heart? Perhaps I could pass your preference on to Jackson before the shoot-out."

Koop's sure smile faded, and Catalina knew she had at least dented his confidence.

But soon that smug grin was back. "The Kid's soft. He's always been soft. Hell, I'll empty both guns into the sonofabitch while you watch, and then I'll collect on that bet."

Catalina would have fallen over if she hadn't been tied to the chair. Her head swam, and she closed her eyes against the sudden dizziness that engulfed her.

Koop wore two six-shooters. He'd just threatened to shoot Jackson a dozen times.

"He's not dead!" Harold Goodman pushed his way through the batwing doors, and Catalina snapped her head around. Goodman's face was beet red with anger, and his hands were clenched at his sides.

Koop remained seated, apparently unconcerned. "Who's not dead?"

"Doc Booker! Some damn farmer found him on the road, still in his buckboard, wounded but still *alive*."

Catalina closed her eyes and sighed. Relieved, frightened, angry, all at the same time, she tried to hold onto her sanity.

"Where is he now?" Koop asked casually.

"At the preacher's house, with Reverend Preston watching over him."

"I'll take care of him later, when I'm done with the Kid."

"That's going to be difficult for you," Catalina said sweetly. "You'll be dead."

Alberta and Milo watched from a distance, having the sense to stay away from the emotion-charged Goodman and the calm and deadly Koop.

"You were paid to do a job," Goodman insisted, his anger making him foolish. "I insist that you take care of Doc Booker first."

"See?" Catalina cooed, egging Koop on. "Even this boy knows you can't beat Kid Creede. Why else would he insist that you finish the job now?"

Koop shot her an angry glance. "Am I gonna have to gag you, woman?"

Catalina leaned back and was silent, but her smile—forced as it was—remained.

Her arms and her hands were numb, but her boots kept the rope at her ankles from doing any damage. She could run, if she was free. She could flip Koop and take his guns, if she wasn't tied up. Of course, she hadn't been able to flip Milo, but

319

he was even bigger than Koop, and she'd been drunk at the time.

Goodman and Koop continued to stare at one another, and she could see the younger man growing angrier and more frustrated with each passing moment. Had he expected a man like Koop to obey him—to respect him—because he was paid to?

Catalina could see what Goodman could not—that Koop's hand rested on the butt of his gun, easily, almost casually. But not quite casually. The fingers flexed, jumped almost, as Jackson's had on occasion.

"Damn it, Wynkoop," Goodman shouted, stepping forward. He raised his fist, in what could have been seen as a blow coming, though Catalina suspected the young man was simply raising his fist in impotent anger.

They would never know. Koop drew his weapon and fired directly into Harold Goodman's chest. Catalina flinched and closed her eyes. As much as she hated Harold Goodman, as much as she felt the man deserved to die at the hand of his own hired gun, she didn't have the stomach to watch a man die, to see more blood spilled.

She heard Koop order Milo to take away the body, in a voice more amused than remorseful. Harold Goodman might have been a pesky fly, or a spider beneath Koop's heavy boot. He didn't care that a man was dead, that he had taken a life. Not in the least.

Catalina didn't open her eyes until she felt

those thick fingers beneath her chin, rough fingers caressing her skin.

"Did I scare you, blondie?" he asked gruffly.

She lifted her head to shake his fingers away. "I feel ill," she admitted, and it was the truth. "Do you think you could . . . untie me? I mean, where am I going to go? How far could I expect to get?" Catalina forced her eyes wide and gave Koop her best vulnerable woman stare, scared and helpless. The scared part wasn't an act.

Koop actually looked as if he was considering her request, and then Alberta appeared at his elbow. "Watch your step with this one, Koop," she confided. "She tossed Harold flat on his back one night a while back. Grabbed his arm and threw the boy over her shoulder. Damnedest thing I ever did see."

Koop tilted his head and gave Catalina what amounted to an oh-you-naughty-girl lift of his eyebrows, accompanied with a crooked smile, and Catalina knew that if she were free the first thing she would do was pop Alberta right in her big mouth.

"Maybe I should leave you right where you are, for the moment." Koop nodded his thanks to Alberta, leaving a frustrated Catalina to tug at knots that refused to give.

He didn't push his bay, but rode slowly into town. Rushing without thinking had almost gotten him killed the last time he was in Baxter. It took all his strength, all his resolve to push down the emotions that made him want to barrel headlong into town to find Catalina.

Kid Creede didn't act impulsively. Ever.

They were expecting him. It was the middle of the day, not yet noon, but there was not a soul on the street. Straight ahead, at the opposite end of the single street, a door slammed shut. A gust of wind brushed across the dirt path, and for a moment Baxter looked like an abandoned mining town. A ghost town. There were plenty of those in Arizona Territory.

Catalina had been wrong. He'd been wrong. He couldn't leave Kid Creede behind and start a new life as if the first thirty-one years hadn't happened. He couldn't be reborn. There would always be a Koop out there, waiting. He wouldn't ask Catalina to live like that.

Koop stepped out of Alberta's and onto the boardwalk. Alberta and Milo were right behind him, and they held between them a bound Catalina. Her hands were tied behind her; even her legs were lashed together. Koop was taking no chances with his hostage.

The fury that welled up inside him was quickly squelched. It wouldn't help Catalina. It would probably get them both killed. His eyes searched the windows and balconies above his head and found them as deserted as the street.

Koop stepped onto the street as Jackson dismounted and tossed the reins over a hitching post.

"The woman almost had me convinced you weren't coming, Kid," Koop said with a tight smile.

Jackson spared a glance at Catalina, but he returned his eyes quickly to his opponent. She was too white, her eyes too wide, and there wasn't a damn thing he could do but kill Koop, and probably Harold Goodman as well. What then? Even if he could escape, the sheriff would be on his tail. Alone, he could get away, but he couldn't leave Catalina behind.

Koop stood in the middle of the street, his hands twitching, hovering over his pistols. The man thought he was fast, but he had a catch in his draw that would slow him up just enough. It was the reason Koop would never be one of the great ones. It was the reason Jackson knew he could outdraw the gunman who had taken Catalina.

Without turning his head or taking his eyes from Koop, Jackson knew the boardwalk was filling up. Whispers reached him, muted footsteps, a swinging door. He heard a footstep on a balcony above Koop's head. No one said a word . . . as they settled in, he couldn't even hear them breathe.

They had come to watch someone die. Bloodthirsty bastards, all of them.

Catalina bit her lip to keep from screaming. It would only distract Jackson, and he needed to keep his attention on Koop. But inside she was screaming; her heart was about to burst, her lungs about to explode with the scream she held back.

Her heart had stopped when she'd been pushed onto the boardwalk and she'd seen Jackson atop his horse, just as she'd seen him that first day. Cold. Stoic. He'd dismounted without so much as a glance in her direction, without a word to her.

Standing on the street, he was Kid Creede once again, with that hat so low over his eyes that she couldn't see them, and that duster billowing about his legs. There were silver spurs on his boots that danced and sang with each slow step he took, and with a smooth motion he pushed the duster back so the two Colts he wore were visible.

She wanted to wrestle against the grip Alberta and that goon Milo had on her, but she didn't dare. It wouldn't do to make any move that might call attention to her and away from Koop. He was the real threat to Jackson . . . and to her.

Koop was ruthless, and he was looking to make his reputation . . . to make himself a legend. Otherwise, he would have shot Jackson down at Doc's ranch. It would have been simple enough, once Jackson had dropped Doc's ancient rifle.

There wasn't a sound, except for the beating of her heart, which she was certain Jackson could hear, it was so loud. Everyone . . . everything waited. The wind was still, a cloud covered the sun, and even Alberta held her breath.

It happened quickly. Koop drew first, and in spite of her resolve, the scream Catalina had been withholding burst free.

Koop didn't get off a single shot. Jackson drew, so fast his hand was nothing but a blur, and as his Colt fired Koop crumpled to the ground.

He turned to her then, ignoring the murmurs of the staring crowd. Alberta and her bartender released Catalina and backed away. Jackson hadn't reholstered his weapon, and it hung at his side. No one who had just seen the gunfight would doubt that whoever Jackson wanted dead would soon *be* dead.

"Are you all right?" he asked in a low, smooth voice, free of emotion.

Catalina nodded her head. "Yes," she whispered. She could see his eyes now, cold as ice. Withdrawn and . . . alone. "Hurry. We've got to get away from here."

He holstered his Colt and dropped down to untie the rope Koop had wrapped around her legs, his movements unhurried. It was already too late. The sheriff was approaching with quick steps down the boardwalk. Catalina wanted to shout at the lawman. Surely he had known what was happening. He'd ignored it, until the threat was over.

"It was self-defense," she said, looking down at Jackson's hat. He didn't seem at all concerned at the sheriff's approach. Didn't stand until the ropes fell at Catalina's feet.

When he did stand it was with a slow deliberation, like a snake uncoiling. He didn't even look at her, but glared over her shoulder to Alberta.

"Untie her hands," he ordered in a low voice, and Alberta jumped to do as she was told.

Jackson turned to the sheriff, and the man's step slowed. He was afraid of Jackson . . . of Kid Creede . . . Catalina could see that in his eyes.

"I'll be happy to turn myself in and hand over my weapons."

Linda Jones

"No," Catalina yelled, but he continued as if she wasn't even there.

"If you'll grant me one last request."

Her hands were free, and Catalina let her arms fall to her sides. She wanted to wrap them around Jackson, but he faced the sheriff stiffly, hard as a rock, and she didn't dare step forward even to lay a hand on his arm.

The sheriff had stopped several feet away from Jackson, eyes flitting from his holsters to his eyes. He didn't have to wonder who would win if he were to make the mistake of drawing on Jackson. But he didn't answer right away.

"We can do this hard or we can do it easy," Jackson said silkily. "Your choice."

"What kind of request?" the sheriff asked wearily.

"I want to be married," Jackson said, no emotion in that low voice, "and then I want you to let my wife leave Baxter, with your word that she won't be followed."

"No," Catalina whispered. "I won't leave you."

He must have heard her . . . he was only a couple of feet away . . . but he said nothing, didn't even turn his head to acknowledge her.

"Turn over your weapons first," the sheriff said.

Catalina moved forward, a single step, and she saw the half smile creep across Jackson's face. There was no humor in that smile, and it chilled her to the bone.

"I'm not stupid, Sheriff," Jackson answered.

The sheriff shuffled his feet, dragging his boot heels across the boardwalk. "All right. Reverend

326

Preston can perform the ceremony in my office."

"In the church," Jackson amended. "And then Catalina leaves town on my horse, and you give your word that no one will go after her."

"A woman alone . . ." the sheriff began. "It's not safe."

"I want your word," Jackson all but whispered.

The sheriff thought it over, but not for long. "All right. You have it. No one will follow her."

Catalina reached out and placed her hand on Jackson's arm. He did turn his head to her then, and looked down at her face with those cold eyes.

"I meant what I said," she whispered. "I won't leave you here."

She could see no emotion in his eyes, no regret, no indecision. He didn't lay his hand over hers or smile, or give her a conspiratorial wink. He had nothing up his sleeve, no plan to get them out of this one. Jackson intended to hand himself over to the sheriff and turn her away.

"You have no choice," he answered in a whisper even lower than her own.

And it was the certainty in that voice, the determination in those pale blue eyes, that finally convinced her. He was sending her home.

They walked to the church, Jackson's step stiff and sure as Catalina gripped the sleeve of his duster. She told him how Koop had killed Harold Goodman, and the news that Doc had survived the attempt on his life.

He showed no reaction to either of those bits of news, no satisfaction or relief. She could tell that he had distanced himself again, shut himself off from emotion, buried his soul deep.

The sheriff allowed no one but himself and Reverend Preston in the small church, shutting the heavy doors on the crowd that had followed them from Alberta's.

"How's Doc?" Catalina asked the preacher, as soon as the doors were closed.

The solemn preacher nodded his head slowly. "Gravely injured, but still strong. I believe he'll make it." He glanced over her shoulder to the sheriff. "The man that was killed . . ." He paused, "The gunman who apparently kidnapped Miss Lane. . . . You are aware, are you not, Sheriff Ross, that the man ambushed Doc Booker with the intention of killing him?"

Catalina twisted her head slowly. Sheriff Ross? Wilson's great-grandfather, perhaps. Great-great? She tried to do the math in her head as she looked for a resemblance. Perhaps. Sheriff Ross was as cowardly as Wilson. More.

Sheriff Ross made it clear that he didn't care what Koop had done. Taking Jackson would make his reputation, just as Koop had been looking to do. Neither of them were half the man Jackson was. They were empty shells, not men at all.

Her head swam, and Catalina closed her eyes. A tear slipped down her cheek, and she felt Jackson's warm fingers on her face.

"Don't cry, Catalina," he whispered, his soft words for her alone.

Chapter Twenty

It was a somber ceremony, with none of the joy and promise for the future Catalina had expected to feel on her wedding day. Sheriff Ross stood behind them, in the middle of the aisle, their only witness. Reverend Preston, Doc's friend, performed the ceremony without a smile, without a spark of hope in his voice.

Jackson stood stiffly beside her, his eyes straight ahead, his hand covering her trembling fingers, resting on his arm. He had removed his hat and deposited it on a pew, but he wore his gunbelt and his duster. His face was covered with black stubble, and he looked as forbidding and deadly as Kid Creede was expected to look.

It wasn't supposed to end like this. They were supposed to have a lifetime together, a new start. She was going to teach Jackson how to be a good father to their baby, how to make friends, how to trust.

Instead of the satin-and-lace wedding gown she had been wearing on the day Jackson found her in the desert, Catalina was wearing a faded blue calico that had belonged to Doc's late wife. Her fingers twitched, and the pressure of Jackson's hand increased, just enough to let her know that he was aware of her.

Catalina listened to the words that finally made her Jackson's wife. It was what she'd wanted . . . but not like this. The price was too high.

He could have gotten away, as soon as he'd shot Koop. He could have run to his horse and taken off . . . but she had never expected Jackson to do that. For her, he had tried to leave that part of his life behind. He hadn't wanted to kill Koop. He had broken his promise and come to Baxter to save her.

And now he was sending her away.

He took both her hands in his and she looked up into his impassive face as the preacher pronounced them man and wife. He hadn't been this cold when she'd first met him. Not hard like this. Did he, somewhere deep inside, blame her for his downfall? She knew she would always blame herself. All she'd wanted was to save him, to keep him alive. She had failed miserably.

Jackson kissed her, a brief, passionless kiss to seal the pact.

"All right," Sheriff Ross said testily. "Let's go."

Jackson turned his head slowly to the lawman. "Give us five minutes. Alone."

"I don't . . ." the sheriff began.

"Five minutes," Jackson said again.

The sheriff hesitated, but he left with the preacher, and Catalina was at last alone with her husband.

"I'll come back for you," she promised Jackson in a whispery voice that shook just slightly. "I'll break you out of jail."

"You can't come back."

They stood silently at the altar, there where they'd been legally wed. All her plans—for a fresh start in Texas, for a chance to show Jackson how wonderful life could be—wiped away in a single morning.

Jackson took her hand and led her to the front pew. Catalina sat, and he stood before her, twining his fingers through hers, studying the hand he held.

"I swear, I'll get you away from this place . . ." she began.

"They won't be putting me in jail, Catalina." Jackson didn't raise his voice, and there was no emotion in that statement. Only harsh assurance. "They'll either shoot me or hang me before the day is out, and I don't want you here when that happens."

Catalina felt physically ill. Her stomach churned, her vision blurred, and she clasped Jackson's hand tightly. "That's why you insisted on the ceremony."

Jackson nodded.

"I can't . . . I won't . . ."

Jackson sat beside her, and with his free hand he reached into the inside pocket of his duster to grasp the two pieces of wulfenite. "You'll need this," he said softly, holding out the piece of the stone that was still attached to Qaletaqa's braided leather. She refused to take it, so he placed it around her neck. "You know what to do."

The other piece he placed around his own neck, closing his fingers around the stone until she could no longer see the golden crystal. "I'll keep this, if you don't mind. It's as good as any wedding ring. Better, I reckon."

He leaned forward then and kissed her, tender and hungry and touched with the finality of a forced good-bye. His lips lingered, pulling away and then drawn to hers again, soft and warm as he showed her a tenderness she knew no one else had ever seen from him.

"I'm going to stay here with you," Catalina insisted. "You can't force me to go back."

She saw it then, the softening of those cold eyes, the melting of the ice there. "Do it for me, Catalina. You won't be safe here, without me to protect you."

"But . . ."

Jackson laid a finger over her lips, stilling her protests. "Listen to me. I know we didn't have much time, but it's a miracle we had even that. I'd never known love until I found you. I didn't believe in love or miracles or magic until you showed me they existed."

Jackson pulled her head against his shoulder and held her so tight she could barely breathe. But it wasn't tight enough. Catalina knew then that his emotionless face and words, the iciness that set him apart, was only a shield. That he was holding on to his sanity as desperately as she was.

"And we have to think about the baby." His voice almost broke. "A baby, Catalina." There was wonder in his voice, the voice of a man who had never before known wonder. "I've known my time was coming. I certainly never expected to see the twentieth century. This baby . . . this child . . . will grow up in the twenty-first. It's the only thing you can do for me now. The only gift I'll ever ask you for. To take care of this baby. That can't be done here, Catalina."

"So to show how much I love you, I have to leave?" Catalina pressed her face against his shoulder. Her lips against the dusty fabric, her every breath a sharp reminder that she would never be next to him again, never again taste his lips. Never lie next to him, breathless and happy, their hearts beating in a synchronized rhythm. "I can't."

Jackson took her shoulders and pushed her gently away. "For me. Remember what you said? Two halves of the same soul. Maybe . . . if the soul survives . . . I'll be in 1996, waiting for you. Another body, but the same soul. I promise you, Catalina, if it's possible, I'll be there. And I'll find you."

"I don't want another man; I want you." She didn't want to cry. Since she'd watched him ride into town she'd fought the tears—had allowed only that single tear Jackson had brushed away. She didn't sob, but the tears welled up in her eyes. "I can't believe I came all this way just to find you, and now I have to give you up."

Jackson kissed her, a slow melting of their lips that could only break her heart, and he held his hand over her belly. His fingers stroked her gently, strong brown fingers brushing against faded blue calico. "Maybe, if there has to be a reason, this is it. The baby. A part of us, Catalina."

A part of us, she thought bitterly. It didn't ease the pain.

"Look for me," Jackson whispered. "When you get back to 1996, look for me."

The door opened slowly and bright light spilled onto the church aisle, across Jackson's face and hers. The sun warmed her cheek, but it did nothing to chase away the chill. The sheriff appeared in the doorway, silently demanding his prisoner. There were a handful of armed men behind him, ready to take on the infamous Kid Creede if they had to.

The shield closed back over Jackson's eyes and they were cold once again. "Take my horse," he whispered. "And leave. Now. You know where to go."

Catalina closed her fingers around the wulfenite that dangled from her neck. Yes, damn it all, she knew where to go.

Jackson distanced himself from her, mentally and physically. She knew he was attempting to keep her from harm, but she wasn't ready to let him go. Not yet.

But she walked down the street, alone, while Jackson stood on the church steps facing a hostile crowd.

She turned away from him and didn't look back. Not as she walked away from the church, unable to be oblivious to the stares that followed her, not as she walked down the middle of the street, passing the bloodstained site where Koop had died. Someone had already taken the gunman's body away.

Jackson's horse was still tethered in front of Alberta's. The madam and her employees weren't a part of the crowd at the church. They watched her over the top of the batwing doors, as silent and as hostile as the sheriff and his men. Milo frowned. Winnie looked more annoyed than anything else. Alberta was seething—angry because she was losing her new girl? Angry because Catalina was getting away from Baxter, while Alberta never would?

There was a touch of pity in Juanita's dark eyes. Pity and what could have been envy, though it was hard to tell.

Catalina stepped into the stirrup and swung a leg over Jackson's bay, seating herself in the saddle. Maybe he was right. Maybe it was all for the child she carried. Maybe. At the moment that thought didn't diminish the ache in her heart. She was simply angry, and strangely empty.

She had to look back. She couldn't leave without one more look, one more image to burn into her brain. It would have to last her a lifetime.

Jackson was walking down the street, coming straight toward her. His step was slow and even, his back stiff, his head high. The sheriff and the rest of his men stayed well back, forming a wall behind Jackson. They were afraid of him, still. Afraid of Kid Creede with his cold eyes and his lightning draw. Afraid of the fearlessness within him.

He came straight to her. His face gave away nothing, no regret, no indecision.

"There has to be another way," she said as he neared her, and her heart quickened as he came closer. "Jump on. Hurry!" she hissed.

Jackson raised his hand and slapped the horse's rump smartly before Catalina knew what

335

he was planning. He never said a word as the bay took off. Catalina held on as the town around her, the buildings and the people, became nothing more than a teary blur.

He watched her ride away, her head low, her hair whipping in the wind.

It was the only way.

He waited until she was out of sight, but not so far away that she couldn't hear.

Jackson drew both guns in a smooth, practiced motion, and fired into the air. He waited, half expecting to feel a bullet slam into his back, waiting for the explosion of the guns to his rear, but there was nothing but the roar of his own Colts.

He fired into the air until his weapons were empty. Eleven times. Not Catalina's dozen, but she probably wouldn't be able to tell the difference, not when so many of the shots came one on top of the other.

It would be best if she was convinced that he was dead, shot a dozen times as the history book she had told him about had said. He knew he'd be dead, one way or another, soon enough. But he didn't want Catalina coming back to Baxter. He didn't want her to watch him die, and he didn't want her trapped in town. He wanted her to move on.

He spun the Colts easily on his fingers and slipped them back into their holsters. They were emptied, and he was now defenseless.

He turned back to the sheriff and the morbidly curious townspeople, and unbuckled the gunbelt that held two empty Colts and a healthy store of ammunition. He swung it aside, discarding the weapons that had kept him alive up to this point. Weapons Catalina had always detested.

The sheriff said nothing.

"Well?" Jackson snapped. "Let's get on with it."

She was passing the gnarled tree just past the edge of town when she heard the shots, and she closed her eyes tight. History couldn't be changed, after all. She fixed a tearful, fuzzy stare on the red rocks and didn't look back, didn't attempt to slow the horse that galloped toward Doc's ranch.

Maybe Jackson was right about the survival of the soul. She would look for him in 1996, but the thought didn't ease the pain inside her. If anything, it made her feel worse.

She couldn't imagine ever loving anyone again.

Except the baby. Their baby. If not for the child, she would have fought to stay with Jackson. Maybe then they could have found a way to escape together.

But now it was too late. Jackson Cady—Kid Creede—was dead. Shot a dozen times, just as history had written. The short paragraph she had read had said nothing about defending his wife from Koop, about leaving a pregnant wife behind. There had been nothing there to indicate that he had been a good man who'd wanted nothing more than a normal life with the woman who loved him.

Jackson paced in front of the tree, the sheriff—gun in hand—dogging his every step. Why

337

couldn't they just get this over with? They had turned it into an event, bringing out the women and children, making a holiday of the hanging of Kid Creede. They ate and drank and laughed, and it seemed as if the day dragged on forever. It was as if they didn't want the festivities to end.

Reverend Preston had tried to talk to him, but Jackson had nothing to say. In spite of Jackson's indifference, the preacher had launched into a lengthy prayer. A plea for the soul of a condemned man, a prayer for a killer who was certainly damned. The crowd had listened piously, while Jackson impatiently fingered the stone that rested against his chest. His life was over. Catalina was gone.

Finally they tied his hands behind his back, and the cautious sheriff helped him into the saddle of a sorry-looking horse. Sheriff Ross expected trouble—Jackson could see that in every nervous move, in those twitching eyes—and he didn't see fit to ease the lawman's worry by mentioning the fact that Kid Creede had given his word that there would be no trouble.

They placed the noose around his neck. Was she already gone? She'd had time to reach the spot where he'd seen her almost disappear, where he'd first felt the pain and fear of losing the only person he'd ever loved. Time for her, and the baby, to travel forward to 1996. There, they would be safe.

And nothing else mattered.

Catalina stepped forward, the wulfenite grasped tightly in one hand. It was the only way.

It was what Jackson had wanted. What he'd demanded.

She stepped back and turned her head to take a last look at Doc's house. Another last look. She'd been happy there in that ramshackle house, happier than she'd ever thought possible.

Three times she'd tried to go, and each time, at the last moment, she'd pulled back. *I'm not ready*, she told herself again and again. Not ready to leave.

There's no reason to stay.

She closed her eyes and stepped forward once more, filling her mind with images of Indian Springs, the library, Kim, her Mustang. Unbidden, Jackson was there. It was so very clear, her last image of him walking down the street toward her. To send her away.

The dust rose at her feet, swirling, engulfing her, blinding her, and Catalina clutched the wulfenite so tightly it cut into her palm. She was falling, floating, lost. And then she couldn't find her breath.

The man on horseback beside him, the man who had placed the noose around his neck, started to cover Jackson's head with a black hood, but Jackson shook him off with a turn of his head and a harsh glare. No words were necessary, and he had none left. Nothing to say in his own defense, no last-minute prayer.

He stared at the red rocks in the distance—Catalina's rocks—and realized that she'd been right all along. They were alive, somehow. Vibrant.

If there was a way for the soul to survive, he would find her. It was a promise he made to himself, as solemnly as he'd promised Catalina.

His hands were bound tightly behind his back, so he couldn't clutch the golden crystal that lay heavily against his chest. He knew it weighed almost nothing, but as he waited to die the wulfenite seemed to become heavier, and he could feel the heat it emitted through his shirt.

He closed his eyes and saw Catalina's face. In his mind she was smiling, and he grinned himself. The man beside him swore under his breath, a prayer, a curse, a whispered mention of Satan, but Jackson paid him no mind. He concentrated on Catalina's face, on the dancing flecks of gold in her eyes.

He heard the slap of a heavy hand on the nag's rump, the gasp of the crowd, felt the startled nag jerking away beneath him, and then Jackson fell.

Chapter Twenty-one

Catalina took a deep breath, when she could breathe again, and opened her eyes to find herself just a few feet from the highway. The same two-lane road she had been on the day her Mustang had died, and she had found herself wishing to live in the past.

Without thinking, without knowing exactly where she was, she started walking. She did her best not to think of Jackson. It hurt too much. There were so many plans to be made. A job to find, a place to live, a pregnancy to deal with. A child to raise.

She certainly couldn't tell anyone where she had been. No one would believe her, anyway. If she tried to convince anyone of the truth, she'd most likely end up in a psych ward somewhere, strapped to a bed, telling her tale to a woman who had been Cleopatra or Marie Antoinette in a past life.

The pickup truck approached from behind, and she was so lost in thought she didn't hear the rumbling engine until it was right behind her. It came to a shuddering stop, and the driver, a teenager wearing a ball cap and a T-shirt with the sleeves ripped out leaned over to throw open the passenger door.

"You need a ride?"

Catalina stepped into the truck, dragging her calico skirt with her. She didn't normally accept rides from strangers, but the kid looked harmless enough.

"Thanks," she muttered halfheartedly, staring straight ahead.

"What's the costume for?" the boy asked, taking off so suddenly Catalina's head jerked back. "Didn't they finish filming a while back?"

Catalina shook her head, and the kid didn't seem to take offense that she didn't care to speak. "Name's Chris. Chris Booker. My folks have a gas station out here, and I swear, we never see anybody out this way. It was kinda spooky to see you walking down the street in that old costume. I thought for a minute I was seeing a ghost. I've heard stories about ghosts out here, you know."

He stared at the road ahead.

"Booker?" Catalina asked, leaning forward to get a better look at his face. Chris looked nothing like Doc. Coincidence, certainly.

"My name's Catalina. Catalina Cady."

He nodded his head and took one hand off the wheel to offer it to her. They shook hands, and the truck veered to the side, almost leaving the road.

"Where you headed, Miss Cady?"

"Mrs. Cady," Catalina said softly. "Is your mother's name Allie, by any chance?"

"Yeah; you know her?" Chris turned his head, and the pickup truck veered again.

Catalina nodded and grasped the door handle. She decided to hang on for the duration. "I met her once. Is that where you're headed? Your parents' gas station?" Coincidence, that she had come full circle?

Chris nodded.

"Then that's where I'm going."

Catalina was silent for the remainder of the short trip, not wanting to distract Chris from his driving. It was a good thing this road was so infrequently used, if Chris spent much time on it.

The station appeared just as it had before, deserted, neglected, yet still inviting. But one fixture was missing: The old Indian who had given her the moccasins and the wulfenite was gone. There wasn't even a chair there, in the spot where she'd seen him before.

Allie was as surprised to see Catalina as she'd been the first time, and recovered just as quickly.

"Well, I'll be," she muttered. "He said you'd be back."

"Who said I'd be back?"

Allie took a moment to take in Catalina's strange dress, shook her head slightly, and offered Catalina a cold drink from the refrigerator. "That Indian. What was his name? Kelly something?"

"Qaletaqa?" Catalina asked softly.

"That's it." Allie took a drink for herself and plopped down on the stool in the corner.

Catalina leaned against the edge of Stu's desk. Qaletaqa, the traveler. She would have thought it impossible, but nothing was impossible, she

343

had learned. "I don't suppose you still have my Mustang?"

Chris piped up. "That's yours? I love that car. I begged Dad to let me drive it . . ."

"Did he?" Catalina twisted her head to look at the young man in the doorway.

"No," Chris answered, totally disgusted.

Catalina had to bite her tongue to keep from saying thank goodness. Instead, she turned back to Allie. "So you do still have it? And it's running?"

Allie smiled and slid from her perch. She slipped past Catalina and opened the middle drawer of Stu's desk. She took out a ring of keys, selected one, and opened the bottom drawer, a smug smile on her face.

"That old Indian, Kelly, Kalla . . ."

"Qaletaqa," Catalina said softly.

Allie repeated the name twice, until she was certain she had it. "Anyway, he showed up here just a couple of days before you did, plopped his chair right out front, and sat. When I asked him what he did, he said he was a fixer."

"A fixer?"

Allie lifted her head so Catalina could see her over the top of the desk. "A fixer. I'm not sure exactly what he fixed. When I asked him if he repaired, you know, televisions or toasters or cars, he just said he fixed whatever needed fixing."

She lowered her head again, and Catalina looked up as Chris left the office, drink in hand. Their conversation had evidently turned too boring for him.

"Here it is," Allie said, and she popped up with a thick envelope in her hands. She offered the envelope to Catalina with a smile on her face. "I'm so glad you came back. I don't know what I would have done with this if you hadn't."

Catalina took the envelope and opened it. Money. Cash. More than a librarian ever saw at one time.

"This isn't mine," she breathed.

"Qaletaqa gave me a huge diamond ring, said it was yours. He said I should sell it, use whatever was necessary to fix your car, and save you the rest."

"How could he know I'd be back?" The whispered question was for her own benefit, but Allie answered.

"I sure don't know, but he said you wouldn't be coming back alone."

Catalina's head snapped up. Could she have brought Jackson with her? No. It was the baby. How had Qaletaqa known that?

A fixer. If she could travel back a hundred years and forward again, surely others could, too. Qaletaqa was an experienced traveler, someone who had gathered the knowledge to control where and when he went. Could she do the same? Could she travel back once again—to a time before Jackson was shot?

She'd proved to herself once that history couldn't be changed. Would she be a fool to try again? And how would she start? How could she be certain she'd travel to the right time? She'd traveled back a hundred years before. Glancing at the calendar on the wall proved that time here had moved forward as it had in 1896. If she could travel back again, would it be to a time after Jackson's death? Could she somehow control where . . . when she would arrive?

Catalina left the envelope on the desk and ran out the door, around the building and into the sand. She ran forward, knowing exactly where she was going this time. If she was too late, she'd find Qaletaqa, young or old, and make him teach her, make him take her back to a time when it wasn't too late.

She reached the spot where she had stopped before, where the sandstorm had engulfed her and taken her back. She clasped the wulfenite and closed her eyes and thought of Jackson. His touch, his smell, the sight of him smiling at her. Catalina waited for the breathless sensation, but nothing happened. She stepped forward, concentrating so desperately on Jackson's face that she saw nothing else. Thought of nothing else.

Nothing. No swirls of sand, no sensation of flying, no breathless wonder. She dropped the wulfenite and spun around, only to see Allie watching her from a distance. Was that why it hadn't worked?

She knew in an instant that Allie's presence had nothing to do with her inability to go back. She couldn't go back because Jackson wasn't there for her anymore.

Catalina returned to the station, passing Allie silently, saying nothing to the woman who followed her closely. How would she ever accept that it was too late?

Her Mustang was running, and she had some

cash to get her new life started. If only Jackson was here, her life would be perfect.

But life wasn't supposed to be perfect.

"Tell me, Allie," Catalina lifted the fat envelope from the desk and grasped it in her hands. "Do you know much of Stu's genealogy?"

"A little." Allie seemed slightly wary of her, but she didn't ask about her frantic race into the desert sand, or her dejected trip back to the station. Catalina was grateful for that. She wasn't good at lying, and she knew no one would believe the truth.

"I didn't know until I met Chris that your last name was Booker. Is there, by any chance, a Doc Booker among Stu's ancestors?"

Allie lifted her eyebrows, a bit startled but not shocked. "You've heard the stories?"

Catalina nodded. "A few. But I didn't think Doc had any children."

"He and his first wife didn't have any, but after he married Helen Dunston, they had three."

Catalina shook her head. "I can't believe it."

"He was on up there in years," Allie said, reclaiming her stool. "As the family tells it, he was shot, and Helen nursed him back to health. They were married a few months later. . . ."

"He waited until her year of mourning was up," Catalina muttered.

"What?" Allie leaned forward.

"Nothing."

"Anyway, Helen was a quite a few years younger than he was, and they shocked everybody when Jackson was born."

Catalina dropped her half-filled bottle of soda,

and it landed on its side, spewing bubbles all over Catalina's skirt. She didn't care.

"Jackson?" she whispered.

Allie reached down and scooped up the soda bottle, then dropped a rag over the clear puddle. "Yeah. Stu's grandfather, Jackson Booker."

Catalina closed her eyes. Jackson had promised her that if there was a way . . . if the soul survived . . . he would be waiting for her. Could it be so simple? Was there a Jackson Booker out there somewhere with pale blue eyes searching for her?

"No," she breathed deeply, trying to remain calm. That wasn't what she wanted. She wanted Jackson. Her Jackson. No substitute, no recycled soul. *Her* Jackson.

"She married him right before he made that big strike, found that mine. The last profitable gold mine in these parts."

Doc had finally found something worth taking a risk for, something—someone—to change his own life for.

"Chris said you were here," Stu called, and Catalina opened her eyes to see the man almost upon her, wiping his hands on a greasy towel. "I'll be damned. Your Mustang's out back, and she runs like a beauty. I just cleaned up the engine a little, replaced a few worn parts. I still don't know why it died on you that day."

"Thank you. Certainly I owe you more for storing it for such a long time." Catalina reached into the envelope and withdrew a few bills, but Stu shook her off.

"It was no trouble at all," Stu assured her with

a genuine smile, and that was when she saw Doc. His smile had been infrequent, but he had passed it on to his great grandson.

She heard squealing tires and saw a blur of white, and then Chris brought her Mustang to a stop in front of the office.

"I thought I'd bring it around front for you," he shouted, a wide grin on his face.

Allie muttered, in that universal way mothers have, "Christopher Jackson Booker," and Stu rolled his eyes.

"I told that boy to keep his hands off . . ."

"It's all right," Catalina said with a smile. And it was. "I need to get on the road. There's . . . something I need to do in Indian Springs."

Something that suddenly seemed terribly important.

Catalina pushed her way through the double glass doors of the Indian Springs Public Library. She had so many things to do, she told herself as she headed for the staircase. Kim was first on the list. What explanation could she give her best friend? The truth? Even Kim wouldn't believe that. How would she explain disappearing for more than two months and coming home pregnant?

She tried to fill her mind with practical thoughts, plans for the future, so she wouldn't have to think about Jackson. That hurt too much. He was gone.

Of course he was gone. It was 1996, after all, and Kid Creede and all of his kind were long dead.

The stairs seemed incredibly long, winding to the second floor. A young woman with a baby in her arms passed Catalina on the stairs, and the girl smiled and stared at Catalina's calico dress.

At the top of the stairs Catalina turned and looked down into the lobby. There was someone new at the main desk. The person they'd hired to replace her, no doubt, watching the desk while Kathy took one of her infamous long, late lunches. Catalina had known all along that she'd have to find a new job, but the money from Wilson's ring would take the immediacy out of that search. She had time.

She walked slowly down aisle nine, all the way to the end. Nothing had changed. She could reach out and touch the spines of all these history books. Tell anyone who asked what was in most of them. But what she knew now was that just because it was history, that didn't mean it was the truth. History had not been kind to Jackson, after all.

At the end of the row she stopped and laid her hands on the books. Why was she torturing herself like this? Nothing had changed. Kid Creede had died in Baxter—shot a dozen times. In the book he was nothing but a footnote in history; a minor character, she'd called him. But in her heart and her mind he was real. Still with her. Flesh and blood.

But she had to see. To prove to herself that he was lost in the past.

She dropped to the floor, sitting cross-legged in front of the section that held the book on Arizona history, and the paragraph on Kid Creede.

The long skirt of the first Mrs. Booker's calico pooled around her, reminding her that she was out of place, out of time.

The book stood on the bottom shelf, and it was almost always there. It was an obscure book, written years ago by a local author, and was usually checked out only when the kids at the elementary school did their year-end reports in the spring. But Catalina had read it, front to back, and she knew right where the paragraph on Jackson was.

She slid the book from the shelf and held it in her lap for a moment, running her fingers over the paper cover that had been torn and taped. Why was she doing this to herself? Why couldn't she just convince herself that it had all been a dream? A hallucination? A brief madness?

She opened the book and flipped the pages to the chapter on the land wars in Baxter. It looked just the same, and she started to read the paragraph at the end of the fifth page. She read it, and then read it again, laying her fingers over the words.

Disappeared. Not shot a dozen times, not ambushed on the street. The words swam before her eyes as she read the paragraph again. Had Jackson survived? How? She'd seen the mob behind him, had heard the shots.

Disappeared. Nothing else had changed. The article touched on Jackson's part in the land wars in Baxter, but instead of the sentence that had coldly recorded his death there were the words— *Scheduled to hang, Kid Creede mysteriously disappeared and was never heard from again.*

351

Catalina couldn't rest until she knew for certain what had happened to Jackson after she'd left Baxter. She wrapped her fingers around the wulfenite that swung from her neck. She had to go back. Damn it, there had to be a way!

It was a distant jingle, at first, a familiar sound that broke her concentration as she stared at the page and read the paragraph once more. A jingle, and a heavy step on the stairs. Catalina lifted her head and closed the book. She knew that sound.

With every heavy and slow step on the stairs, they jangled lightly. Spurs. Silver spurs.

Catalina didn't move. She stared at the books on the shelf and held her breath. It wasn't possible. She was going to look down the aisle and find a fat old man with a pocket full of change, or a woman with a heavy step who was wearing too many gold chains around her neck.

She covered her face with her hands and took a deep breath. It wasn't possible.

The steps were coming closer, down her aisle now, and Catalina dropped her hands slowly. She would have known that step anywhere . . . any time.

"Catalina?" He dropped down beside her, and she turned to stare into his face and his pale blue eyes. "Are you all right?"

Catalina threw her arms around his neck, and Jackson wrapped his arms around her. "You're here," she whispered. "How?"

"I'm not sure." His voice was low, husky and full of wonder. "I was thinking of you, and I fell with that noose around my neck, and my boots hit a . . . a hard black road."

"They hung you?" Catalina brushed her hand over his neck, saw a small red abrasion there and traced it with her finger.

"They tried."

"How did you find me?"

Catalina pulled away from him so she could see his face and assure herself that he was real. She laid her hands on his shoulders and ran them slowly down his arms, over the black duster he still wore. He was real, and warm, and somehow he was here with her.

"The only place I could think to look was this library. A lady picked me up on the road." He pulled her onto his lap. "They don't give a man much room to walk these days, do they?" he added. "She almost hit me, so she stopped to make sure I was all right, and she gave me a ride in her . . . her car. It was like flying, Catalina." There was real amazement in his voice, and Catalina thought of all the magic she could show him. The fact that he was here was the best magic of all.

Catalina laid her hands on Jackson's stubbled face. "I'm glad you found me," she whispered, laying her lips on his. "I thought . . . I thought I was going to have to live without you."

The clicking of high heels on the wooden floor interrupted her, and reminded her that they weren't really alone. Catalina lifted her head and saw, standing at the end of the aisle, a hussy with long bare legs, high heels, and a very short skirt beneath a snug blouse. Her dark hair was tossed back artfully, and she was staring at Jackson with a near pout of her full lips. She looked, incredibly, something like Juanita.

"Did you find your . . . your wife?" she asked.

Jackson pulled away from Catalina just slightly and smiled at the scantily dressed woman. "Yes. Thank you, ma'am."

"So you don't, like, need a ride anywhere else?"

The tramp was so obviously disappointed that Jackson had found his wife that Catalina wanted to strangle the dim-witted, much too attractive hussy who had almost run Jackson down on the highway.

Jackson shook his head. "I think we'll just sit here for a while, ma'am. You see, my wife's had a difficult day, and she's in the family way, so she needs to take it easy for a bit."

The bimbo nodded her head several times as she backed away, her eyes never leaving Jackson. "That's too bad. I'm headed for San Francisco for a couple of weeks. I coulda used some company."

The woman turned and walked away, and Catalina melted against Jackson, folding into him, and then she took his face between her hands and kissed him, and kissed him again. She would never be able to get enough of him.

"I want to take you to the movies," she whispered when she pulled away from him, leaving her lips so close to his that they were almost touching. "And show you airplanes and television and . . . so many wonders. We can get in my Mustang and take off. Wherever we want to go."

"Will you teach me to drive?" Jackson asked, resting his hand at her back and leaning her backward over his arm. "I think I'd like that."

"Yes."

Jackson kissed her throat, and Catalina let her head fall back. "Oh, Jackson, I have so many things to show you."

He ran his hand under the hem of her dress and rested strong fingers against her calf. "Good," he whispered huskily. "I still have a few things to show you, myself."

Epilogue

"That doesn't look like me at all," Jackson whispered.

Catalina lifted the paperback book carefully from the shelf. It was just one of many, but she'd waited a long time for this.

"At least his hair's the right color," she said.

"He's got no hair on his chest, and there's not a scar on that body. Dammit, Catalina, I can't believe you told everything."

She smiled at her husband and tugged on a long strand of black hair. This was the Jackson she'd fallen in love with. He'd let his beard grow back, and his hair grow long. "No one will believe that it's true. It's a romance, Jackson. Fantasy, remember?"

"But it is true." He continued to whisper, even though the bookstore was deserted but for the clerk who sat near the register at the front of the store.

"Daddy!" Booker screamed, throwing himself at Jackson's leg and holding on. Jackson lifted his son, swinging the two-year-old effortlessly to his shoulders. "Buy me a story," Booker demanded. "A doggie one."

"You have a hundred doggie stories at home,"

Jackson said, but he turned away from the romance section and strolled to the children's books.

"I need another one," Booker whined.

Catalina stood back and watched as Jackson and Booker carefully examined each and every doggie book. Booker was the picture of his father, black-headed and blue-eyed and stubborn. Smart, too. And beautiful. Of course, all mothers thought their children were smart and beautiful, even when to others they obviously weren't.

This one should be a girl, Catalina thought as she unconsciously touched her flat stomach. And maybe this time Jackson wouldn't freak out in the delivery room and threaten the poor obstetrician.

Booker decided, very forcefully, on his story. It had a picture of a purple dog with a silly grin on the front, and he clutched it against his chest like a true treasure. At least there was one trait he'd inherited from his mother.

Jackson paid the clerk and left the store with Booker still perched on his shoulders. Catalina had to take quick steps to keep up with him, but as soon as he realized that she was practically running he slowed down and smiled at her.

"I still can't believe you told *everything*."

"Are you mad at me?"

Jackson gave her a devilish grin and offered up his palm. "Not if you let me drive home."

Catalina slipped the keys to the Mustang from her pocket and tossed them through the air. Jackson snagged them by the ring and twirled them on one finger. He loved to drive, but he tended to go too fast, and when he was distracted he was all over the road.

If he was going to drive, then she really should wait until they got home to tell him about the new baby. Nothing fazed Kid Creede, but she never knew how Jackson Cady would take big news.

Guardian Angel

LINDA WINSTEAD

Despite her father's wish that she marry and produce heirs for his spread, Melanie Barnett prefers shooting her suitors in the backside to looking them in the face. Then a masked gunman rescues her from an attempted kidnapping, and Mel has to give him the reward he requests: a single kiss.

Everybody in Paradise, Texas, believes that Gabriel Maxwell is a greenhorn dandy who has no business on a ranch. Yet he is as handy with his pistol as with a lovely lady. To keep Mel from harm, he disguises himself and protects her. But his brazen masquerade can't hide his obvious desire. And when his deception is revealed, he will either face Mel's fierce wrath—or her fiery rapture.

_51970-4 $4.99 US/$5.99 CAN

Dorchester Publishing Co., Inc.
65 Commerce Road
Stamford, CT 06902

WEST WIND

Linda Winstead

Annabelle St. Clair has the voice of an angel and the devil at her heels. On the run for a murder she didn't commit, the world-renowned opera diva is reduced to singing in saloons until she finds a handsome gunslinger willing to take her to safety in San Francisco.

A restless bounty hunter, Shelley is more at home on the range than in Annabelle's polite society. Yet on the rugged trail, he can't resist sharing with her a passion as vast and limitless as the Western sky.

But despite the ecstasy they find, Annabelle can trust no one, especially not a man with dangerous secrets—secrets that threaten to ruin their lives and destroy their love.

_3796-3 $4.99 US/$5.99 CAN

Chase the Lightning

LINDA WINSTEAD

"A captivating tale not to be missed!"
—Raine Cantrell

Renata Parkhurst can't believe her luck. The proper daughter of a Philadelphia doctor has run away to her cousin's Colorado spread hunting for love, and the day she arrives, a wounded rancher falls right into her arms.

Although everyone in Silver Valley believes that Jake Wolf is a cold-blooded murderer, no one would accuse him of being a lady-killer. Yet even as he grudgingly allows Renata to tend to his healing, he begins to lose himself in her tender caresses.

The townsfolk say that Renata has a better chance of being hit by lightning than of finding happiness with Jake. But to win the heart of the man of her dreams, the stunning beauty will gladly give up all she possesses and chase the lightning.

_52002-8 $4.99 US/$5.99 CAN

TIMESWEPT

BITTERROOT

VICTORIA CHANCELLOR

Bestselling Author Of *Forever & A Day*

In the Wyoming Territory—a land both breathtaking and brutal—bitterroots grow every summer for a brief time. Therapist Rebecca Hartford has never seen such a plant—until she is swept back to the days of Indian medicine men, feuding ranchers, and her pioneer forebears. Nor has she ever known a man as dark, menacing, and devastatingly handsome as Sloan Travers. Sloan hides a tormented past, and Rebecca vows to use her professional skills to help the former Union soldier, even though she longs to succumb to personal desire. But when a mysterious shaman warns Rebecca that her sojourn in the Old West will last only as long as the bitterroot blooms, she can only pray that her love for Sloan is strong enough to span the ages....

_52087-7 $5.50 US/$7.50 CAN

FRANKLY, MY DEAR... SANDRA HILL

By the Bestselling Author of *The Tarnished Lady*

Selene has three great passions: men, food, and *Gone with the Wind*. But the glamorous model always found herself starving—for both nourishment and affection. Weary of the petty world of high fashion, she heads to New Orleans for one last job before she begins a new life. Then a voodoo spell sends her back to the days of opulent balls and vixenish belles like Scarlet O'Hara.

Charmed by the Old South, Selene can't get her fill of gumbo, crayfish, beignets—or an alarmingly handsome planter. Dark and brooding, James Baptiste does not share Rhett Butler's cavalier spirit, and his bayou plantation is no Tara. But fiddle-dee-dee, Selene doesn't need her mammy to tell her the virile Creole is the only lover she ever gave a damn about. And with God as her witness, she vows never to go hungry or without the man she desires again.

_4042-5 $5.50 US/$6.50 CAN

Dorchester Publishing Co., Inc.
65 Commerce Road
Stamford, CT 06902

Please add $1.75 for shipping and handling for the first book and $.50 for each book thereafter. NY, NYC, PA and CT residents, please add appropriate sales tax. No cash, stamps, or C.O.D.s. All orders shipped within 6 weeks via postal service book rate. Canadian orders require $2.00 extra postage and must be paid in U.S. dollars through a U.S. banking facility.

Name _____

Address _____

City _____ State _____ Zip _____

I have enclosed $_____ in payment for the checked book(s).

Payment <u>must</u> accompany all orders.☐ Please send a free catalog.

TIMESWEPT

Don't miss these passionate time-travel romances, in which modern-day heroines fulfill their hearts' desires with men from different eras.

Traveler by Elaine Fox. A late-night stroll through a Civil War battlefield park leads Shelby Manning to a most intriguing stranger. Bloody, confused, and dressed in Union blue, Carter Lindsey insists he has just come from the Battle of Fredericksburg—more than one hundred years in the past. Before she knows it, Shelby finds herself swept into a passion like none she's ever known and willing to defy time itself to keep Carter at her side.

__52074-5 $4.99 US/$6.99 CAN

Passion's Timeless Hour by Vivian Knight-Jenkins. Propelled by a freak accident from the killing fields of Vietnam to a Civil War battlefield, army nurse Rebecca Ann Warren discovers long-buried desires in the arms of Confederate leader Alexander Ransom. But when Alex begins to suspect she may be a Yankee spy, Rebecca must convince him of the impossible to prove her innocence...that she is from another time, another place.

__52079-6 $4.99 US/$6.99 CAN